"Do that again."

He put his hand on the back of her neck and tilted her head back so he could see her better. He found her hat pin, pulled it out and lifted the hat from her head, then pitched it onto the chair with his.

She knew she should struggle and protest. So why didn't she? Kissing Mr. Hart would be dull and tedious. Totally forgettable. Wouldn't it? Her loosened hair seemed to be flying everywhere. "Do what again?"

"Stick out your bottom lip. Pout."

"I don't under—"

"Just do it."

With a gulp and a deep breath, Trina stuck out her bottom lip.

Gabriel sucked that pouty lip into his mouth and felt her shudder from the crown of her head to, he suspected, her dainty little toes. If she was going to slap his face and report his behavior to Papa, she'd do it now....

Dear Reader,

March is the time of spring, of growth, and the budding of things to come. Like these four never-before-published authors that we selected for our annual March Madness Promotion. These fresh new voices in historical romance are bound to be tomorrow's stars!

Among this year's choices for the month is *The Maiden and the Warrior* by Jacqueline Navin, a heartrending medieval tale about a fierce warrior who is saved from the demons that haunt him when he marries the widow of the man who sold him into slavery. Goodness also prevails in *Gabriel's Heart* by Madeline George. In this flirty Western, an ex-sheriff uses a feisty socialite to exact revenge, but ends up falling in love with her first!

Last Chance Bride by Jillian Hart is a touching portrayal of a lonely spinster-turned-mail-order-bride who shows an embittered widower the true meaning of love on the rugged Montana frontier. And don't miss *A Duke Deceived* by Cheryl Bolen, a Regency story about a handsome duke whose hasty marriage to a penniless noblewoman is tested by her secret deeds.

Whatever your tastes in reading, you'll be sure to find a romantic journey back to the past between the covers of a Harlequin Historical.

Sincerely,

Tracy Farrell, Senior Editor

Please address questions and book requests to:
Silhouette Reader Service
U.S.: 3010 Walden Ave., P.O. Box 1325, Buffalo, NY 14269
Canadian: P.O. Box 609, Fort Erie, Ont. L2A 5X3

GABRIEL'S HEART

MADELINE GEORGE

Harlequin Books

TORONTO • NEW YORK • LONDON
AMSTERDAM • PARIS • SYDNEY • HAMBURG
STOCKHOLM • ATHENS • TOKYO • MILAN
MADRID • WARSAW • BUDAPEST • AUCKLAND

ISBN 0-373-29005-5

GABRIEL'S HEART

MADELINE GEORGE,

a country girl through and through, is a native Texan who found her Texas drawl a perfect basis for writing Western historical romance. A former elementary school teacher, she now loves the freedom of traveling with her husband—and writing partner—in their travel trailer, doing research for new books.

If you'd like to receive her newsletter, *Madeline's Heart,* and notices of upcoming releases, the author would appreciate hearing from you. Please write to her: Madeline George, P.O. Box 543, Rising Star, Texas 76471.

This book is dedicated
to my husband, Chuck,
forever and always my dearest love.

Prologue

August 1881

Gabriel Hart spied the cabin when he crested the hill. No sign of Hannah anywhere. He frowned. She usually heard him coming and hurried to meet him.

He grinned. Napping. Had to be it. Now that they were expecting a baby in a few months, she had to rest more often.

When he passed the well and saw the bucket spilled, the dipper in the dust, Gabriel's gut tightened and his blood raced. Something wasn't right. The house and yard were too quiet. Too empty.

He stepped down from his horse, let the reins drop and reached for the Colt on his hip—but he'd waited too long.

A flash. Thunder in the still afternoon.

The first bullet tore a ragged hole in his right wrist. Pain jolted through his gun hand.

Another flash. More thunder.

The second bullet gouged into his side and lodged

beneath his left lung. Fire spread through his chest like a bolt of lightning, taking his breath away.

Gabriel dropped to his knees and glared at the man who'd just shot him. Otis Blackburn. The bastard was holding Hannah the same way he'd hold a rag doll.

"Gabriel…"

Her bruised face, and her clothes, torn and bloody, told him what had happened.

"Hannah!"

A knife. Sunlight flashed off the blade as it ripped her throat. Her scream slashed through Gabriel like a dagger. Blood soaked into her dress, draining her life away.

Hatred gave Gabriel the strength to stand. If only he'd gotten home a little sooner. Five minutes earlier, and this snake of a man, this waste of skin he thought he'd put away forever, would be bleeding out his life in place of the woman who made Gabriel's life complete. The woman who carried his child.

Hannah's brown eyes glazed over and her bruised, bleeding lips mouthed Gabriel's name as she sank to the ground at his feet.

Otis Blackburn laughed while Hannah died.

The hammer clicked back. "I won't kill you, Hart. I want you to live at least ten more years. I want you to know what it's like to be in prison all those days and nights. In prison in your own body." He took aim at Gabriel's right knee.

With his last strength Gabriel lunged at the filthy murderer and drove his head into Blackburn's gut. The gun fired into thin air. Gabriel pounded his good fist into Blackburn's face and gouged at his eyes until he felt blood trickle between his fingers.

Blackburn smashed the butt of his gun into Gabriel's temple.

Gabriel sank into the dust, pain burning through him.

"*Adiós*, lawman." Blackburn mounted and rode off toward the ridge.

Gabriel dragged himself forward until he could touch Hannah's limp hand. Already cold. He balled his left hand into a fist and raised it to the vanishing image of the killer.

"Someday, Blackburn, I'll find you. You'll die. So help me, God. You'll beg to die."

Chapter One

October 1882

"Geoffrey, I have to get to the depot. The train won't wait for us if we're late."

"But, Katrina, I have something really important to tell you. To give you, actually."

Trina McCabe thrust one of her brown leather traveling bags at Geoffrey Monroe in an attempt to budge him from the spot in the hall outside her bedroom door. He'd arrived at the ranch half an hour ago, but she hadn't spoken to him until just now. She wasn't ready to talk to Geoffrey yet. She knew the thing he had to show her was an engagement ring, but she wasn't ready to address that subject. To be truthful, she didn't know if she'd ever be ready to discuss it. So she'd made him wait, hoping he'd get the idea she was too busy to talk today. But it hadn't worked. Couldn't he take a hint just once?

In the looking glass above her chiffonier, her cheeks seemed a trifle pale. She touched the tips of two fingers to her tongue, then scrubbed at one of the pink roses on the wallpaper. With a few practiced strokes she transferred the pink dye to her cheeks. Satisfied, she straightened her blue feathered hat.

"Please listen, Katrina. Aren't you curious to see what I brought you?" Geoffrey shined the toe of one boot on the back of his freshly pressed nankeen trousers, then straightened his vest nervously. "Can't you stand still?"

"No, I can't. Papa will be calling any minute now that it's time to—"

Amos McCabe bellowed from downstairs. "Trina! We're leaving right now. Are you coming or not?"

"I'm coming, Papa!" Trina called back. "Now, Geoffrey, there'll be worlds of time to talk once I'm back from Silver Falls. Come for supper then. I promise I'll listen to every word you say." Every dull and tedious word, she wanted to add, but Geoffrey was, after all, her beau. Wasn't he?

Geoffrey grabbed her bag and reached for the valise, but Trina beat him to it. For some reason, demonstrating her independence seemed terribly important. Geoffrey clutched the bag as though it contained silver or gold.

"You shouldn't be carrying heavy things, Katrina." Geoffrey grabbed the valise from her hand. "I'll carry this, too. Maybe I ought to go with you to Silver Falls."

"Nonsense!" She said it too emphatically and knew it. She gave him her sweetest smile as placation to turn his protests into thin air, as always, and scanned the room to see if she'd left anything essential. The valise had been heavier than she'd thought, so she decided not to argue with Geoffrey and let him carry it, too. Traveling without a trunk was terribly inconvenient. She usually packed three trunks for a trip this long. But there would be no one she knew in Silver Falls. Praise the Lord for that.

Her father's voice boomed again from downstairs.

"Trina! We're going without you if you aren't down here by the time I count to five!"

"Papa's going to have apoplexy. Come on!" Trina hurried down the stairs with Geoffrey close behind, lugging the baggage. She needed a couple of days to herself, without Geoffrey six inches away, panting around her like a lonesome puppy.

And she had to look after her father. Something wasn't right about this business trip. He'd protested her coming in such a way she'd been genuinely alarmed at the idea of him going to Silver Falls at all, much less alone. Then there were those dreadful men who'd come to the house last week. Well, there was simply no way she'd allow him to go without her.

Geoffrey practically stepped on her skirts all the way down the stairs, and even bumped her behind with the baggage a couple of times. If Trina didn't get away soon, she'd pitch the biggest fit any of them had ever seen!

Outside, Amos McCabe waited in the carriage, along with Trina's oldest brother, Tom, who was going to drive them to the depot in Denver. The icy air hinted at snow, while the wind felt like icicles against her bare skin.

"There you are at last. Geoffrey, we'll see you when we get back. I'll wire Tom from Silver Falls when my business is complete. He'll let you know when to expect us in Denver." He took a look at Trina. "What kind of a dress is that to be wearing on a train? Shouldn't you be wearing wool in the winter—and a dark color? Bright blue in the wintertime—"

"But this *is* wool, Papa. It's a new kind of wool, as warm as the heavy kind. It came in last week. I ordered it last spring, don't you remember?" Of course he didn't remember. If she reminded him of the cost, he would no doubt remember that. "I couldn't wait another minute to wear it."

"It'll be covered in soot and cinders five minutes after we get to town. And that ridiculous hat, with feathers and flowers. It looks like you're wearing a flowerpot."

"That's exactly what it's called, Papa. A flowerpot hat."

Amos snorted his opinion. "There's no time for you to change. I hope you brought something sensible to wear once we get to Silver Falls."

"Yes, Papa, I did. Don't worry."

Tom shook his head at her, then cast a look of disgust at Geoffrey. "I'll send word. Let's go." Tom helped Trina into the seat, handed her a lap blanket, then climbed in after her. Before Geoffrey could add anything, Tom slapped the horse's rump with the reins and the carriage lurched forward with a squeal.

"I'll see you when you get back, Katrina!" Geoffrey ran along beside the carriage for a dozen yards or so, puffing great billows of steamy breath, before stopping to wave.

Trina waved halfheartedly. For a month of Sundays Geoffrey had been talking about buying her an engagement ring, begging her to say she'd accept one. When she'd put him off the fourth time, he'd gone ahead and picked it out. Red and green stones set in gold filigree.

Mr. Filby at the general store had told everyone in town about it, figuring their engagement was a sure thing. Only two hours after the stage had come through and left the box at Mr. Filby's store, Trina had heard from Alissa who had heard from Fanny who had heard from Sarah that the ring had arrived. Practically everyone in town had seen the ring since then. Except Trina.

She sighed. A ring was exactly what she'd been wanting him to give her, wasn't it? An expensive, gaudy ring that would catch everyone's eye? Once she'd accepted it, they'd be officially engaged and a date could be set for the wedding.

Weddings were so much fun. There would be parties given in her honor and so many gifts they wouldn't have room for them all. And all three of her brothers would have to be fitted for new suits and she'd get to see them all dressed fit to kill at the same time. So why had she stubbornly refused to give poor, pitiful Geoffrey an answer?

Trina stuck out her lower lip and pulled the blanket tighter around her neck. She knew now that a ring wasn't what she wanted at all. The problem was, she didn't know what she wanted instead. Geoffrey was nice enough, and his father did own a prosperous haberdashery in Denver. If she and Geoffrey were married, she'd have all the beautiful clothes she could wear. But clothes weren't everything. Just what *was* everything, she couldn't say. She just knew Geoffrey wasn't it. She'd never intended to lead Geoffrey on or give him false hopes about their being married someday. How on earth had it come this far?

Amos nudged his daughter's elbow. "Trina?"

"Yes, Papa?"

"What was Geoffrey all riled up about?"

"He wants to give me an engagement ring."

Amos hesitated. "Are you going to accept it?"

"I don't know. Perhaps I'll know when we get back

home.'' He had enough on his mind. She could tell him after they got back that she'd thought about it and decided marrying Geoffrey simply would not make her happy.

Amos patted her arm. ''Want to talk about it?''

''Not really.'' She smiled and squeezed his hand. ''Let's forget all about Geoffrey and the ranch while we're on this trip, all right? I think we both need a diversion.''

''Agreed. I only hope you won't be bored.''

''Why, Papa, of course I won't be bored. After all, I'm with my favorite fellow, aren't I?''

It was the truth. Trina suspected it would continue to be the truth, whoever she married. She sighed and stared at a piñon pine up ahead. If only the prospect of marriage could be more exciting. It seemed to be the only thing she knew of that could leave her completely bored. She gathered the blanket closer around her chin. The wind was absolutely wicked.

Amos dug in his pocket, then handed a derringer to Trina.

''Put this in your pocket. You never know who you might meet on the train or in Silver Falls.''

''But Papa, I've never fired a gun in my life.''

''It isn't that hard. You probably won't need it, but it can't hurt to have it, just in case.''

''In case—''

''Just take it without a big argument, for once in your life.''

Stung by the reproach, she stared at the derringer for a moment, then pushed it deep into her pocket. A worrisome little thought skittered through her mind. She recalled the day those dirty men had come to the house.

They'd left angry. Just afterward, her father had announced the trip to the mining town.

"Papa, are you sure we ought to go to Silver Falls? Maybe we should—"

"What? But you said—"

"I know. I'm not talking about that."

"Then what? I don't—"

"I'm thinking about those men who came to the house last week. They sounded angry. It worries me."

"It's nothing for you to be concerned about."

"But what if they—"

"Enough! This is business and doesn't concern you. Settle down and enjoy the trip."

"But Papa—"

"Katrina...hush!"

She hushed. But she didn't like it one bit.

Gabriel heard the train whistle when it rounded the last bend, just west of the Denver depot, where he'd been waiting for the past hour.

Through a flurry of feathery snowflakes mixed with cinders, and soot belching from the smokestack, the locomotive chuffed its way into the depot like an iron monster, creaking slowly to a stop. People waiting to board the train stepped back to avoid the expulsion of steam from the engine, then inched forward while arriving passengers poured from the cars.

Gabriel got up from the hard wooden bench and stretched his back muscles, then rubbed at a spot on his rib cage. Better than fourteen months since he'd been shot and it still ached. He knew it wouldn't stop completely until he killed Otis Blackburn.

Passengers gathered their baggage. A line formed, heading out the door. Just ahead, a woman wearing a silly-looking hat with blue feathers and flowers turned her head to allow a young man to kiss her cheek. Gabriel inched past. "Excuse me, ma'am."

She nodded and stepped back an inch or two to let him pass. He went outside to the platform.

Trina watched him go, leaning over a bit to get a better look.

Tom narrowed his eyes. "Remember Geoffrey?"

Trina smiled sweetly. "How could I ever forget Geoffrey? Goodbye, Tom. I wish you'd change your mind and come with us." The last thing she wanted on this trip was a fussy older brother hanging around, but she had to be polite.

"Can't. Too much to do at home. I'll see you when you get back."

She leaned toward the door to see if she could spot that man again, but he was already out of sight. So handsome. Could he possibly be going to Silver Falls? On the same train? For a moment Geoffrey's face flashed through her mind and she felt a twinge of guilt for admiring another man. But she'd decided their engagement wasn't going to happen. That meant she was single and unattached—and free to admire handsome men when they happened along. She smiled, pleased with her decision.

She saw her father's puzzled look but ignored it, as usual. He shook his head, then went out to the platform, leaving her to catch up on her own. She took her time, trying to think of some reason to speak to the handsome stranger. She could pretend to recognize him from a social function in Denver. That usually worked quite well. He would tell her his name and perhaps even be interested in a conversation sometime during their journey.

"Trina! Are you coming?"

"Yes, Papa, I'm coming." Mercy. It was so bothersome to rush.

Outside, the conductor came to the railing of the first car, squinted when the wind stung his eyes, then cupped one hand around his mouth and shouted, "Silver Falls! Board! All aboard!"

Gabriel paused to allow several ladies and a couple of children, flushed with the cold and chattering like a flock of magpies, to enter in front of him. He dug into his pockets for his gloves and pulled them on. Their rabbit-fur lining eased the sting of the wind. His fingers tingled with warmth. The handrail, colder than the air and rough with rust and flaking paint, wasn't touchable in winter. Likely as not, a bare hand on that rail would leave skin behind.

The acrid stench of coal smoke and fumes stung his nostrils and left a bad taste in his mouth. After one last look around, he went inside the car, surveying the group of milling, babbling passengers. Pushing his way past a gentleman with a bristly mustache and a rotund belly, he slid into the third seat on the right, all the way over next to the window. To kill time, he stared out into the rail yard.

Cattle milled about in a nearby pen, awaiting transfer to the slaughterhouses in Chicago. The stink of them invaded everything, but Gabriel hardly noticed. There'd been a time when that herd might have been his, but those days were long gone. Only one animal occupied Gabriel's mind now—a two-legged, one-eyed animal he aimed to slaughter personally.

The grimy window glass barely allowed him to see outside the train. Soot coated everything. The sun, had it been able to burn through the cloud cover, could not have penetrated to the gloomy interior of the passenger car. But that hadn't dimmed the enthusiasm of the ladies and children finally getting settled in their seats.

Gabriel had waited a long time to board this train. He'd ground his teeth in expectation of catching the man who'd laughed when he slaughtered Hannah. Blackburn wouldn't laugh when Gabriel caught up to him in Silver Falls. No, that would be the last thing he'd do.

"Ticket, mister?"

The conductor bumped his shoulder, then held out his hand.

Gabriel handed over the ticket, waited for the pale writing to be scrutinized, then took it back and stowed it in his inside coat pocket. The conductor moved on down the car, asking to see tickets as he went. Gabriel watched him for a moment, then stared out the window again, impatient to leave the station. Silver Falls was just about a day from Denver. Now that the winter snows had started collecting in the passes, keeping the tracks cleared had become a constant battle and made train schedules a joke. They'd be there when they got there, snow and slides permitting.

"Excuse me, sir?"

Gabriel heard the woman's voice, but didn't think she was talking to him. She tapped his arm.

"Sir?"

He stared at her for a minute before answering. The lady with blue feathers. Dressed in such finery, she had to be rich. Blue dress to match the feathers. Fancy toilet water. And, he'd guess, miles of that thick, red hair cascading down her back from under that boxy hat. The young man who'd kissed her cheek didn't seem to be with her.

"Ma'am? How may I be of assistance?"

Old habits died slowly. Service had been his job—his life—for too many years. Years after ranching. Years after facing every upstart in the state of Texas eager to try his luck at beating the fastest gun in the territory. Or so they'd thought.

"I know we've met before. Aren't you—"

"No, ma'am. We haven't. And I'm not."

"I see. Well. I must be mistaken."

"Trina! Over here!" The man with the brushy mustache motioned for her to join him, then held up his hand in greeting. "Sheriff Hart? Good to see you again."

Gabriel nodded.

Trina smiled. Sheriff Hart. Her mind whirled with the possibilities of this revelation. She went to the seat where her father had already made himself comfortable, pulled a hankie from her sleeve and dusted the seat before perching on the edge.

"Let's go back to the Pullman, Papa."

"Not yet, Trina. I have some business to tend to."

Well, that was that. She'd have to wait to question her father about the handsome Sheriff Hart.

Gabriel recognized Senator Amos McCabe after a bit of thought. The redhead must be his daughter. And the young man in the depot... His son-in-law?

Gabriel's brow wrinkled. He'd never met her before today. He would have remembered. He settled into the seat, squirmed until he'd attained the best possible position for dozing, and pulled his hat down to his eyebrows to catch a snooze. It was a long way to Silver Falls. He intended to be fresh when they arrived tomorrow afternoon. Later, he'd go on back to the Pullman. Now, though, he had to be alert and observant, in

case one of Blackburn's men was on board, heading for
a rendezvous with his miserable boss. A pain in his back
prompted another adjustment in his position. He'd pretend to take a nap and study each man in the car. Mem-
orizing a face now could mean the difference between
being dead and alive in Silver Falls.

Trina was also squirming. There wasn't a way to get
comfortable in these hard contraptions they called seats.
She glanced around to see if everyone else was having
the same trouble. Of course, she wasn't actually interested in everyone. Just a certain man her father called
Sheriff Hart.

Trina couldn't decide how to continue her conversation with this sheriff. She listened surreptitiously to
her father's conversation. Boring. Glancing back at the
sheriff, she fanned her face with one hand, warding off
some of the cinders floating around, feeling warmer just
from thinking about speaking to him again. She'd have
to come up with an excuse, though.

The train pulled out of the station, throwing her off
balance. She struggled against the jerking motions of
the lumbering locomotive, watching Sheriff Hart shifting position in the rigid seat, trying to get more comfortable. Didn't he know it would be impossible to sleep
in all this confusion? He'd likely choke to death and
never wake up again if the air didn't clear up soon.

She pulled the lace-edged hankie from her sleeve
again and covered her mouth and nose with the side she
hadn't used to dust the seat, filtering some of the smoke
and cinders clogging the air, but it was no use. By the
time they reached Silver Falls, she'd have succumbed
to asphyxiation, too.

If the atmosphere didn't improve soon, she'd have to
retreat to her quarters in the Pullman car, with or with-

out her father. He was still talking to someone about that business matter he'd mentioned. Her first thought had been to suggest he invite the man to their quarters, but, after taking a good look at the man—dirty face, dirty clothes, bad teeth, something in one of his eyes making him blink constantly—she thought perhaps her father was right to speak with him here. Whew! The stench of cattle penned up too long permeated the air. She fanned her face and let her eyes wander across the car.

Sheriff Hart's eyelashes had to be as long as hers. His beard, dark brown, had been neatly trimmed, probably with sharp scissors. And his mustache didn't curve over his top lip into his mouth, like some she'd seen. His neatly trimmed beard and mustache said something about the man. And his hair didn't seem to be matted and dirty, the way some men seemed content to tolerate theirs. His thick hair had a bit of curl to it and lay nicely on his collar, just the right length in back. She wondered what it would feel like to run her fingers through it, slowly and carefully, massaging his scalp as she went....

Her father coughed and nudged her with his elbow. "Trina, hand me that bag."

She fetched the heavy leather case for her father and noted again how he wheezed when he talked. He was too heavy, that's all there was to it. She'd been trying to get him to cut down on fat meats and gravy for the longest time, but he stubbornly refused. The bigger he'd gotten, the more trouble he'd had breathing. This thin mountain air didn't help one bit. When they got to Silver Falls, where it was much higher still, what would he do then? She didn't want to think about it, but she had to. If something happened, she would be the one responsible for finding help. Tom should have come with them, but he'd stubbornly refused. Her father wouldn't hear of it, anyway. Too much work to be done at the ranch—as always. Never a slack minute.

Trina coughed. Her nose stung and her eyes watered fiercely. Something had to be done about the air or they'd all perish.

"Conductor! Conductor!" She fanned her face with her hankie until he got there. "We simply must open some windows. The air—"

"Winders! Are you out of your mind?"

"I most certainly am not. I'm deeply concerned—"

"But, ma'am, it's cold outside. If we open them winders, you're likely to freeze solid before we reach the first pass." His wrinkled face twisted into an expression of sheer disgust.

"It's stuffy and smoky in here. I can hardly breathe."

"Well, then, I 'spect you'd better stick your nose outside that door and cool off a mite. I ain't openin' them winders. Not for you or anybody on this train."

"Well, I never...!"

The conductor stuck his nose in the air and stalked off down the car.

Gabriel grinned at the exchange. The wind and a swirl of snow from the door when the conductor left sent a shiver through him. It was just like a woman to want to open a window in winter on a train going thirty miles an hour. Gabriel studied the feisty Miss McCabe for a moment. And feisty she was. Now she was railing at "Papa" to do something about the stuffiness. Spoiled. Pampered. Nothing but a beautiful child.

The senator finally interrupted her tirade. "Go stand on the landing, Trina, if you're that all-fired hot. I have business to tend to before we get to Silver Falls. I can't get it done with you caterwauling about how thick the air is.''

Gabriel almost laughed out loud when Trina's bottom lip stuck out. Pouting. Poor little rich girl. She spied him watching her. He should have looked away, but didn't.

Trina squared her shoulders, tucked in her bottom lip and glared at him. Then she stood, whirled around and headed for the far end of the car. She pulled the heavy door open, then held it there, standing behind it out of the wind, until everyone in the car hooted and hollered and the car filled with snow and cinders. Then she slammed the door, went back to her seat and perched there, stiff as a tree trunk.

Gabriel kept right on grinning. Her cheeks flamed with anger and she deliberately looked away. Gabriel knew how mad she was, but couldn't help being amused by it all. He'd enjoyed her little display, even though it had chilled him to the bone. She had spunk, a man had to give her that. In fact, there were a lot of things a man would like to give her.

The thought disturbed him. During the fourteen months he'd spent healing and getting his strength back, he'd never even looked at a woman. The pain from losing Hannah to that scum had blacked out any thought other than stringing the son of a bitch up by his tenderest parts, and torturing him until he screamed in agony, the way Hannah had screamed. The memory made him shiver, but not from cold.

Now here he was, swapping howdies across the room with a spoiled senator's daughter. Gabriel decided a walk might not be a bad idea. He knew every face now. Sitting in this contraption they called a seat had made him stiff, even though he shouldn't be having such pains. He wasn't that old. Twenty-nine. Or was it thirty? He'd missed one birthday, delirious with fever and pain, thanks to that sorry bastard Blackburn.

She was still glaring at him from time to time. Well, he'd just have to apologize. But not too much. Gabriel smiled and tipped his hat at the poker-faced lady when he strode past, then stepped out on the platform between the passenger and Pullman cars, careful to close the door securely behind him. That ought to get her fired up, for sure.

He shuddered in the frigid wind, then took a deep draft of mountain air. Damn, but it smelled good. Nothing like it in all the world. The fragrances of ponderosa and limber pines, aspens, maples and spruce mingled with the frosty aroma of fresh snow. How snow could have a smell, Gabriel didn't know, but it did. A clean smell. New. Unblemished. It covered the ugliness with unmatched beauty. Only when people walked through it and muddied it up did it lose its virgin whiteness and turn to slush and slop in the roadways. Signs of progress.

Cities had come to smell like pigsties, with all the newfangled machinery and trains belching smoke all over the place. He preferred clean mountain air anytime. And snow without boot prints.

Gabriel took a long, slow breath and drank in the spectacle around him. Mountains held their heads up fourteen thousand feet overlooking valleys, broad and fertile, and lofty bluffs exposing layers of sandstone in a dozen colors. Magnificent. Gabriel had come to love this country during his search for justice and revenge, yet he still longed for Texas—and home. Someday, after Blackburn was dead and left to rot, Gabriel would go home.

The door bumped open behind him. Gabriel knew without looking who it would be. Only, she didn't seem to be riled.

"Mr. Hart, I believe? My father told me about you. I am Katrina McCabe."

So, she wasn't married after all. Gabriel amended his previous assumption. Future son-in-law, perhaps?

"What can I do for you, Miss McCabe?"

Gabriel looked sideways at her. She'd already begun to shiver hard. He wondered how long she'd last before having to run back inside the car, stuffy or otherwise. The cape she wore would be fine if she weren't out in the wind. Out here, she needed a heavy coat.

He supposed he should get her out of the cold, but somehow he also figured she wouldn't want to talk in the same car with her father. This lady had something stuck in her craw, but he didn't really want to know what it was. He had enough to think about for one train ride. Her cheeks flushed red with the cold, matching the color of her pouty lips.

"I'm c-con-concerned about something. I h-hoped you might be able to h-help." Trina clutched the cape tighter around her but it did nothing to stop the bite of the wind. She might turn to a pillar of ice right where she stood.

Gabriel wanted to curse out loud. His only concern was his own business. Damn, but this woman was getting to be a bother, in less time than it took to take a decent nap.

"I was about to inspect my quarters in the Pullman, Miss McCabe. You might want to check on yours, also."

"A splen-splendid idea, Mr. Hart."

Gabriel helped her across the walkway and onto the next platform, then held the heavy door open against the wind while she hurried into the Pullman car oppo-site. He stepped inside after her and pulled the door closed behind him with a loud clang.

Their breaths puffed steamy in the cold air of the Pullman. Baseboard heaters, warming the compartments with heat from the locomotive's furnace, didn't warm the corridors very much. It took her a while to stop shivering.

Gabriel thought about offering her his fleece-lined coat, then changed his mind. No use being cold just because some flighty female decided to take a walk. She'd warm up if she stayed inside.

"Feelin' better, ma'am?"

Trina patted her cheeks, swept the snow and cinders from her skirt, straightened her pleats and tried to as-sume a dignified air before answering his question. "Somewhat better, Mr. Hart. Thank you kindly."

"You wanted to talk to me about something?" He hoped it was worth hearing. He could see that her mind was conjuring up something. In spite of it all, he was curious to see what she wanted.

"I'm concerned about my father's welfare on this journey. I...uh...I think he may be in some danger."

"I see. What makes you think so?" Best let her talk until she ran down. That is, if it didn't take too long.

The outside door, caught by the wind, slammed open, and two men came into the Pullman. They managed to push the door closed, then "beg-pardoned" their way between Gabriel and Trina. They departed the car at the far end.

Trina watched every step they took, then looked up and down the corridor before she spoke, in whispers this time. The delay had given her time to concoct her story. "Have you noticed the men on this train?" Her eyes widened.

Gabriel swallowed hard. Brown. Her eyes were brown. Just like Hannah's. The knot in his gut tightened. "Which ones, ma'am?"

"Those men in the front car. Sitting just behind my father. The men who just came through here. I think—" she checked the corridor again "—I think they want to harm him."

Gabriel burst out laughing. Just like a stupid little kid, playing cowpokes and Indians. Worse than that, he was standing here listening to this nonsense.

"Mr. Hart! I assure you—"

"I'm sorry, ma'am. I guess you caught me off guard, that's all." He sobered his face. "Why do you think they want to hurt your father?"

She whispered again. Gabriel had to lean forward, just inches from her nose, to hear what she said. A shooting pain across his ribs made him want to curse out loud. Damn that Blackburn!

"Because of the land," she whispered, her eyes getting rounder by the minute.

"The land?" He whispered, too, and felt plumb foolish doing it. "Which land?"

"The land in Silver Falls. The land that's being given to the state of Colorado."

"I'm afraid I don't follow, ma'am."

She gave him a look of sheer impatience, then leaned back and practically shouted, "They don't want the state to have it. I should think that would be perfectly clear. I overheard their arguments with my father at home last week. They aren't happy, believe me."

Gabriel winced with the abrupt change in volume. This little conversation had already gone on longer than he'd intended.

"I really don't think you have anything to worry about, Miss McCabe. If you'll excuse me, I need to check my sleeping quarters.'' He tipped his hat to her and went on down the corridor, leaving her fuming behind him.

"Well, I never…!"

Gabriel didn't doubt she'd "never." He sort of suspected she'd enjoy it if she did, though. A stirring in his loins surprised and bothered him. Such feelings were best left alone until Blackburn was half-dead and left rotting on an anthill somewhere.

How long since he'd had such feelings? Too long. Fourteen months. He felt guilty. And empty inside. Best stay away from her. Especially if the young man really was her intended.

Gabriel wasn't ready for activity of the sort Miss McCabe inspired. Killing Blackburn. Now, that would be an activity he'd enjoy.

Chapter Two

While Trina continued to fume, muttering to herself under her breath, standing with her back to him by the grimy window in the forward door, Gabriel retreated into his compartment. He shook his head, latched the door and stretched his back again. Damn, but this cold weather was enough to crack bones.

The compact compartment had only one purpose—to provide a horizontal place to sleep when a train ride extended overnight. A narrow cot folded down from the wall. He stashed his leather case beneath it on the floor. One low chair squatted next to the door while its mate, opposite, sat next to the outside window. The chair was just big enough to hold his hat. The only door not opening on to the corridor led to the water closet, which was so cramped Gabriel figured he'd have to leave the door open to wash his face—or bump his butt when he leaned over the sink.

With its shades of tan and pale green, the whole room exuded drabness. The worn places on the green chairs showed through tan, and the scratches in the tan paint, oddly enough, revealed a coat of green beneath.

The solitary window—after he'd wiped away some

of the soot—provided all the color a man needed, though. Only one was missing—the deep, dark red of Blackburn's blood. Gabriel would add it to the blues and greens of the landscape just as soon as the train got to Silver Falls.

Men's voices from the other end of the car, loud and angry, cut through the steady rumble of the wheels on the tracks. Garbled. Nothing clear. None of his business.

A few seconds later the door to his compartment swung open and Trina McCabe rushed inside, closed the door carefully and squatted down, hiding.

Gabriel leaned down and whispered directly into her ear.

"May I help you, Miss McCabe?"

Trina jumped up and her cheeks burned as crimson as pokers. She obviously hadn't realized she'd chosen his compartment to hide in. He couldn't resist goading her. "Did you drop something, ma'am?"

"Quiet! They'll hear you!" If this didn't get his attention, nothing would! She'd pulled a lot of foolish stunts in the past to get a man to notice her, but this one had to be the prize.

"Who?"

"Listen!"

Gabriel thought about escorting her back into the corridor, but the voices got louder. Two men stopped just outside.

"He's got to be stopped, and you know it!"

"But he's a senator! Do you know what you're saying? We can't—"

"There's got to be a way. We can't let him—"

"Quiet!"

Gabriel stood perfectly still. Trina hadn't moved a muscle.

"Did you hear someone coming?" one of the men said, quieter this time.

"Naw. They're all up front, which is where I'm headed right now. You comin' or not?"

"I'm comin', but I'm tellin' you right now that I ain't gonna be a party to no killin'."

Trina drew in a sharp breath and Gabriel saw her start to turn around, her mouth opening to speak. To keep her from giving them away, which didn't seem like a very good idea right now, Gabriel mashed her back against the wall and clamped one hand over her mouth.

Trina struggled, then realized she was making too much noise. She settled down, nodded acquiescence, and Gabriel let her go, but didn't move away.

The voices faded as the men went on down the corridor. Then the forward door opened and closed and Gabriel stepped back.

Trina tried to catch her breath. What those men had said—coupled with being so close to a man's chest she could have counted the hairs if she'd been so inclined—left her breathless. She thought she'd exaggerated the story about her father being in danger.

"Now do you believe me?"

"Ma'am, I don't rightly know what to believe. But I will say you seem to be right about your father's well-being on this trip." Her toilet water made his head swim a little. Before long, the whole room would be filled with it.

Trina took a deep breath. "Thank you."

"For what?"

"For believing me."

Gabriel smiled. "Beggin' your pardon, ma'am, but it wasn't you I believed. It was those two men, talkin' about your father and about killin' somebody in the same breath.''

Her face turned red again and she started to say something, but whirled around instead, stamping on Gabriel's toe.

Swallowing an oath, Gabriel decided to let it go. ''Is somethin' else wrong, Miss McCabe?''

She turned slowly and glared at him. ''Wrong? Other than several men on this train wanting to kill my father, what else could possibly be wrong?''

''Not anything I can think of, ma'am. Now, if you'll excuse me, I need to wash up a bit.'' He nodded toward the door.

She didn't budge. ''I'd like to know what you intend to do about protecting my father. After all, you are a sheriff.''

Gabriel started to say just what he was thinking—that he couldn't care less about her father—but his background as a peace officer prevented him. ''Exsheriff. It depends, Miss McCabe, on whether or not an attempt is made to harm your father while he's on this train. Should I be present if that happens, I will, by all means, do my best to see that he isn't harmed, even though I am no longer an officer of the law. Now, if you'll excuse me...?''

He leaned past her, opened the door and waited until she left, nose in the air. Gabriel watched her all the way to the end of the corridor. Her skirts swished back and forth across the dusty floor.

Damn fool woman. It was enough to make a decent man want to throw himself off a train. Or into her compartment come nightfall.

Gabriel rubbed his chin, shook his head, then looked

at his watch. Ten forty-five in the morning. It had already been a long day.

Outside the car, a man yelled something Gabriel couldn't decipher. Trina screamed.

Gabriel ran into the corridor. Trina stood at the end of the car, gaping in horror at something outside on the landing.

"Papa! Oh, dear God...!" she muttered.

Gabriel pushed past her and jerked the door open. He scanned quickly back and forth before stepping onto the snowy platform next to Senator McCabe. The passenger car door opposite slammed back and two men came outside.

"What happened? We heard a man yell, then somethin' that sounded like a wildcat!"

Gabriel looked carefully at their faces. One appeared to be stunned, but the other watched Gabriel warily. A twitch winked one eye.

"I didn't see anything." Gabriel held on to the rail and leaned out into the wind, trying to see down the track behind them. It wouldn't have surprised him to spot a body dragging from the undercarriage, but there was no sign of anyone, dragging or otherwise.

Trina came out of the Pullman, grimacing and holding her handkerchief over her nose, her eyes red and moist. She began to shiver immediately.

"Papa? Are you all right?"

He didn't answer right away, just stared at Trina as though trying to decide what to say or do next. Gabriel sensed the senator was hiding something.

"I'm fine, Trina. Get back inside before you catch your death." He turned to Gabriel. "Hart, you were out here mighty fast. You must've seen something."

"Sorry, Senator."

Senator McCabe ushered everyone except Gabriel back into the passenger car. Trina wasn't happy, but she minded her father.

Gabriel went back into the Pullman. Something had happened out there and he didn't like it. Trina had seen something, but she wasn't telling anyone about it. He thought again about the two men talking outside his door. Maybe one of them had decided the other was about to break, or that he wasn't going along with the plan, whatever that might have been. Maybe, just maybe, one of those men had met with an unfortunate accident and had "fallen" off the train. If that proved true, then someone else might have a similar "accident" before the train reached Silver Falls.

Gabriel watched Trina tiptoe sneaky-like out of the passenger car. It didn't surprise him at all. She fought the wind, managed to get back into the Pullman and closed the door with Gabriel's help. He thought she might shiver into pieces right there in front of him.

"Miss McCabe, it's cold out there, in case you hadn't noticed." He reached into his compartment, fetched his coat, then slung it around her shoulders. When he pulled the front together, she stumbled up against him, surrounding them both with that intoxicating fragrance.

She looked up into his eyes, her bottom lip still quivering with cold, and Gabriel had the sudden urge to kiss her. He pushed her away instead, cursing under his breath at such a blame fool notion.

"You needn't curse at me, Mr. Hart. I'm not the one who pushed that wretched man off the train."

"How do you know what we heard was a man departing the train?" Gabriel went back into his quarters, leaving the door open, knowing she'd follow him inside either way.

"Not departing, Mr. Hart. Pushed. There's quite a big difference."

"And you saw him get pushed, did you?"

Trina hesitated. "Well…" She looked all around the small room, at the ceiling, at her shoes, everywhere except at Gabriel.

He turned to the window and watched the snowy trees marching steadily past. Now the lady was hiding something. She'd called her father's name at the window. Who else had she seen on the platform? Why would she protect the person who'd pushed a man off the train unless…

Trina decided to lie. "No, I didn't see that man pushed off the train. But it doesn't take a scholar to know that's exactly what happened." She came over to the window where he stood and touched his arm. "If you could…"

Gabriel stiffened.

She removed her hand, embarrassed by his reaction, and cleared her throat. "Excuse me, Mr. Hart, but I have every reason to believe that my father could be the next man thrown from this train. Are you going to wait until that happens before you do something? What sort of sheriff were you, anyway?"

Gabriel released a long sigh and wished the pounding in his temples would stop. "A good one. All right, Miss McCabe. I'll see what I can find out. From your father."

"My father! Certainly you aren't going to alarm him—"

"If there's someone on this train who wants to kill your father, then he sure as shootin' has a reason for it. I've never seen the time yet where the object of another man's hate wasn't aware of that hate. Your father knows. He just hasn't decided to tell me yet. If he wants my help, he'll have to trust me with the truth."

"What you say makes a good deal of sense, but I doubt you're going to learn anything from my father. I assure you he's as upright and honest a man as you'll find in these days of scoundrels and renegades." She squared her shoulders and lifted her chin to emphasize the words.

So, the lady didn't want him to talk to her father. He thought he knew why. Her bottom lip stuck out just a fraction. The impulse to kiss that pouty lip swept through him again. Damn! What could he be thinking of? "All right, ma'am. Now, if you'll excuse me... again..."

Trina handed his coat back to him, straightened her skirt and her ruffled shirtwaist blouse, sniffed once, then left, feathers bouncing.

Gabriel closed the door and wished like hell Senator McCabe and his bothersome daughter had chosen a different train to Silver Falls, or that whoever it was who had kissed Trina's cheek at the depot had come along. Then her husband-to-be would be up to his eyebrows in this mess.

Everything in his gut told him he had no business messing around with the senator and his troubles. Ex-sheriff or not, Gabriel was a passenger on this train just like everyone else, and what he wanted most in the world right now was to be left alone with his thoughts of killing Otis Blackburn. That woman had a way of distracting him from the business at hand. If he played his cards right and stayed out of everyone's way, maybe he could avoid any complications with the senator or the feisty Miss McCabe. In fact, he had a mind to...

Loud voices. An argument. Then a gunshot.

"Damn." All his good intentions shot to hell.

Gabriel pulled out his Colt and checked the chamber. He eased over to the door, cracked it open just an inch and peered out.

A man lay crumpled on the floor not ten feet away. Standing over the body was none other than Senator McCabe himself, holding a smoking gun.

Chapter Three

Trina came out of the compartment across from Gabriel's holding the derringer in front of her with both hands, like a dead rat she intended to throw into the garbage. When she saw her father, she dropped the gun and ran into his arms.

"Papa! You killed him!" Tears streamed down her cheeks. She stared at the dead man in horror and shock.

Gabriel knelt beside the body and turned it over. One shot, straight through the heart. The senator hadn't taken any chances. "Senator, maybe you'd better tell us what happened."

Others arrived, from both ends of the train. In the midst of the confusion, Gabriel called for quiet.

"Senator?"

"He tried to kill me. But I didn't shoot him. Wilson did. He was defending me, just as I hired him to do. I took his gun for protection while he followed this scalawag's sidekick back to the passenger car."

"I'm just grateful you weren't injured, Papa."

"How did he try to kill you, Senator?" Gabriel watched faces in the crowd while he waited for the answer. That twitch again, on a man returning from the passenger car. The bodyguard?

"He tried to push me off the train! I was coming back to find Trina and he was waiting for me between the cars."

The story didn't make sense. "How did the two of you get in here, then?"

Trina turned on him. "Mr. Hart, your tone would indicate that you don't believe what my father just told you."

"No offense, ma'am. I just—"

"Now, Trina, let the man do his job. Gabriel Hart is one of the finest sheriffs I've ever met. No offense taken, Mr. Hart. I managed to get away and ran inside the car. He followed me in. I tried to reason with him, but he wouldn't listen. He pulled a gun. Wilson, here, came in behind and shot him."

"I see." Gabriel looked around. "I think all you folks should get to wherever you're going. There's nothing else happening here."

The crowd thinned out, leaving Gabriel, Trina and her father. Gabriel still didn't know anything about the bodyguard or the other men who seemed to show up whenever the senator got into a ruckus, but he decided he ought to find out more about them.

"Now what, Sheriff?" Amos wheezed from exertion.

"First of all, I'm not a sheriff anymore. I'm a passenger, same as you. I just don't want to see anyone else 'fall' off this train."

Senator McCabe's eyes darted from Gabriel to Trina as he nodded agreement. "Let's get on to our quarters, Trina. You've had quite a scare. For the remainder of this journey, I suggest we spend the majority of our time under lock and key."

Trina sighed and picked up the derringer from where she'd dropped it. McCabe took it from her and stowed it in his pocket.

"Thank you, Mr. Hart, for your help in convincing my father that he should be more careful."

The senator frowned. "Trina, you didn't—"

Gabriel cleared his throat noisily. No use in getting her in Dutch with her father. "Your daughter asked me earlier if I might be on the lookout for your welfare, Senator. She cares for you a great deal."

"Yes, thank God, she does. I've been mother and father to her since she was born. Raised in a house with three older brothers, it's a miracle she's turned out to be the lady she is today."

Flustered, Trina pulled at her father's arm. "Papa, I should think Mr. Hart has better things to do than listen to our entire life history. Thank you again, Mr. Hart. We shall appreciate your protection for the remainder of our trip."

She flashed her brown eyes at Gabriel, and he was amused to see her embarrassed to have been discovered in clandestine antics. Her cheeks blazed.

"I'll be glad to help in any way I can, ma'am." Now, why in tarnation had he said that? The last thing in the world he wanted was to protect the McCabe family. Damn!

The conductor arrived, huffing and puffing, excited with the news of a killing on his train, and solicited help in taking the body back to the baggage car behind the Pullman. Gabriel saw his chance to escape the scene, and volunteered.

Trina watched him go. She'd never met a man in her life she couldn't stare down. Until now. A challenge, if ever she'd seen one.

"Now, Papa, you must rest. Let me help you."

"Dammit, Trina, quit fussin' over me like I was some doddering old fool! I'm perfectly capable of making it ten feet to my bed."

Trina's lower lip quivered. "I just...I'm sorry, Papa, but I..." She managed to squeeze out one tear.

"Now, Trina, darlin', don't cry. I didn't mean it like it sounded. I appreciate your concern for me. I just don't like bein' pampered in public, that's all."

Trina sniffed and dabbed at her nose with her hankie. "I'm sorry, I forgot. You only like being pampered at home." She hid a smile behind the hankie.

He gave her a look that silenced her—for the time being, anyway. "Now I'm gonna rest awhile. I suggest you do the same."

"I shall. Thank you, Papa. Lock your door."

"I will, I will. You'd think I was ninety years old and feebleminded, instead of being a representative of the great state of Colorado, and the father of this young whippersnapper."

He locked the door behind him. Trina thought about going to her own compartment, then changed her mind. Something wasn't right. She could tell by the cold gleam in the ex-sheriff's eyes that he knew something he wasn't telling. She wanted to know what it was.

She tiptoed to the end of the car and tried to see through the windows of both the Pullman and the baggage car behind. The glare from the snow outside made it impossible. She'd have to make herself known if she were to discover what was happening where they were stowing away the dead body. A shiver reminded her she'd left her cape in her compartment. She'd get it, then she'd try to ease into—

The door slammed open, pushing her back against

the wall. Tarnation! She'd have to be more careful. Caught spying by the sheriff. Careless, that's all there was to it. Careless.

"Miss McCabe, was there somethin' else you needed?"

"Absolutely not, Mr. Hart. I was merely..." Her mind went blank—something that had never happened before. She'd always been able to conjure up believable stories to match whatever situation presented itself. Until now. That same amused expression, which had angered her clear to the bone before, perched on his face again. Why, he actually enjoyed seeing her squirm.

Instead of covering up what she'd been doing, she decided to turn the tables and make him do a little squirming instead. In control of the situation. That's where she'd always been and where she intended to be now. "What, may I ask, is so amusing?"

Gabriel debated whether to tell her he knew exactly what she'd been doing at that window. If he did, though, she'd be spittin' mad at him again. But then, if she stayed spittin' mad, she might leave him alone for the rest of the trip. Just what he wanted. Or was it? He chose the middle path.

"Nothing is amusing, Miss McCabe. I've just boxed up a dead man who got shot even though he wasn't carrying a firearm of any sort, and I'm late for a nap. Now, if you'll excuse me..." He shouldn't have told her that little piece of news. He shook his head. Damn female. Making him act like somebody else.

"No gun? But my father said—"

"I know what your father said. He lied."

"Lied! You take that back this instant! My father is not a liar!"

Now he'd done it. He'd have to smooth those fancy

feathers again. "I didn't mean to call your father a liar. I just said he lied. I assume he had good reason."

That took all the fire out of her next attack. Just when Trina thought she'd taken control, he'd snatched it away again.

"But what possible reason could there be for him to lie about such a thing? Didn't he know you'd check the body?"

"I'm sure he did."

Voices again. Gabriel grabbed Trina's arm, pulled her inside his compartment and closed the door.

"No noise this time, understand?"

"Of course I understand. Do you think I'm—"

He held up his hand in a silent threat to clamp her mouth shut if she didn't do it on her own.

Trina's first instinct was to slap his face, but she pressed her lips together instead, hating to admit he was right. They listened to the conversation in the hallway.

"Chet's gone. Now Lurvy. Watch your back, partner. We could be next."

"He wouldn't dare."

"He's already dared twice. Let's get into those trunks before someone else does." They left without another word.

Trina turned around and drew a long, slow breath. Gabriel was right up against her, not two inches away.

"Those men—"

"Seem to think your father was responsible for pushing that first man off the train." Which was exactly Gabriel's conclusion, along with the suspicion that Trina had witnessed the deed.

"But that's ridiculous." His breath on her face made her slightly giddy. Along with his eyes, his dark brown, beautiful eyes. And his lips, soft and kissable, surrounded by his beard and mustache, neatly trimmed. "Unless he had a good reason."

Gabriel knew if he didn't back off he was going to kiss her, right here and now. A thoroughly improper thing to be thinking about, much less doing. Any minute now, he expected her to bolt. To change the tone of the way things were going. To rail at him to find the culprits who were actually responsible for these killings and do something to exonerate her father. But she didn't. She didn't move an inch. If anything, she relaxed a bit toward him, putting herself even closer. The blue feathers on her hat swayed and fluttered.

That damn perfume made his head swim. What was it, anyway? Lilac. Hannah had worn lilac perfume. Hannah…

Gabriel cleared his throat and backed up. Feeling guilty as hell for betraying Hannah's memory, he took a deep breath and studied the rock formations passing by the window.

"You'd best be gettin' back to your quarters, ma'am. Be sure you lock the door."

Trina didn't know whether to feel angry or disappointed or both. She'd been kissed once or twice in her life. Why, Geoffrey had kissed her just last week when he'd proposed to her for the fifth time. It had not felt exciting in the least. But she ought to be excited, shouldn't she? The way she felt right now, for instance.

The excitement of kissing Geoffrey had been entirely one-sided. Trina had considered it dull at best. And tedious. Just what she found attractive about Geoffrey was getting to be harder to identify with each passing day. Geoffrey was sweet enough, but he did everything she told him to do. Staring down Geoffrey was no challenge at all. And he'd certainly never backed away from kissing her when she'd let it be known she was willing to be kissed. Had she ever felt this excited, this eager to be kissed, when Geoffrey was the man just inches away? She couldn't remember.

Kissing Mr. Hart would no doubt be dull and tedious, in spite of the fact that looking into his eyes caused little tingly things all up and down her spine.

Trina shook herself. A well-bred young lady shouldn't be thinking such thoughts. Why, it was practically indecent to want to kiss a man before they'd at least talked about engagement. And she had no intention of ever being courted by such a man as Gabriel Hart. Why, what would Aunt Francis and Cousin Bertha say? And Aunt Sophie! She'd never be able to live down such a thing, even if she lived to be sixty-eight. Just because Trina never had a mother to tell her how a lady should behave didn't mean she hadn't had plenty of instruction from the other women in the family.

Trina sighed. How dull it was to be proper. How tedious. A thought struck her. Of course. That had to be it.

"Mr. Hart, are you married?"

Such grief appeared in Gabriel's eyes that she gasped, staggered backward a couple of steps and reached for her throat.

"I'm sorry, Mr. Hart. I obviously have overstepped the boundary of good taste by asking such a personal question. I sincerely beg your pardon, sir."

Gabriel stared out the window. He had to get his emotions—his hatred—under control. Any reminder of Hannah brought it back as if it were yesterday. The grief and the hatred burning in him sometimes threatened to blank out his mind entirely. He couldn't let it run free. Not until he had Blackburn in front of him, pleading for mercy—which he wouldn't get. But this woman couldn't know that.

Gabriel closed his eyes. "It's nothing you've done, Miss McCabe."

"Are you sure? I—"

"My wife died over a year ago." The words bit into him like a rattlesnake and refused to let go, pumping venom into him, poisoning his very soul. "Your question was a reminder, that's all. There's no harm done."

How could she have been so thoughtless as to blurt a personal question that way? Trina scolded herself soundly, wishing she'd had the good sense to keep her thoughts and curiosity to herself.

"I'm dreadfully sorry."

"Yes, ma'am. Now, if you'll pardon me..."

In spite of what he'd just said, she knew she'd let her headstrong tendencies get out of hand again. She owed him another apology.

"Of course, Mr. Hart. I apologize again for my... thoughtless question. I...I'll speak with you again later...about my father."

Gabriel nodded but didn't look at her. He had to push the venom away so he could be in control again.

Hesitating in the corridor, Trina berated herself for hurting him so terribly. He must have loved his wife dearly for her death to still be such a dagger in his heart. She wondered how Mrs. Hart had died, but knew she could never ask. It wasn't any of her business, anyway. He'd said it was over a year ago. By now he should have accepted her death and decided to get on with his life, shouldn't he?

Trina slapped her cheeks, punishing herself for being so nosy. Shame on her! What must she be thinking to want to pry into this man's life and affairs? She had to forget the incident and hope he would do the same. If she never mentioned it again, perhaps he'd forgive her impertinence.

She knew she should go straight to her compartment, lock the door and stay there until the train arrived in Silver Falls tomorrow. But something niggled at her like a bird trying to pluck a stubborn worm from a hole in a tree trunk. She had to see for herself why her father had lied. Seeing his bodyguard push that man off the train while her father watched had almost made her heart stop beating. He'd supposedly killed that second man because he was threatening to kill her father—and that couldn't have been true, since the man had not been carrying a gun. None of it made any sense.

Trina eased out the back door of the Pullman, shivered over to the baggage car and went inside, then stopped for a minute to let her eyes adjust to the darkness.

The car was piled haphazardly with boxes, traveling bags and trunks of all sizes and descriptions. There seemed to be no pattern to the jumble at all. Luckily, each parcel dangled a label with the owner's name and destination. On the left was a platform. Anything previously there had been moved to make room for the unexpected baggage now occupying the space.

There he lay. Deader than a doornail. Trina shivered, but not from the cold. If she were to inspect the body, looking for a gun, she'd have to touch—

The door slammed back with a loud thud. "Are you lost, Miss McCabe?"

Trina jumped about a mile and let out a yelp.

The conductor latched the door and shook his head at her. "This is the baggage car, ma'am. I don't believe whatever you're lookin' for will be in here, unless you mean to get into one of those trunks you brought on board.''

"Trunks? I didn't bring any trunks. You must have me confused—''

"Two of 'em. Heavy. I figured they was chock-full of your fancy clothes and doodads. Your father saw to the loading hisself.''

"My father? Are you sure?''

"Yes, ma'am. Now, if you'll tell me what you're lookin' for, maybe I can help you find it.''

"Nothing. I'm…lost…just as you said. I guess I got turned around and went out the back door instead of the front. I'll go back to my quarters now. Thank you kindly.''

The conductor shook his head again and watched her go, muttering under his breath about foolish females.

Trina went straight to Gabriel's door and knocked lightly.

Gabriel came, hesitated when he saw it was her, then opened the door. "Miss McCabe—''

"Shh! I have to talk to you. It's important.'' She pushed past him.

There didn't seem to be any escaping this woman. He closed the door and waited.

"Mr. Hart, I have just learned something extraordinary.''

"I see.'' Gabriel was back on an even keel. He didn't want to lose the edge again, but if anyone could make him do it, it was Trina McCabe. "Who?''

Trina stopped. "I beg your pardon?''

Was she slow or stupid or something? "Who told you whatever it is you're so all-fired excited about?''

"No one. The conductor. You did!''

Gabriel didn't like the sound of this. "Miss McCabe..."

"Let me start again. May I sit down?"

Gabriel threw up his hands. "Sure! Why not? *Mi casa es su casa.*"

Trina stopped halfway down and stood again. "What was that? Spanish?"

"Never mind. Just get it said."

"Back in the baggage car just now—"

"What were you doing back there?"

"Looking at the dead body."

"You enjoy looking at dead bodies, do you?"

"Of course not. I just wanted to see if he had a gun."

"I told you he didn't."

"I wanted to see for myself."

"Humph." Gabriel didn't cotton to being doubted.

"Anyway, the conductor startled me. He thought I was looking for one of the trunks I brought on board the train."

"How long are you plannin' to be in Silver Falls, Miss McCabe?"

"Two days. Why?"

"Just wonderin' why you'd bring trunks for such a short stay."

"But I didn't."

"Didn't what?"

"Bring any trunks."

"Wait a minute. You just said—"

"The conductor thought they were my trunks, but they weren't."

Gabriel sighed. She was determined to make him pull the story out of her word by word. "Whose were they?"

"My father's."

Gabriel's head started to hurt. "Is there a point to any of this?"

"I was getting to the point when you interrupted."

"Pardon me, ma'am, for interrupting."

"You're pardoned."

"Can we get on with this little recital?" He rubbed his forehead tiredly.

"Certainly." If he wanted her to hurry, why was he asking so many questions? It must be the nature of an ex-sheriff. "It seems that my father brought two heavy trunks on board the train in Denver. I wasn't aware of it until now."

"So?"

"So I don't know what's in those trunks. What could it be? My father's bodyguard pushed a man off the train, then killed a man who was trying to shoot my father, only the man had no gun, and...and...Mr. Hart, I'm so confused, I don't know what to think next!"

"You and me both, ma'am." He'd been right about her seeing something earlier. But it brought him no satisfaction to have figured it out. Gabriel just wanted to be alone. Trina was giving him the granddaddy of all headaches and he needed a drink and some shut-eye to get rid of it. "I'll think about it for a while and let you know later what I decide, all right? You really must go to your quarters now. I think part of your confusion is due to lack of rest."

Trina could see the pain in his eyes when he reached to massage his temples. She stifled the impulse to massage them for him. "I'm sorry, Mr. Hart. I've caused you more distress than I have a right to. I won't bother you again, I promise."

"Thank you, ma'am." He opened the door for her and smiled thinly when she walked past him. He waited until she entered her compartment and clicked the lock into place before he closed his door and lay down on the bed.

Distractions. He had to rid himself of distractions and get back to the task at hand, which was to find Blackburn and kill him. Nothing else could hold any importance for him.

In his mind he saw Trina's face, shining with excitement. Her lower lip, stuck out in a pout. The dismay and regret he'd seen in her eyes when she'd asked if he was married. He'd never seen a woman with as many different faces as she had.

Damnedest woman he'd ever met.

Hannah had been as predictable as night and day. Not Trina McCabe. Guessing which face she'd show him next was like trying to guess when it would rain in Texas. Or when it would quit.

He rubbed his temples and tried to blank his mind of anything except his primary thought—kill Blackburn.

He'd forgotten to have that drink.

Gabriel got up, grabbed his coat and headed for the dining car. The scent of lilac perfume lingered on the collar of his coat where it had touched her face and neck. A hollow feeling opened up in the pit of his stomach.

Damn woman.

He stalked off down the hall.

Trina watched him go, then left her compartment. Tiptoeing, looking back over her shoulder at every noise, every bump of the train, she headed for the baggage car.

Chapter Four

Inside the dank baggage car, Trina took a long, slow, deep breath and tried to stop shivering. The dead man lay there, as cold as the mountain outside. He was already starting to stiffen. His arms stuck out like those on a porcelain doll, and one boot cleared the shelf an inch. She shivered again, less with the cold than with revulsion.

It was stupid for her to be here, but she had to know the contents of those trunks her father had brought on board, and she had to get to them before those men did. With all her heart she hoped it would be something she'd laugh and scold herself about later.

She picked her way among the baggage carefully, having difficulty standing erect with the swaying and lurching of the cumbersome car as it climbed the mountain. Boxes tied with string...leather bags...canvas bags...trunks with other names on them... There they were. The tags tied to the locks had McCabe written on them. She tried to open the nearest trunk.

Locked. She'd suspected they would be, otherwise those two men would have stolen whatever was in them. How was she going to get into one of them?

The answer was obvious. She'd have to have the key. She knew, as surely as she knew Gabriel Hart was the most attractive and maddening man she'd ever met, that dear old Papa would have the key in his pocket.

The only other alternative would be to break one of the locks, but then her father would know someone had gotten into the trunk, and she certainly didn't want that.

With her lip stuck out, she went back to the Pullman...and met Gabriel Hart just inside the door.

"You must be really curious about dead men, Miss McCabe, to spend so much time back there inspecting the body."

Trina bristled. "I did not go back there to 'inspect the body,' Mr. Hart." Caught. In spite of all her sneakiness. Her heart fluttered like a little bird.

"Well, then, why were you in that car?"

It wasn't any of his business what she did. Then again, he might know a way to get into those trunks without leaving any trace of the entry.

"If you must know, I was inspecting the trunks my father brought on board."

"I see. Did you satisfy your curiosity?"

"No. They're locked and I have no way to unlock them." She stuck out her lip again.

Gabriel couldn't stand to let that lip go unkissed.

"Come in here."

"What?"

"I said, come in here."

Gabriel took her hand and dragged her into his compartment, closed the door, then pulled Trina into his arms.

She didn't protest. In fact, her eyes widened until he could see the whites all the way around. Afraid? He didn't think so. Shocked? Surprised would be closer. Her lips were mashed together in a straight line.

"Do that again." He put his hand on the back of her neck and tilted her head back so he could see her better. Those blasted feathers fluttered between them. He found the hat pin, pulled it out and lifted the hat from her head, then pitched it onto the chair with his.

She knew she should struggle and protest. So why didn't she? Kissing Mr. Hart would be dull and tedious. Totally forgettable. Wouldn't it? She reached to see if her hair stuck out where the hat pin had pulled loose. It seemed to be flying everywhere. "Do what again?"

"Stick out your bottom lip. Pout."

"I don't under—"

"Just do it."

With a gulp and a deep breath, Trina stuck out her bottom lip.

Gabriel sucked that pouty lip into his mouth and felt her shudder from the crown of her head to, he suspected, her dainty little toes. If she was going to slap his face and report his behavior to Papa, she'd do it now.

Trina, startled beyond words, wound her arms around his neck. The kiss was neither dull nor tedious. Mercy! Those other boys she'd kissed—whatever their names had been—had no idea whatsoever how to kiss. No wonder it had been so dull. Gabriel Hart, on the other hand, knew exactly what kissing was all about. If he thought she was going to push him away…

Gabriel smiled through the kiss. He could tell she hadn't been kissed—really kissed—before. She might have let her young man press his lips to hers, but he'd bet she'd never opened her lips and…

He pushed his tongue into her mouth.

Surprisingly, she opened wider, inviting what was undoubtedly new to her, and started making noises in her throat—little kitten noises—that drove Gabriel crazy. Never in his life had he kissed a woman who really knew how to kiss back. Not even Hannah—

He stiffened. And pulled away.

Trina knew exactly what was going on in his mind, and she wasn't about to stand for it.

"No, you don't, Gabriel. I'm not her. I'm me. You're kissing me. And you'd better keep kissing me until I say when."

Now he was shocked. So much so, he was able to push Hannah out of his mind for the moment.

"What happens if I don't keep kissing you, Miss McCabe?"

"You don't want to know. Just do it."

"Yes, ma'am."

He let her come to him this time. She didn't disappoint him. She seemed eager to taste him again, so he obliged. She ran her fingers up through his hair, along his scalp, and he trembled with the delicacy of her touch. When she put her tongue into his mouth he decided she was game for just about anything, short of hiking her skirts and joining him in bed. In time, though...

Gabriel moved one hand between them and tentatively placed it beneath her left breast, just to see if she'd stop him.

She didn't. In fact, she leaned back just a mite to give him more room.

He took advantage of that room and covered her breast with his hand. Damn, but women wore a lot of clothes. It was more like touching a saddle than a woman's curvy parts. But who was he to complain? Could she feel that, he wondered?

Trina squirmed a little, wishing she could actually feel his hand touching her. Too many underclothes, she decided. Still, it was nice, all the same, and devilishly naughty.

Trina knew she was acting like a hussy, but what the hell? as her brothers would say. The train would reach Silver Falls tomorrow and she'd never see Gabriel Hart again as long as she lived. Might as well add to her education the best she could while she had the chance. She wondered what else she might be able to learn....

"Buttons," she muttered against his mouth.

Gabriel looked straight into her eyes. "Buttons?"

Trina sighed in disappointment. He'd broken the spell. Why did he have to look at her? Why couldn't he just take the hint and...

Gabriel looked at the front of her blouse and saw the row of buttons down the front. Could she possibly want...

"You mean you want me to—"

A loud knock at the door made both of them jump.

Trina turned away to the window, grabbed her hat and straightened her skirts even though they didn't need straightening. She checked her left breast to see if his hand had left a telltale print. It hadn't. Thank goodness. She plopped the hat back on her head and frantically stuffed wayward curls beneath it. There wasn't time to ask Gabriel what he'd done with the pin.

Gabriel opened the door. Senator McCabe looked past him to Trina and nodded with a tight pinch to his mouth.

"I should have known I'd find you here. I apologize,

Mr. Hart, if my daughter has been bothering you again with all this protection nonsense.''

"It's quite all right, Senator. I think…" He ventured a glance at Trina, who had straightened her back into a poker and regained her composure. The hat sat slightly skewed to one side, feathers fluttering. "I think I've convinced her that everything is going to be fine now. Once we get the little things taken care of and out of the way."

Trina almost burst out laughing. Instead, she gave him a look that she hoped would say, "If you think you're going to get my buttons out of the way…" Then she stopped to consider what that would mean—and the fact she'd been the one to draw attention to her buttons in the first place. Her cheeks warmed until she knew they must be flaming.

"Absolutely, Mr. Hart. I can see now that I was silly to worry. I'm sure you're quite capable of taking care of any…little thing…that gets in your way."

Gabriel stifled his laughter by coughing. "Coal dust. Awful stuff," he mumbled.

Senator McCabe looked from his daughter to Gabriel and back again with a thoroughly puzzled expression. "Come on, Trina. I'm sure Mr. Hart needs to rest."

Trina offered her hand to Gabriel—just the fingertips—and squeezed lightly when he reciprocated. "Thank you, Mr. Hart, for your assistance in this matter. I'm sure we'll be seeing more of each other later." She left with her father, babbling something about being starved.

Gabriel closed the door behind her. Damnedest woman he'd ever known. The idea of seeing her again—seeing more of her, kissing her again—made him uncomfortably anxious.

Hannah's face chided from deep in his mind. He felt guilty as hell. Yet, thinking more about Hannah, he wondered if she might not encourage him to get back to living again.

Gabriel sank into the empty pale green chair, propped his elbows on the ragged spots and closed his eyes. Would life ever be normal for him again? Could it be, without Hannah? Without their child? His hands tightened into fists until his fingers ached from the pressure. Blackburn had murdered an unborn child. No man capable of such an act deserved to share the earth or breathe the same air as decent folk. Gabriel intended to see to it that Blackburn wouldn't for much longer.

A light tapping at the door brought Gabriel back to the present. Miss McCabe again? If so, she'd chosen a bad time to come for more kisses.

Gabriel didn't get up. "Who is it?"

"Amos McCabe. I beg your pardon, Mr. Hart, but there's a matter of the utmost importance I must discuss with you."

First the daughter, now the father. Gabriel wished again he'd chosen another train. He pushed himself out of the chair and opened the door.

The senator hurried inside. "Close the door. What I'm about to tell you shouldn't be heard by anyone but yourself."

Chapter Five

"All right, Senator, spit it out."

"This won't take long, Mr. Hart. May I sit down?" He sank into the chair by the window and tried to catch his breath. The altitude was already hindering his breathing. He sighed and shook his head. "It's gotten out of hand. I'm not sure I'm going to be able to keep things together much longer."

Gabriel matched the senator's sigh with one of his own, picked up his hat and sat down in the other chair, knowing it was a mistake. The senator might drone on for an hour if they got too comfy. He propped one ankle on the other knee and rested the hat in his lap. One blue feather fluttered from the hat to the floor. He decided to ignore it—and take up the matter later with Trina.

"I don't follow you, Senator. To tell the truth, I'm not sure I want to. Your business is yours. I don't aim to interfere or get mixed up in it." If he could just convince a certain redhead that was the case, his life would be a lot simpler.

McCabe nodded. "It's unfair of me to involve you, I know. But, as I said, things have gotten out of hand.

I'm not sure there's anyone else on this train I can trust.''

''What makes you certain you can trust me?''

''I know you. I know of you. After you've heard what I have to say, if you decide you don't want any part of it, I'll shake your hand and honor your wishes. Fair enough?''

A trap. If he said no to whatever the hell was stuck in McCabe's craw, Gabriel would come out a coward, or, at least, an uncaring son of a bitch. There was no way out he could see.

''Spill it, Senator. I'm listening.'' Gabriel reached for his watch and flipped open the cover to give the idea he didn't want to spend all day jawing.

''Thank you, Mr. Hart. You won't be sorry.''

''I already am.''

The senator looked a bit guilty at that, but it didn't stop him. ''The two men who've been killed—''

''Do you admit you pushed a man off this train?''

McCabe stopped. ''I...pushed him?''

''Your daughter saw it happen.''

''She told you that?''

''I saw her face when she was standing at that window. Nothing else would have disturbed her that much.'' He figured he'd protect Trina's little indiscretion for the time being. No use in getting the senator riled at his daughter.

McCabe nodded. ''Very well. I watched while Wilson pushed him—before he could push me.''

''So it was self-defense.''

''Yes, indeed.''

''Just as it was with the man Wilson shot. The man without a gun.''

"No gun? That's nonsense. Of course he had a gun. If Wilson hadn't shot him—"

"No gun, Senator. Why don't you cut the bull and tell the truth? Why did you let him kill those two men?"

McCabe hesitated, running one hand over his mustache. "You want the truth? Here it is." McCabe licked his lips, looking everywhere in the room except at Gabriel.

"Those men have been threatening me for the past month—since Lucias Cobb decided to deed his land to the state of Colorado. They're Cobb's sorry kin, and they claim the land is rightfully theirs. Cobb wanted to make sure they never got their filthy hands on it, so he decided to give it to the state. I was told—weeks ago—that if I showed up in Silver Falls to accept the land on behalf of the state, they'd kill me before I could do it. When they tried, they were killed—in self-defense. It's as simple as that."

Gabriel didn't buy it. The story was too pat, and it didn't explain why McCabe had let an unarmed man be shot. Something wasn't right, and Gabriel knew McCabe wasn't telling him the whole story.

"What do you want me to do about all this, Senator?" Gabriel uncrossed his legs.

"Protect me from these scoundrels until we get to Silver Falls. And, when we get there, be my bodyguard until I've had a chance to secure the deed. Once that's done, Cobb's kin will be powerless." McCabe dug deep in his coat pocket. "I don't expect you to do it for nothing." He pulled out a small roll of bills and peeled off several. "I intend to pay well for your services."

"Senator, I—"

"Don't say no right off. Think about it." He got up and laid the bills on his chair. "Consider this payment for services already rendered. If you decide to take me up on the offer, there'll be more, I assure you. Much more.'' He extended his hand. "Think it over. I'll be in my quarters.''

Gabriel shook his hand, then stood silent while the senator left.

"Damn.'' Gabriel stared at the money on the chair. Better than a hundred dollars, from the looks of it. McCabe was desperate. If what he confessed was the truth, he had every right to be. Yet a gut feeling told Gabriel the senator had lied through his teeth, beginning to end. Something in his eyes... If Gabriel agreed to provide protection, and the senator was caught up in something illegal, then Gabriel would be involved, as well. Yet if his story—far-fetched as it sounded— proved to be true, and Gabriel didn't protect him...

Gabriel stared out the window at snow-covered pines whizzing past, and tried to decide what to do. If ever he'd been between a rock and a hard place, this was it.

Trina saw her father entering Gabriel's compartment. Luckily, he didn't catch her spying. This was her chance to get that key—if her father didn't have it in his pocket.

Trina tiptoed down the corridor and into her father's compartment. She closed the door then stood with her back against it, surveying the room. Where might he have put it? Methodically she went through everything piece by piece: his valise, which contained a bunch of papers, but no key; his overcoat pockets—nothing there to shout about; and finally the chest of drawers in the water closet. Nothing. Hell's bells! He had it in his pocket for sure.

She was about to go back to her own quarters when

she spied something in the corner between one of the chairs and the baseboard heater.

"Absentminded old fool," she muttered. "Why, this could've caught on fire and burned up the whole train." She reached for the leather case and pulled it into the center of the room. It was hot on the side touching the heater. Locked. Just like the trunks. What could her father be carrying that had to be locked up?

A noise in the corridor reminded her to hurry a bit. She replaced the leather case, taking care it didn't lean against the heater this time, and went back to the door.

Easing it open just enough to peek out, she waited until a woman with two noisy children disappeared into a compartment at the far end of the car, verified the corridor was empty, then tiptoed back to her own compartment as the door to Gabriel's quarters opened and her father emerged. Trina leaned against the door, puffing a little from the excitement of her clandestine activities, and listened for conversation, but there was none.

What did her father want with Gabriel? Obviously, protection. But what about the trunks and that strange case? She couldn't remember ever seeing that case in his study at home. Those items might indicate other doings afoot. If only she could get his keys so she could see what was hiding in those mysterious parcels....

When Gabriel woke from a restless sleep, the sun had slipped behind the mountain. Shadows enclosed the train in gloomy darkness.

His stomach rumbled. A steak would go down mighty good right now. Rare, with juices running out when he sliced through. Some fried potatoes and onions would taste pretty good, too.

Gabriel washed his face and hands and tried to wake

up a little more. Sleeping in the daytime had become a habit while he was mending. He'd have to quit it pretty soon. It didn't look good at all for a grown man to take naps like a little kid.

He decided to change his shirt while freshening up. The one he'd been wearing all day—and sleeping in for the past couple of hours—had wrinkled badly.

Gabriel pulled on a fresh shirt, tucked it in, then made his way forward to the dining car, hooked on in front of the passenger car. A steward met him at the door.

"Ah, Mr. Hart. Senator McCabe requests that you join him for dinner."

Great. Just great. How could he refuse without seeming rude? He followed the steward to where the senator and Trina sat on opposite sides of the table.

"Senator. Miss McCabe." He noticed she'd left the feathered hat in her compartment. Wise decision. Her hair was as red as a Hereford calf, falling down her back, almost to her waist.

Trina indicated the chair next to hers. "So glad you could join us, Mr. Hart."

Gabriel sat down, acutely aware the table was so small and the chairs so close together that their elbows touched.

Senator McCabe gave Gabriel a questioning look.

Gabriel ignored it, answering silently that he hadn't made up his mind yet.

Trina studied both of them carefully, wondering what all the unspoken communication was about, then launched into a lively spiel concerning the china and silver on the table.

Gabriel hardly listened. Who cared about the dishes? Or the pink and purple broomstraw flowers in a glass vase? Or the linen tablecloth and napkins?

McCabe commented occasionally, but his mind clearly wasn't on the table setting, either.

The steward took their orders. Gabriel asked for a rare steak and fried potatoes with onions, the senator took the same and Trina selected some sort of fancy chicken dish with sauce on top and vegetables on the side. The steward filled their glasses with water and left.

Gabriel wished for a more substantial beverage, but decided he could wait until later, just before bedtime. And only a short one then. The senator's actions demonstrated an undercurrent of fear and anxiety Gabriel didn't like one bit. Even though things had settled down considerably since the senator had disposed of those two men, Gabriel knew better than to relax.

When their food arrived, Gabriel cut into the steak, then almost dropped his knife. Under the tablecloth Trina's hand tightened on his knee.

What the devil was she up to? Was she trying to alert him to danger of some sort? He ventured a sideways glance at her, but she chattered merrily to her father about some sort of society something Gabriel knew nothing about. Her hand left his leg and reappeared holding her napkin. She dabbed at her lips daintily and looked squarely at him.

"How is your meat, Mr. Hart?"

Gabriel looked off down the car, at his steak, anywhere but at her. "Fine, ma'am. Just fine."

She replaced the napkin in her lap.

Her hand squeezed his thigh this time and Gabriel choked on his steak. He hacked until his throat was clear, then gulped water until he could breathe again.

"Something wrong with your steak?" Senator McCabe frowned with concern.

"No, Senator. Just...hard to swallow." He gave

Trina a look meant to embarrass her, but it had the opposite effect. She squeezed his thigh again, letting her fingers dance around a little.

What a tart she was! Gabriel decided to shock her into being the lady she was supposed to be. He dropped his left hand to his lap, took her hand in his and brought it higher on his thigh until her hand touched—

Trina jerked her hand away and choked on a bite of chicken. Gabriel slapped her on the back.

"Now you, Trina?" Senator McCabe looked back and forth between Gabriel and his daughter, who was so red in the face she could have been suffering a stroke. "Perhaps I should speak to the chef. Something is causing both of you to strangle."

"I don't think that'll be necessary, Senator." Gabriel patted Trina on the back again and smiled. "She'll be fine. I think she may have bitten off more than she could chew, that's all."

Trina gasped for breath and glared at Gabriel. How dare he do such a crude thing to her, right in front of her father? Why, he'd practically...practically...as a matter of fact, he'd actually...put her hand... She sputtered again and reached for her water glass.

"Confound it, Trina, are you all right, or aren't you?"

Gabriel picked up his napkin and handed it to her, thinking she might need an extra. "She's fine, Senator."

When she took the napkin, Gabriel thought about squeezing her knee, but it would set her to choking again, as sure as shootin'. He decided to leave well enough alone.

They finished the meal with little conversation.

Gabriel enjoyed Trina's discomfort immensely. In fact, it made him happier than he'd been in months.

Trina could hardly wait for the meal to end. She wanted to wring Gabriel's neck! That's exactly what she intended to do, just as soon as the train was quiet and everyone else was asleep. She'd teach Gabriel Hart a thing or two about embarrassing Katrina McCabe!

Chapter Six

Midnight. As far as Trina could determine, the entire train—with the exception of the engineer, of course—was asleep. No one would hear when she gave Gabriel Hart a piece of her mind. No man would embarrass Katrina McCabe and get away with it unscathed.

Trina eased into the corridor and looked carefully up and down, making sure no one was out and about at this hour. Even the excited, rowdy children at the end were sound asleep. The train's motion had slowed considerably, now that they were higher in the mountains. The gentle swaying and rhythmic clicking of the machinery locking the cars together proved extremely conducive to sleep. But Trina had no intention of sleeping.

She tiptoed to Gabriel's door and listened. No sound within. Dreaming, no doubt, of how he'd humiliated her in front of her father. Just because she'd squeezed his leg a couple of times was no excuse for what he'd done. Why, all she'd wanted was to shake him up a little—show him that she was in control of the situation. He'd spoiled it by...

A noise. Footsteps inside. A door bumping. The water closet? Trina waited a minute, then straightened her spine and knocked lightly. She certainly didn't want to wake her father. No response.

She knocked again, harder this time.

The knob turned and Gabriel looked out.

Before Trina could say anything, he opened the door wider, grabbed her arm and pulled her into the room. With one smooth motion he closed the door and turned the lock.

"Mr.—"

"Shut up." He leaned toward her stammering mouth.

"But—"

"Shut up." He clamped his mouth over hers and pulled her hard against him.

Trina couldn't move, his hold on her was so tight, and she couldn't breathe because he was kissing her...kissing her so...deliciously. She gave in and kissed him back.

Gabriel took a step toward the bed he'd fallen into over an hour ago, and pulled Trina along with him. Her tongue in his mouth made his head swim, and the feel of her against his bare chest conjured up pictures in his head—and sensations in his loins—of her bare skin next to his. But she was trussed up like a turkey, and it would take at least ten minutes of dedicated work to loosen all the stays and laces associated with that confounded corset she was wearing. How did women tolerate such a torturous device? Was she so fat she had to hold in the rolls in order to appear slender? He decided, right then and there, to find out for himself.

"Buttons..." she mumbled against his lips.

Gabriel laughed out loud.

Trina couldn't believe her ears. He'd wake the whole train if he didn't stop all that noisy laughing! Trina clamped her hands behind his neck and brought his mouth down to hers again to shut him up.

Gabriel didn't mind. He fumbled with the small, round buttons, but they frustrated him completely. He took hold of each side of the blouse and ripped the rest of the buttons off.

Trina let out a little shriek, but decided what was done was done. Hungrily she pulled him closer, amazed he could produce such a fever pitch in her. Never had she felt so...well, so alive! So excited! So anxious. It wasn't what she'd come for. Was it? Perhaps it was. Perhaps— Oh, dear God. Oh...dear...oh...

Gabriel found her breasts beneath the blouse and camisole. Even though they crowded upward because of that infernal corset, he could tell there wasn't an extra ounce of fat on this woman. No, indeed. She didn't need a corset. Or any clothes at all, for that matter. In fact, he suspected, buck naked she might be the most beautiful thing he'd ever laid eyes on, bar none.

Trina gulped and gasped and tried to breathe, but found it impossible with sensational new feelings skittering through her. The corset squeezed the life out of her with every shuddering breath. He'd started to work on loosening the laces, but he'd never manage it by himself. Should she help? Did she dare? Could she stand it if she didn't?

Gabriel withdrew and sighed. "I give up. How do I get rid of this...this dadblasted thing?"

Trina swallowed and wished her head would clear. What to do? What she *should* do? Or what she *wanted* to do?

"In the back. Let me."

Gabriel looked into her eyes with nothing more than a question.

Not wanting to give a straight answer, Trina ignored the question and slipped her blouse out of the skirt and off, so she could get at the laces. But she couldn't reach far enough.

"Turn around."

Gabriel's voice had dropped at least two tones. Anger? She didn't think so. Passion and desire? A definite possibility. Trina knew it was time to make up her mind exactly what she wanted to happen next.

"Turn around!"

"Mr. Hart?"

"What is it...Miss McCabe?"

"I...that is...I didn't come here to..." Her face colored dark red and she wondered if he could tell it, even in the near dark.

"Why *did* you come here?"

"To give you..." Her eyes had finally adjusted to the pale moonlight in the room. She saw clearly, for the first time, that Gabriel was naked. At least, what she could see of him was. His chest was covered with dark hair, curled and tangled over smooth muscles. She'd always assumed a man's skin would be rough where a woman's skin was soft. But Gabriel's...

Gabriel saw how she looked at him, and took advantage of her hesitation. He leaned forward until his lips touched the satiny curve of her neck, then filtered her hair, now in disarray, through his fingers and over her shoulder out of the way, to breathe into her ear ever so lightly until he felt her shiver. "Give me what?"

"A piece..."

He sucked her earlobe into his mouth and twirled his tongue around it until she shivered again.

"Of...my...mind..."

"Your mind?"

"Oh, to hell with it!" She whirled around so suddenly, he almost fell to the floor. "Those laces at the bottom. Pull them and the whole thing will come off."

Gabriel laughed out loud again and did as she instructed. When the offending garment finally gave up and came loose, Gabriel tossed it into a corner and circled her waist—bare, slender, soft as a kitten—with his hands. She inhaled so deeply, his fingers almost touched.

"Why do you wear that thing, anyway?"

"Ladies always wear corsets, Mr. Hart."

Still stuck on calling him "Mr. Hart," was she? He'd see what he could do about that. Gabriel gave her other ear the same attention he'd bestowed on the first one. Her fingers explored their way through his chest hair and around his neck and continued over his scalp until he shivered, too.

Damn, but this woman knew exactly what made him crazy. When she leaned over far enough to pull his earlobe into her mouth, he settled back to enjoy, and tried not to think about how long it had been since he'd made love—and to whom. It had been much too long. Trina was too near and too available to let himself give in to any guilt attacks that would deprive him of the pleasure he'd been without for better than a year.

Gabriel pushed Trina back on the bed and pulled the skirt and petticoats off her long legs, leaving only her bloomers. Her breasts protruded from her slender frame even though she lay flat. He had such a hunger for them, he couldn't wait another minute. With a smile and a featherlight kiss to her lips, Gabriel bent to kiss and touch and caress the skin he suspected had never been kissed or touched or caressed before. Her reaction when he licked her nipples told him he was right. When he alternately pulled the now-erect points into his mouth, the noises she made told him he hadn't lost his touch in pleasing a woman.

Trina couldn't believe what was happening to her body. Instead of pleasure just where he was kissing, the exquisite sensations went all through her. Right down to her toes, and little tingly whirls on top of her head. And her fingers seemed ten times more sensitive as they explored his back and neck and scalp. In fact, it was so wonderful, she thought she might die of pleasure if he didn't stop soon. But, please God, she prayed, don't let him stop. Nothing could feel as good as what she was feeling now. Nothing.

Several loud knocks at the door interrupted.

"Hart? I have to see you. Now."

Amos McCabe.

Gabriel held up one hand to silence Trina's gasping, then motioned her quiet and still. He went to the door, but didn't open it.

"What is it, Senator? I'm trying to get some shut-eye."

"I apologize for disturbing you this late, but I must speak to you."

Trina's eyes got as big as the moon. She shook her head violently and held her hands together as though praying. Gabriel waved her fears away.

"Give me a minute to put some clothes on."

Trina couldn't believe it! Was he actually going to let her father in? How on earth could she explain? Her father might try to kill Gabriel on the spot. Hell's bells!

Gabriel took his time putting on his pants and shirt, then went back to the door. In one smooth motion he opened the door and went out into the corridor.

"With the bed made down, there's not much room

for entertaining guests, Senator. Let's go to your quarters.''

Amos McCabe hesitated only a moment before agreeing that was a good idea. He led the way, with Gabriel close behind. Gabriel paused at the door and glanced toward his own compartment. Trina peeked through the cracked door. He motioned toward her quarters, then went inside and closed the door behind him.

Trina didn't waste any time. She gathered her clothing into a wad, then, wearing only her bloomers, praying no one else would decide to take a middle-of-the-night stroll, made a dash for her room and safety.

It was all she could do not to slam the door after she made it inside. Her chest heaved so violently, one would have thought she'd run from the house to the barn and back. Mercy. When she'd decided to tell Gabriel exactly how she felt about him insulting her, she'd never in her wildest dreams pictured herself running practically naked across the train, clutching her clothes across her naked bosom.

Trina's breathing slowed somewhat and she finally managed a deep breath. There were other things this night had brought that she'd never have dreamed of, as well. She closed her eyes and tried to recall every precious moment. Then her mind cleared.

If only her father hadn't come to the door, what might have happened....

She thought about letting Geoffrey touch her the way Gabriel had. It made her shiver. And cringe. She knew that very instant she could never marry Geoffrey.

He simply wasn't Gabriel.

Poor Geoffrey. Would he cry when she told him she couldn't see him again? Probably not. He might plead

with her to change her mind. But she wouldn't. Now
that she'd met Gabriel, her life had changed forever.

A door opened and closed in the corridor.

Trina peeked out and saw Gabriel at his own door.

She waggled her fingers at him. Then, with a feeling
of sheer wickedness, touched her palm to her lips and
blew him a kiss.

Gabriel smiled and shook his head, then went into his
quarters and closed the door.

Trina closed hers, too, and flopped onto the bed,
which she'd made down before going to give Mr. Hart
a piece of her mind. My, but what she'd given him
instead! She started to giggle and couldn't stop.

Gabriel took off his clothes—again—and stretched
out on the bed, wrinkled and slightly damp. Would he
ever get any sleep tonight?

He'd promised protection for the senator while they
were on the train, but he hadn't promised anything after
they reached Silver Falls.

He thought about Trina. Alive in his arms. Loving
the way he'd touched her, kissed her.

Damn. What could have possessed him to do such a
thing? He had to be crazy. In the morning she'd feel
ashamed and guilty, and would probably be madder
than a hornet, to boot. She'd tell "Papa" that mean old
Mr. Hart had dragged her into his room and molested
her. When they got back to Denver there'd be three
brothers to deal with. Gabriel wouldn't be able to say
a word in his own defense, because it would mean calling Trina a floozy.

Gabriel laughed and turned onto his side. She'd acted
like a floozy tonight. The only difference was that a
floozy pretended to like sex, and Trina had loved it—

what she'd experienced of it, anyway. She'd like the rest, too. He'd bet his Sunday buttons on it.

Damnedest woman…

Well, whatever happened would happen, and he'd deal with it when it did. He had to have some sleep so his shooting hand wouldn't shake tomorrow when he aimed his Colt at Blackburn's heart. No. Knees first. Then elbows. Then the hand that had held the knife. Then his gut. Blackburn didn't deserve to die quickly.

Trina. Handfuls of red hair scattered over his pillow. Eyes wide. Bottom lip in his mouth. Nipples that stuck out about a mile when he kissed them. Her tongue in his mouth. What a woman.

Sleep. That's what he needed.

Trina… Trina… Trina…

Next morning the steward met Gabriel at the door to the dining car with the request that he join Senator and Miss McCabe at their table.

Gabriel's gut tied itself into a knot. Had she told her father?

The senator grinned and waved.

Not yet, anyway.

Gabriel shook hands with the senator, tipped his hat to Trina, then sat next to her, just as he had the evening before.

"Did you sleep well, Mr. Hart?" Trina beamed at him over a plate of fried eggs, biscuits and a thick slice of ham.

"Uh…yes, ma'am. Thank you kindly. After I finally got to sleep, I hardly moved till morning."

Amos cleared his throat noisily. "My apologies again, Mr. Hart, for disturbing you so late. I couldn't sleep until we'd reached an agreement."

"You didn't awaken Mr. Hart too late, I hope."

"Long after you were in bed, my dear."

Gabriel almost choked on his coffee. Trina had been in bed, all right. It just hadn't been her own.

With a jolt Gabriel felt Trina's hand on his thigh under the table. She inched her way upward—

He spilled his coffee on the linen tablecloth.

"Oh, dear." Trina dabbed at the wet spot. "I hope you didn't burn yourself, Mr. Hart."

"I'm fine. Thank you...Miss McCabe."

The senator frowned. "A jinx must have followed us on this train. I've never seen so many accidents in such a short time."

"It's nothing, Papa. Just the bumpy movements of the train, that's all."

The ride seemed unusually smooth to Gabriel. But then, he felt unusually smooth this morning, himself. He watched Trina fork a piece of ham into her mouth and had the urge to kiss her, ham and all.

The steward brought his breakfast and he gratefully commenced eating his own ham and eggs. Damn, but everything tasted good. As he sipped at his cup, the train lurched. Hot coffee spilled over Gabriel's chin.

"Damn!" He grabbed his napkin, but the coffee had already burned all it was going to burn. "Excuse my language, ma'am. Are we stopping, or what?"

"It would appear so." McCabe motioned to the nearest steward, who came immediately. "Why are we stopping?"

"I'll check, sir." He disappeared down the aisle.

Gabriel leaned across Trina to peer out the window, catching the scent of her perfume. Different this morning. More like honeysuckle. The train was slowing.

"I'll be back." Gabriel got up and left the car. He met the baggage man coming forward.

"Why are we stopping?"

"I don't know, sir. I was just on my way to find out. I've looked down the tracks as far as I can see. There don't seem to be nothing in the way to stop us. Someone said it was a snowslide, farther around the bend. If that's what it is, it won't be long before we're goin' again. We brought shovels."

Gabriel waited until the train came to a complete stop, then stepped down to the ground and walked forward. Cliffs jutted straight up and straight down from the area carved from the mountain for tracks, leaving little room for walking alongside the train. Gabriel picked his way carefully, trying to see around the next bend, with no luck.

A hammer clicked back. "Hold it right there, Hart."

Gabriel turned around slowly with his hands half-raised. Wilson. The man with the twitch. Gabriel had had a hunch all along he was up to no good, in spite of his being McCabe's bodyguard. "What's going on here?"

"Just a little delay, that's all. Snowslide. I hear you've agreed to protect McCabe while he's on this train. That right?"

"I don't see it's any of your business what I do."

"When it concerns Cobb's land, it concerns me."

Gabriel stared straight at the man holding the gun on him. The twitch got worse. Gabriel figured he was wound tighter than a rattler, ready to spring. It shouldn't take much to make him strike.

"Cobb doesn't concern me. Suppose you put that gun down and we'll talk about it."

"Sorry, Hart. Can't do that."

From somewhere up the line came a shout. The track had been cleared. The distraction was just enough to give Gabriel the advantage. With a short lunge, he caught the gunman off guard. The pistol went flying down the ravine. One hard chop to the chin, and he lay still in the snow.

Gunshots rang out across the mountain. Gabriel dropped to his knees and slid under the train.

Chapter Seven

The last echo of gunshots faded until only the hesitant chuffing of the stalled locomotive remained.

Wilson lay in the snow, shaking his head, trying to clear his rattled senses. When he finally focused his eyes, Gabriel cocked the hammer of the Colt.

"Don't move. I'd hate to stain the snow bright red."

Wilson froze—all but his eyes. The twitch doubled in speed.

Gabriel rolled hard left just in time to avoid the bullet whizzing past him from thirty feet away, and triggered his Colt three times. A man, kneeling to take aim under the car, slumped into the snow on top of his rifle just as the train lurched and slowly started to move.

Wilson had fled, using the distraction to get away— on board or into the trees, Gabriel had no idea.

Gabriel rolled out from under the train, gave a quick look in both directions, then climbed back onto the Pullman platform. The train picked up speed slowly, laboring to recover momentum. Gabriel stopped outside the door and watched the reflection of the Pullman's window in the baggage car window opposite. A man. Just inside the door.

Gabriel took a slow, deep breath, hunkered down a little to keep from being seen, and reached for the handle—but not in time. The door slammed hard against him. He flinched just enough to keep from being crushed.

He grabbed the man by the collar—Wilson again—dragged the foul-smelling hombre to the railing and dangled him over the side, so he'd land just in front of the wheels of the baggage car if Gabriel decided to let go.

Wilson pleaded with him, terrified. Gabriel lowered him another inch.

"Don't kill me! In God's name—I'll do anything—just don't kill me!"

With a cold smile, Gabriel pulled him up just to the point where his toes could touch the floor.

"Start talkin'."

He wheezed and gasped. "Give me...a minute...."

It was time he and this piece of trash had a private talk.

"Come on."

He cried out again when Gabriel pushed him toward the door of the baggage car.

In the dining car children cried, stewards tried to clean up spilled water glasses, people milled about, asking over and over why the train had stopped. Trina couldn't think about anything except Gabriel. Had he been involved in the shooting they'd heard? Where was he now? She had to find him.

Amos McCabe was too busy shouting orders to take notice of Trina's doings, so she slipped out of the car, hurried through the passenger car to the Pullman—he wasn't among the clutch of confused passengers—and into the baggage car. There was no one there, only the dead body. The train jerked, then began to move. Someone came onto the platform outside. She went to the window.

Gabriel! Dropping a man over the rail! The train moved again, sluggishly. Did he intend to kill that man? Abruptly, Gabriel pushed him toward the baggage car door.

Trina backed up, searching frantically for a place to hide. She spied the trunks. There was barely room behind them, but she managed to squeeze into the space. She flattened herself against the cold wooden floor and tried not to breathe. From the sound of it, Gabriel was furious, and the man with him clearly terrified. She managed to inch over just enough to see through a space between the trunks, then lay perfectly still, listened and watched.

Gabriel picked the man up by his shirt until his heels almost cleared the floor, then glared at him with fire in his eyes.

"I'm listening."

The man said nothing.

"All right. Have it your way." Gabriel dragged him back toward the door.

"Don't throw me under them wheels! I'll talk."

Gabriel dropped him on the floor. The breath rushed out of him. "I'm listening."

"Cobb. I work for Cobb." His eye twitched so violently, he seemed to be winking, over and over again. "I'm Wilson. James Wilson."

"And?"

"I was sent to keep the senator from gettin' to Silver Falls. I tried to get in good with him so's I could find out what he's plannin' and report back to Silver Falls to warn 'em aheada time. He hired me as bodyguard.''

"And?"

"That's it. McCabe hired you to protect him, so we figured he was on to us. You had to go."

Gabriel got that itchy feeling again. The senator had lied. "Senator McCabe told me he was accepting Cobb's land for the state. You don't seem to agree with that."

A strange, high-pitched laugh escaped Wilson's cracked lips. "That senator's a sly one, all right. Makes everybody think he's doing the state's business, when in truth he's only out for hisself. When a man like McCabe starts doing business with the scum he's been associating with lately, then it ain't hard to figure out he's in business for somebody other than the state of Colorado."

"What scum?"

"In Silver Falls. Been there since last spring. Scum's too good a name for him. A killer. A heart that's nothing but cold stone. Uglier 'n sin. I'd like to shake the hand of the man who gouged out one of his eyes."

Gabriel's chest burned until he could hardly take a breath. Blood roared through him, hot and angry. His hands tightened into fists, his knuckles white with the strain. Wilson slid away across the floor, terrified of the hatred he saw in Gabriel's face.

"You know him, don't you?" Wilson put one hand over his twitching eye.

Gabriel nodded.

"Blackburn. Otis Blackburn," Wilson whispered, apparently afraid to say more.

The sound of that name being spoken aloud was almost more than Gabriel could endure. He stepped forward, grabbed Wilson by the front of his shirt and hauled him to his feet. Wilson whimpered in fear.

"You know where he's holed up in Silver Falls?"

Wilson shook his head. Sweat poured from his face in rivers. Silent, he waited, gulping for air and shaking with fear.

Gabriel's mind started to clear. He had to stay calm. "Tell me what you know about McCabe and... Blackburn. Don't leave anything out if you want to leave this car walking and not flying."

Wilson nodded and started to talk. Ten minutes later Gabriel turned and left the car. Wilson slumped to the floor and ran trembling hands through his greasy hair. There was going to be big trouble when they got to Silver Falls, and McCabe's part of it was going to be a slight annoyance compared to what Wilson suspected would happen to Blackburn when Gabriel Hart caught him.

Wilson got up from the floor and shuffled out the front door of the car, stepping over trunks and boxes that had shifted when the train stopped.

Trina waited a full minute after Wilson left the car before she moved. She stood up carefully, shaking with cold and with the impact of what she'd seen and heard.

Could it be true? Her father a thief? Working with such an evil man? Why did Gabriel hate Blackburn so? She had to have answers. Without a doubt, those answers couldn't come from her father. She had to talk to Gabriel.

She hurried back to the Pullman and paused for a moment to soak up some warmth. Her skin flushed with the sudden change in temperature and she wished she could take off a couple of layers of clothing until she adjusted, but there was no time for adjustment. Wilson must have gone on to the passenger car. Thank heaven!

Gabriel's door was closed. Had he gone back to his quarters? Or had he— The thought made her shiver harder. If, in his present state of mind, he'd gone to confront her father about his association with Blackburn, he might—

Trina hurried to Gabriel's door, praying he'd be there. She knocked. No response. Then she heard the water closet door just as she'd heard it the night before and released a long, relieved sigh. He'd come here to cool off first. She knocked again.

The door cracked open an inch. Gabriel looked out and, just as he'd done last night, reached out, pulled her into the compartment and locked the door.

That's as far as the similarity went. Gabriel's face, wet from being splashed with water, still bore all the signs of hatred and anger she'd witnessed in the baggage car.

Gabriel's emotions slowly settled into the realm of logic and reality. Learning that McCabe was working with Blackburn had almost pushed him over the edge. He couldn't let that happen again.

"Gabriel—"

"Shut up."

"But I—"

"I said, shut up!" Gabriel's grip on her arms tightened until he realized he was hurting her. He eased up a little. "I can't play games with you, Trina. Not anymore."

"I know. I heard."

"Heard what?" Gabriel peered into her eyes. What he saw wasn't fear. He pushed her away and strode to the window, trying harder to calm himself, to save the anger.

"I heard...that is, I was in the baggage car when—"

Gabriel jerked around. "You were where?"

"In the baggage car. I went looking for you when the train stopped. I didn't mean to spy, Gabriel. It just happened. I swear to you, I was there by accident." Would he believe her?

"What did you hear?"

"Everything you said to that awful man. And..." She stopped and closed her eyes. The reality of the situation was finally starting to soak in. "And...what he said to you. But it can't be true, Gabriel. It just can't."

What was he to do now? Gabriel couldn't tell her he believed Wilson's story—at least, part of it. It made more sense than anything he'd heard so far. He didn't think Wilson would have risked lying. If he'd been told to betray his own mother, he'd been scared enough to do that. No, he'd told the straight story. Or, what he believed to be the straight story, anyway. If he hadn't, and Gabriel ever caught up with him again...

Trina tried to touch Gabriel's arm, but he stepped back, just out of reach. She folded her arms in front of her, embarrassed, then let them drop to her sides in dismay. "I just can't believe my father is a thief. There has to be some other explanation. I can't ask him straight out if what I heard is true."

That much was sure. Gabriel realized, right then and there, that Trina had to keep quiet about this whole messy business. If she told her father what Wilson had said, and it proved to be the truth, then McCabe would decide Gabriel had to be killed in order to protect his deal with Blackburn. Damn. What a hell of a day this had been.

Gabriel's rage subsided. He had to get back to cold, hard facts. The first fact at hand was comforting Trina and convincing her to keep her mouth shut.

"Come here, Trina. It's going to be all right."

They were exactly the words Trina needed to hear. She went straight into Gabriel's arms and held him as tightly as she could. "Is it true, Gabriel? About my father?"

He kissed her lightly. "I don't know. I have to find out, though. Whatever I learn, I'll have to do what's required. I want you to know that."

"I know. But you wouldn't…that is, he won't be—"

"I'd never shoot a man without cause, Trina. If he gives me no choice…"

She knew she should be furious with him for such a statement, but she couldn't do anything but hold him.

Chapter Eight

Almost noon. Gabriel eased Trina back to her own quarters to lie down for a while. She wasn't wild about the idea, but Gabriel needed time to think and decide what to do next.

Curiously, no one had come looking for him after he shot that man. Wilson seemed to have disappeared, too. What was the senator doing? The train ought to be crawling with people trying to find out what had happened, yet life perked along as usual. Curious. Mighty curious.

Gabriel moved forward to the passenger car. McCabe sat at the far end with three men. He saw Gabriel and motioned him to join them.

Gabriel's gut tightened. One of the men was James Wilson. He'd have to play along and learn as much as he could, then make an accurate judgment as to what the hell was going on.

"Senator." He sat across the aisle, preferring distance between himself and a man who'd do business with Blackburn. Gabriel didn't look straight at Wilson, who had started to sweat.

"Mr. Hart, I trust you weren't injured back there."

"Spit it out, Senator."

"All right. I can see you're a man of no nonsense." McCabe shifted in his chair and glanced at each of the three men sitting with him before he looked back at Gabriel. "There are men on this train trying to kill me. I told you earlier."

"You told me."

"Well, the train was stopped for exactly that purpose. I escaped injury because of these men." He indicated his companions. "I've hired them to protect me, just as I've hired you."

"I quit, Senator."

Wilson's eye twitched violently.

"Now, wait a minute. You agreed—"

"That was before the train stopped. Before a man aimed a gun at me. Before a third man tried to shoot me and ended up dead. Before I learned the whole story."

Wilson coughed so hard it seemed he might choke to death. Gabriel never looked at him. He wanted the senator to sweat a little, just as Wilson was sweating. To wonder what Gabriel knew and what had to be done about it. But the senator didn't sweat. Instead, he seemed curious.

"Just what story is that, Mr. Hart?"

It was just the reaction he wanted from McCabe. "About the land. There's silver, isn't there?"

McCabe sat back and laughed. "Is that what you've learned? That there's silver on the land?" The laughter died. "Of course there's silver. The town wouldn't be there if it weren't for the silver they're finding inside that mountain. That silver is going to mean a lot for Colorado someday. That is, if I accomplish my task in Silver Falls."

Gabriel said nothing. He waited to see how far McCabe would go in the lie.

"That's why I need your help. The men who are out to murder me are no-good, ruthless killers, hired by a low-life slug so he can steal the land for himself—and the silver. You've never met such a man. Sooner kill a baby as an ant under his boot."

Gabriel stiffened.

Wilson ran a shaky hand across his face.

McCabe glanced around as though someone might be listening, then leaned forward and lowered his voice. "A one-eyed snake named Blackburn. Ever heard of him?"

The rage grew in Gabriel again, but he controlled it. "I've heard of him."

"Then you know how ruthless he is. Why, I've heard stories about the man that would keep you awake nights."

Gabriel swallowed the bile rising into his throat, bitter and acrid. "How did you come to know Blackburn, Senator?"

"Know of him. That's all. When I found out he was trying to force old man Cobb off the land, I offered Cobb a way to protect his claim forever. Once the state owns the property, Cobb will continue to live there, and his sons after him, working the mine and sharing in the profits, as long as there's a Cobb to occupy the place. Once I've accepted the land for Colorado, Blackburn will face the entire state if he threatens the Cobb family again. We'll put him away if he's bold enough to make a move. I swear it."

Gabriel didn't reply. The senator hadn't blinked an eye. If Gabriel hadn't already wrenched the opposite story from Wilson, on the verge of passing out right where he sat, Gabriel might have believed it. Now he didn't know what to believe.

"I'll get you to Silver Falls if I can, Senator. But, as I told you before, you'll be on your own from there. My business won't wait."

"I understand. I appreciate your help."

Gabriel went back to the Pullman to his compartment to sort things out. Who was telling the truth? And what should he do to find out?

Hell. Right now he just wanted—

The knock at the door made him smile. Yes, indeed. Exactly what he wanted right now.

When he opened the door a crack and saw Trina standing there, he pulled her inside and locked the door—the third time now, if he'd counted correctly. She came into his arms wanting to be kissed. He obliged.

For a reason he couldn't fathom, Gabriel wanted to forget everything—Wilson, McCabe, Silver Falls, the train and its passengers—and just kiss Trina. For this one moment, Katrina McCabe, soft and willing in his arms, proved to be exactly what Gabriel wanted and needed. Oh, God, how he needed her.

The squeal of brakes announced their arrival in Silver Falls.

Gabriel kissed Trina tenderly, then reached for his coat.

The corridor crawled with people gathering their things, going from one end of the car to the other and back again. The ladies and their noisy children occupied every inch of available walking space. He waited until they passed, then stepped outside and closed the door behind him. The lock clicked into place. Trina would gather herself before going back to her own quarters and her own life, leaving Gabriel alone in his.

The senator stopped him at the end of the car. His wheezing had gotten worse, the thin air affecting him terribly.

"Mr. Hart, I'd like to repeat my request…and offer you double—"

"No, thanks, Senator. I have business of my own to tend to. I won't have time for anything else. Sorry." He pushed his way past McCabe onto the platform.

Icy wind bit his face. He pulled his collar around his ears, his hat tighter on his head, his gloves on his hands, then followed two rowdy children down the steps. No sign of Wilson or other "bodyguards."

"Henry, get out of that man's way. I declare, child, I'm liable to whup the tar out of you before this day's done. Excuse him, please, sir. I declare—"

"It's all right." Gabriel tousled the boy's hair and felt a twinge of pain. His son might have looked like this boy.…

Henry flashed a gappy grin at Gabriel, then jumped down the steps to join his mother.

Gabriel almost let the hatred take him. But he'd need it later to do what he had to do. Until then, it had to crouch low and wait, fangs and talons sharp and poised for attack.

Gabriel stepped onto the platform of uneven, splintery planks and walked into the shack serving as depot for Silver Falls. The dirty little mining town hadn't existed before silver was found, and, in all probability, would die and decay into oblivion someday after the silver played out.

There was nothing inside the shack except a wall with a barred window and a bent old man on the other side wearing a green pasteboard visor over scraggly gray hair. Scribbling in a book with uneven, stained pages, he didn't look up until Gabriel knocked several times on the rough window frame.

"Huh? What is it?"

"I need information."

"Ain't got none."

He returned to his scribbling. Gabriel pulled the book away.

"Hey! Gimme that back! No trains outta here till tomorrow. I told you I don't know nothin' 'bout nobody!"

"Who does?"

"Hell if I know. Try the first saloon. The bartender knows more 'bout this town than most anybody."

Gabriel nodded and handed the book back. "Thanks."

No reply. He went right on scribbling as though Gabriel had never interrupted him.

Back outside, Gabriel noticed Amos McCabe getting off the train. He stopped to catch his breath, glanced around, then nodded at the baggage man down the line unloading the trunks McCabe had brought on board. Gabriel realized neither he nor Trina had learned the contents of those trunks. No telling what the senator was hauling up the mountain. Working with Blackburn, it could be anything.

Trina emerged behind her father and waited for him to help her down from the bottom step, which was a tall one, even for a man. She saw Gabriel, and her cheeks, red from the cold, got even redder. McCabe tugged at her arm, urging her to follow him down the street. With a sigh, she complied.

Gabriel watched them go. McCabe was here to see Blackburn on business. He might lead Gabriel right to him if his wheezing didn't keep him confined to the nearest chair—or bed. The best thing might be to wait and watch.

Saloons lined the main street, as in all mining towns. Other than a hotel and the bawdy houses, the saloons were the mainstay of the economy, with the exception of silver.

In the Red Devil Saloon, Gabriel ordered a beer and struck up a conversation with a man who appeared to have been sitting at the bar quite some time. Before long, Gabriel learned something interesting—and puzzling—about Silver Falls.

The mines surrounding the town had been belching silver ore from the bowels of the mountain for a good many months. It wouldn't be long before big machinery and a lot of cash would be necessary to coax any more from the maze of tunnels gouged from stone and dirt cradling veins of precious ore.

The highest grade of galena silver had been found in the King Solomon mine on the eastern side of the Animas River, where the mines lay at five thousand feet. Here at Silver Falls, the mines were at ten thousand feet, with a lesser grade of galena, and only a fraction of the yield. It all added up to more trouble for less silver. Silver Falls' existence would no doubt be in jeopardy in less than a year.

So why was McCabe here? His story about the state taking over the land for silver didn't wash.

Trina hadn't wanted to let Gabriel out of her sight, but with Papa struggling for every shallow breath, latched on to her elbow like a piece of tight elastic, she'd had little choice in the matter. He'd been angry she'd "disappeared" right before their arrival, and her explanation of feeling a bit ill and standing outside on the platform for fresh air hadn't been all that convincing, considering the weather and all. But he'd get over it eventually.

"Trina, I have business to tend to and I don't want to have to worry 'bout you gettin' into trouble."

"Papa, you know very well I—"

"I don't want to hear any more about it, Katrina!"

The use of her full name silenced her, at least for the time being.

"I expect you to stay right here at the hotel and rest while I'm gone. Ya hear me, now?"

Trina stuck out her lower lip, then smiled, remembering the effect that gesture had on Gabriel. "Yes, Papa. I hear."

"Good. Let's get to our rooms so I can get on with what I have to do. I don't want to be in this miserable excuse for a town any longer than possible. The train leaves at noon tomorrow. I intend to be on it."

"Yes, Papa." She'd wait until he left, then do a little exploring on her own. Curiosity about why Gabriel had come to Silver Falls was burning holes in her. Her father seemed to be adjusting to the altitude somewhat, his face not quite as red as when they'd first gotten off the train, and he wasn't having to stop as often to catch his breath. Hopefully, he'd adjust and be all right until they got back to Denver.

They registered at the desk, then followed the hotel keeper upstairs to their rooms. Her father took it slow and easy, stopping often to rest.

"You can never tell, Trina...what sort of scum might be...roaming the streets out there."

Trina sighed. He was trying to convince her he was right—an old pattern at their house and one she'd learned quite well.

"Yes, Papa."

"If you were to go walkin' alone, you might be dragged off and assaulted. The thought of it makes me want to smash something."

"I know, Papa." He was always wanting to smash something when it came to his daughter's virtue. If he found out what had happened on the train, he'd want to smash Gabriel. She'd have to see to it he never found out.

"Come on, Trina. You're pokin' along like you're puny or something. Are you sick?"

"No, Papa. I'm not sick." She tried to climb the steps a little faster. Her mind didn't poke along. If only Gabriel were to check in to the hotel, too, they might be able to spend more time together. She might as well have fond memories to cherish of the times spent with Gabriel. She sighed and stopped at the top of the stairs to rest. Mercy. No air in this town.

How long would it take to forget the thrill of being held by him? Kissed by him? Touched by him? They'd shared such intimacies, she couldn't even admit silently to herself all they'd done together. Why, just the words themselves—spoken or not—would be scandalous.

"Trina, are you going to wake up?"

"What? Why, Papa, I don't know what you mean. I'm as wide-awake as I've ever been in my drab little life." More so, she thought with a grin, and hurried into her room and closed the door before he could say more.

She hadn't really lived a drab life, but "drab" described this room perfectly. A gray chenille bedspread matched frayed curtains, also gray. The only color in the room came from a blue pitcher and bowl, decorated with white curlicues, on the sideboard. Even the braided rag rugs on the floor had faded to dull shades of gray, and the solitary tintype on the wall featured a family to match the room. Gray and drab, everywhere she looked. She sighed miserably and longed for the train—and Gabriel.

She took off her cape and spread it across the foot of the bed, then went to the mirror on the wall behind the pitcher and bowl to study her reflection carefully.

As far as she could determine, no outward signs existed to betray the fact she and Gabriel had kissed on the train. Her cheeks were just as rosy, her nose the same size and shape, and her lips—were they, perhaps, just the least bit fuller? Could it be that passionate kissing made a girl's lips fuller? If so, what would they look like after ten years of marriage? Or twenty? She giggled suddenly at the thought of a matronly woman with huge, flabby lips.

She sucked her bottom lip into her mouth and thought about Gabriel. The recollection made her warmer all over.

She wandered to the window and drew the dingy curtains. Dust billowed from the folds and made her sneeze. She peered through the panes of grimy glass, scraped the window upward from its niche in the frame and leaned out.

Silver Falls seemed to be arranged in a triangular pattern, necessitated by mountains hovering around the town. The buildings were mostly built of logs, with dirt roofs, a few ambitious frame houses scattered among them, and no brick structures at all. Trina figured residents didn't expect the town to last long enough for such permanence. She certainly wouldn't want to stay here any longer than necessary.

Mountains towering above the town were streaked with orange and rust, glowing red in places where the lowering sun came to rest. On the opposite end of the street the mountains were brown, broken into a jumble of fallen rock, cascading in places all the way to buildings at the base. Aspens, slender and graceful, were interspersed with reigning evergreens. Reddish streamlets, tumbling down the mountain, collected in a basin surrounded by trees. The edges, frozen and dusted with snow, reminded her of face powder on a mirror.

If it hadn't been for the town itself, the scene would have been perfectly wondrous and beautiful, but the presence of people, necessary mining equipment, sludge and trash generated by excavation blighted the majesty of the mountains.

Trina sighed. Was Gabriel down there on the street somewhere, trying to spot her in one of the hotel windows, dreaming about her as she dreamed of him? The only face peering back at her was that of an elderly donkey, laden with a pack which, by all rights, should have crushed him to the ground. The poor beast appeared as melancholy as she.

Trina frowned, remembering the altercation she'd overheard between Gabriel and that awful man in the baggage car. Gabriel despised Blackburn for something he'd done. Something so vile and vicious—

Trina squeezed her eyes tightly shut. Fool! Why hadn't she seen it before? Gabriel was here to find Blackburn!

"Remember, Trina!" she scolded aloud. What made Gabriel that angry—the same intensity of rage she'd seen in the baggage car when he questioned Wilson about Blackburn?

The realization drained all the color from her face. Dizziness swam through her until she thought she might faint.

Gabriel's wife. That same look had twisted his features when she'd asked about marriage. He'd said his wife had died. Oh, God. Had Blackburn killed Gabriel's wife?

Trina sank onto the bed, hoping with all her heart she was wrong. Maybe she'd let her imagination run away with her, as she'd been guilty of doing so many times in the past. If it turned out to be true, Gabriel was here to kill Blackburn. And her father—

Oh, dear God, her father!

She reached for her cape, shrugged it on and ran toward the door.

As she opened it, she heard her father talking to someone in the hall. She left the door cracked just enough to hear. Her heart pounded in her throat until she could hardly breathe.

"Blackburn's at the Golden Eye. He's expectin' you. Did you bring the guns?"

Guns! A picture of the trunks flashed through her mind. Full to the brim with guns—meant for Blackburn? Her throat tightened and her chest felt heavy with dread. Her father answered.

"I brought them. Tell Blackburn I'll be at the Golden Eye in half an hour. He'd better have the deed ready to hand over."

Trina widened the crack just a bit, enough to see the man grin wickedly. His eye twitched nervously. Wilson!

"What're ya gonna do if Blackburn don't have the deed? Shoot him?"

Amos didn't answer for a minute. Trina wished she could see his face. Tears burned her eyes. If her father really was involved in something illegal, Gabriel would have to do something about it. But what? Her father finally spoke, in a voice low and full of regret.

"I don't intend to shoot anyone. But if Blackburn threatens me..."

"You're here for a simple trade, Senator. Nothing more. Just don't be surprised if Blackburn hedges on his end of the deal. But he's more interested in guns and ammunition than a silver mine, which he couldn't hang around to run anyway. He's gettin' what he wants. And you're gettin' what you want. Maybe everything will go just as you expect."

"Maybe. You just tell Blackburn I'm coming."

"On my way." He turned to leave. "Oh, one more thing. Don't be late. Blackburn don't hanker to bein' kept waitin'." He stomped down the stairs.

Trina heard her father's door close. She had to decide what to do. If Gabriel really had come to kill Blackburn, he'd be in town right now, asking around to learn Blackburn's whereabouts. He'd find out, then kill him.

Wait a minute. On the train Wilson had told Gabriel he didn't know where Blackburn was. Either he'd found out after they arrived, or he'd lied to Gabriel. She shuddered. If it proved to be the latter, she certainly hoped, for Wilson's sake, that Gabriel never found out.

Her father would meet Blackburn at the Golden Eye in half an hour. If he and Gabriel got to Blackburn at the same time, her father might be caught between them.

Trina eased the door open again. No one in the hall. She tiptoed out, closing the door as quietly as she could, crept past her father's door and down the stairs.

Somehow, she had to find Gabriel.

Chapter Nine

Gabriel drained his mug of beer and wiped the foam from his mustache with one sleeve. It was time.

It hadn't been hard to find out about Blackburn. The bartender, Horace Greer, and everyone else in the bar seemed to be well acquainted with him. They also feared him. It showed on their faces when they heard his name. Blackburn had made his mark in Silver Falls, just as he had in every town unlucky enough to lie in his path.

Gabriel pulled out his Colt and checked the chamber again. The last thing he wanted was to face Blackburn with less than a full round. The gun slipped back into the holster with ease. Gabriel knew he couldn't beat Blackburn in a straight draw, thanks to the bullet that had shattered his wrist. But he didn't intend to give him that chance. The time for fair fights was long past.

Trina came through the batwing doors.

The whole place hushed and every head turned. Trina scanned their faces, searching, fear and disgust plain on her face.

When she saw Gabriel she straightened her spine and

marched to the bar. A couple of grubby miners abandoned their card game and followed her.

Gabriel waited to speak until she stood two feet in front of him, all the while keeping an eye on the activity behind her.

"Don't you think you turned in the wrong door, Miss McCabe?" Gabriel leaned back against the bar with his elbows resting on the edge. His hand lingered above his gun.

"I came to see you, Mr. Hart. There's a matter of utmost importance that requires your attention." Trina tried not to gulp for air. Her chest felt so restricted, she knew if she tried to take a deep breath she'd probably shudder loudly enough for everyone to hear.

"All right. Let's talk outside. We don't want to disturb these gentlemen any further." Gabriel stared straight at the miners who'd stationed themselves on either side of Trina. The glassy shine in their eyes told him they'd had a lot to drink. He didn't want any trouble.

"Now, mister, this here little lady needs a drink. Barkeep, git the lady some sasperilly. Ma'am, would you care to join me an' Cal at our table?" He pulled off his hat, torn and stained from years of sweat and dirt, and twisted it in his hands. His greasy hair stood up in damp spikes.

Trina wanted to bolt and run, but she knew it would be a mistake. Gabriel would protect her from these... people. The thought gave her courage.

"No, thank you, sir," she said as evenly as she could manage. "My business is with Mr. Hart. If you'll excuse us..."

Cal poked his friend in the ribs. "There, now, ya see, Hank? This lady has 'business' with the other gentleman. You'll jus' havta wait your turn!'' He broke into raucous laughter, as did Hank.

Gabriel laughed woodenly, grasped Trina's elbow firmly and pushed her toward the door. ''Excuse us.''

''Now, wait a minute, feller. 'Business' is conducted upstairs. We'll be waitin' outside the door when you're finished. Shouldn't take more'n a minute or two!'' They almost fell down, slapping each other on the back, laughing and snorting like a couple of boar hogs.

Trina's breath came in short pants and her palms started to sweat. What if Gabriel couldn't subdue both of them? What if they knocked him out? What if they dragged her upstairs and— ''Gabriel…?''

''Fun's over, boys.'' Gabriel pushed a little harder on Trina's elbow, but Hank moved between Trina and the batwings and grabbed her arm.

''Let's take her now, Cal.''

Gabriel moved so fast, Trina barely saw what happened. He punched Cal in the face so hard, he fell over backward. Then he grabbed Hank with both hands and pushed him over the nearest table, scattering cards, whiskey bottles and cardplayers.

''C'mon.'' He grabbed Trina's arm and headed for the batwings, shoving men out of the way with his free arm as he went. He didn't stop until they were halfway down the street and around the corner of Tippett's Dry Goods Store. Once there, he grabbed her shoulders and shook her once, hard.

''What the hell do you think you're doing, coming into a saloon like you belonged there? Didn't it occur to you that you might be in danger, going into a place like that?''

Trina shivered and trembled all over. The stupidity

of what she'd done finally overwhelmed her to the point of hysteria.

"G-Gabriel! I—I'm sorry! I didn't know! I'm s-so sorry!" she blubbered, her breath puffing great volumes of steam into the frigid air.

The sight of tears calmed Gabriel until he actually considered apologizing for being so rough. But, dammit, she'd pulled a ridiculous, dangerous, stupid stunt, and the most practical thing would be to take her right back to her father.

But, with her trembling and shaking, sobbing huge tears, the only thing to do…was hold her.

Trina couldn't believe it. One minute he'd almost shaken her teeth out. Now he was hugging her, stroking her hair, saying silly things like, "Don't cry now, Trina," when he'd been the one to make her cry in the first place.

"Gabriel, I'm sorry I went into that awful place. I didn't know how else to find you. I won't ever do it again, I promise."

A scary thought occurred to him. "You didn't go into any other saloons, did you?"

"Only two."

"Two!" He held her out and stared at her as though she'd lost all of her mind instead of just part of it. "What happened?"

"Nothing. I looked inside, saw you weren't there, and left."

"And nothing happened?"

She shook her head. "Only when I found you. I guess I shouldn't have gone all the way in."

"I guess."

He gathered her close again. Damn, but she felt good. Smelled good, too. Her hands rubbing his back made him want to scoop her up and take her someplace quiet for an hour or two.

"Gabriel?"

"What is it now?"

"My father is meeting that man."

"Which man?"

"Blackburn. The one you've come to kill." She'd know soon enough if she'd figured it out right.

Gabriel didn't have time for games. It made no difference how she knew he'd come for Blackburn. "Where?"

"So you really have come to kill him?"

"That's right. Where are they meeting?"

"But my father—he might be hurt."

Gabriel gripped her arms tighter. "Tell me where they're meeting, Trina."

"Only if you promise my father won't be hurt."

"He won't be hurt by me. Now tell me." The rage settled into coals of hatred in his belly. She'd better tell him or—

"The Golden Eye. He killed your wife, didn't he?"

Grief swept over him again. She couldn't know, yet she did. But it didn't matter. Blackburn was all that mattered.

"Yes. Hannah was pregnant when Blackburn slit her throat." He struggled to breathe normally. "Now, go back to the hotel, Trina. Promise me you'll stay there until it's over."

"But I—"

He shook her again. "Promise!"

"All right! I promise! Gabriel, I'm sorry. I'm so sorry." Her tears came now for Gabriel, for the pain he'd suffered and for the task ahead of him.

Gabriel let go of her, waited until she headed back

toward the hotel, then stopped a miner on the street to ask directions to the Golden Eye.

Trina watched until Gabriel headed north, into the narrowest part of the triangle. Then she followed.

Gabriel's boots crunched through dirty, blackened snow covering the streets of Silver Falls. He focused on one thought, and one thought only—killing Blackburn—encouraging hate and anger, full and hot, acrid and deadly.

For the past fourteen months he'd imagined the feel of Blackburn's scrawny neck in his hands, had imagined slowly squeezing the life from his rancid body. He'd considered shooting his knees, then his elbows and wrists, then his groin before leaving him to bleed to death in agony.

It still wouldn't be enough. Blackburn had caused Gabriel so much pain and grief, it didn't seem right to kill him in less than a month. If he could prolong Blackburn's pain... Yet the earth wasn't a big enough place for Gabriel and this lowlife to breathe the same air for even one more day.

The Golden Eye Saloon stood at the end of the street, away from the other saloons—due to a fairly recent fire that had claimed several buildings, judging from the remains. Boulders crowded both sides, squeezing the town into a point on this end. The relative isolation of the saloon suited Gabriel fine. He'd get everyone out of the way before he faced Blackburn. Having been a lawman and a law-abiding citizen all his life, he had no desire to see anyone innocent get hurt.

That thought brought him to Amos McCabe. Gabriel had to get the senator out of the way, too. That might not be as easy as shooing off the riffraff Blackburn no doubt kept around. After Blackburn was dead, Gabriel would deal with the senator. For Trina's sake, he hoped her father hadn't already done anything illegal.

Trina. Why in tarnation did he have to think about her? She was the last thing he needed while facing down the foulest vermin on the face of the earth. He had to have his head clear and his purpose straight. If he didn't, he might hesitate—the opportunity Blackburn would seize to shoot first, or escape.

Gabriel purposefully remembered watching Hannah die. That image, burned into his mind like a brand, forced everything else away. He was ready.

Trina followed about thirty yards behind Gabriel, staying close to the buildings when she could. If he saw her coming, he'd be furious. He might get hurt yelling at her instead of concentrating on Blackburn.

Trina shivered with cold and the thought of Blackburn killing Gabriel's wife. Gabriel might have watched her die. If so, why Blackburn hadn't killed Gabriel, too, was a puzzle, but he must have had a reason. Or maybe he'd heard someone coming and run. Either way, Gabriel had built up such a hatred for Blackburn, it still festered inside him, devouring him a little bit at a time. If Gabriel didn't kill Blackburn, the open, poisonous wound might never heal.

Gabriel stopped. Trina hid behind a porch support, in case he turned around. He didn't. Changing direction, he headed toward the back of the Golden Eye, fifty yards away.

She spied her father coming up the street on the opposite side. In a few minutes he'd cross over to the Golden Eye.

What should she do? Call to him? Intercept him? If

she let him keep going, he'd get to the saloon just after Gabriel did. He might be shot or killed.

She did the first thing that popped into her mind. She ran toward her father, but didn't call his name for fear Gabriel would hear. Maybe she could get to him in time and stop him from going into the Golden Eye.

The thin mountain air denied her the strength she needed to run even that short distance. After only a dozen steps, her lungs burned and her legs cramped. She wasn't going to make it—

Trina stumbled in the hard-packed snow and fell into a drift piled up between the buildings, curving out into the street. When she managed to get her eyes open and wiped clean, she spied her father ahead. The snow had muffled the sound of her fall, so he hadn't heard.

If only she could shout to him to stop. She could hardly drag enough air into her lungs to keep from blacking out. There was no way she could warn him in time.

Trina watched in horror. Her father climbed the steps of the Golden Eye Saloon and went inside.

Gabriel eased in the back way, careful to reseat the warped door in the frame without a sound. He heard men's voices coming from the front room.

He moved quietly over to the door leading to the front room and pushed it open half an inch. The bartender, wearing a stained dish towel around his ample waist, was wiping the rough wooden counter with a dirty rag. The saloon was empty except for three men at a table in the far corner. The man facing the bar had only one eye.

At the sight of Otis Blackburn in the flesh, Gabriel almost rushed into the room, gun blazing. He held himself in check as hatred and pain doubled, trebled in intensity. He pulled his Colt from the holster and cocked it. Taking a deep breath for control, he got ready to slam the door back hard, but stopped short.

Amos McCabe came into the saloon, hesitated, took a couple of deep breaths, then walked over to the table and sat down opposite Blackburn, right in the line of fire.

"Damn!" Gabriel eased the hammer back.

"Well, Blackburn. I've kept my end of the deal. I'm here to collect yours. Where's the deed?"

Blackburn sneered, revealing brown, rotted teeth and inflamed gums. The senator recoiled from the stench of Blackburn's fetid breath.

"Well, now, if it ain't the senator from the great state of Colorado, come to call. Ain't that a kick, boys?"

The two men seated at the table with Blackburn laughed raucously, obviously drunk. The stench of cheap liquor permeated the room.

McCabe wheezed. Thin air, coupled with nervousness, was taking its toll on him.

"Look here, Blackburn. Bo assured me you could be trusted. Otherwise, I never would've—"

"Hear that, boys? Ain't that just fine and dandy? If Bo McCabe says Otis Blackburn can be trusted, that makes it so, don't it?" Blackburn hooted with laughter and slapped the table, snorting through his nose. A bottle of whiskey tottered, then fell to the floor, where it shattered into a thousand pieces, splashing everyone at the table.

McCabe shot up from the chair and backed away, trying to dodge the whiskey. "Dammit! This suit cost fifty dollars!"

Blackburn's eye gleamed coldly. "My, my. The senator wears fifty dollar duds. We shouldn't be dirtying them up, now, should we?" He leaned forward with his hands flat on the table. "Especially since that's the suit they'll most likely bury him in."

McCabe stopped swiping at the stains on his trousers and looked at Blackburn. "You wouldn't dare..."

Blackburn leaned back and propped one foot on the table. "'Cause of what Bo says? Is that why I wouldn't dare kill you right where you stand?"

Amos McCabe straightened and tried to take a deep breath. "I came for the deed. Once I have it, the guns are yours, just as agreed." Amos's hands shook so badly, he had to clench his fists to steady them.

"Ain't that nice, boys? The senator's givin' us all those guns and the deed to Cobb's pitiful little claim, too. Ain't it strange—I don't see no guns."

McCabe's face got as red as a poker. "Now, see here, Blackburn—"

Blackburn had the senator by the front of his shirt, hauling him across the table, before he could react.

"No. You see. Otis Blackburn takes what he wants and kills whoever he pleases. And right now—" he held his gun under the senator's chin, cocking it slowly "—it pleases me right smart to blow your ugly, son-of-a-bitch face clean off. Right after you tell me where you've stashed those guns."

Gabriel stepped into the room with his gun leveled at the killer. "Let him go, Blackburn."

Blackburn's bloodshot eye bulged. "Hart. You sorry bastard. You didn't die after all."

"Turn the senator loose. Now."

Blackburn grinned in that same disgusting way. "I

think I may just kill him. I been thinkin' 'bout it all day.''

"It'll be the last thought you ever have. Let him go and I might kill you in *less* than a week."

The two men at the table eased back a fraction. Gabriel saw one of them go for his gun.

The Colt blazed once. The man fell to the floor with a grunt and a cry of pain. Gabriel aimed his gun at Blackburn again.

"I said, let him go."

Blackburn licked cracked lips, exposing his rotted teeth. His eye darted around the room, gun hand quivering. He shoved the senator hard across a chair, firing at Gabriel.

Gabriel dived behind the bar, shooting as he fell.

Blackburn cried out when a bullet lodged in his shoulder. Blood soaked his shirt and the front of his vest.

McCabe, on the floor, tried to get up.

"Stay down, Senator!" Gabriel shouted, and fired at Blackburn again over the counter, striking him in the leg.

Blackburn fired, but his aim went crazy. The bullet hit McCabe. Blackburn bolted for the door.

Gabriel took careful aim at Blackburn's back.

At that moment Trina bolted through the front door.

"Papa!"

Blackburn jerked her around in front of him, pressing his arm across her throat.

Gabriel's gut went hollow. Damn woman! Why couldn't she—just once—do what she was told? Gabriel withdrew the gun an inch.

Trina, hysterical, writhed in Blackburn's grasp, but there was no breaking his hold. He shook her once and tightened his grip. "Stop that wiggling, girl, or I'll kill you all, right here."

"No, please! Don't hurt him, I beg you!"

"Shut up!" Using his injured arm with difficulty, Blackburn pointed the gun at Trina's head and pulled the hammer back. "Now, Hart, you're gonna drop your gun on the bar, nice and easy like."

Trina whimpered, faint with fright. If she could pull free—

"That's right, girl. Just be quiet and easy and you and your pa will live a little longer."

Gabriel knew that, before his wrist had been shot, he could have dropped Blackburn right where he stood. Now, though, he wasn't sure. If his aim was even an inch off, he might hit Trina instead. He couldn't take the chance. He laid his Colt on the bar.

"Now you're bein' smart. Back off. I'll turn her loose once I'm away."

"I'll get you, Blackburn."

"I don't think so."

Gabriel grabbed his gun from the bar and dived for the floor, out of the path of Blackburn's bullets.

Seeing an opportunity to escape, Trina whirled around and punched Blackburn's shoulder where he'd been shot, then ran to where her father lay and flattened herself over him.

Blackburn squalled with pain, clutching the wound. He dragged Trina from the floor with his good arm, then fell backward through the open door, stumbling off the porch onto the ground. He grabbed the reins of the only horse tied to the rail outside.

Gabriel tried to get a clear shot, but Blackburn held Trina like a shield, blocking any attempts. Trina writhed like a snake until Blackburn cracked her skull with the barrel of the gun. She went limp in his arms. He draped her over the horse in front of the horn like a sack of flour and stepped up into the saddle behind her.

Gabriel squeezed the trigger, but McCabe caught his ankle, jerked hard and ruined the shot.

''Don't! He'll kill her!'' McCabe shouted.

Gabriel kicked him away. Taking careful aim, he fired at Blackburn, riding north out of Silver Falls into the mountains.

Before the echoes of gunfire faded from the valley, Blackburn and Trina disappeared into a clump of pines.

Chapter Ten

When Gabriel came back into the saloon, the man he'd shot was lying in the corner, moaning. The other men had cleared out, along with Blackburn. The bartender was nowhere to be seen. Lying in the middle of the floor with a gunshot wound in his side, was Senator Amos McCabe, the biggest fool, Gabriel thought, the great state of Colorado had ever produced.

Gabriel shook his head. If Trina hadn't barged in when she had, Blackburn would be dead. Now, with him getting farther away by the minute, and the senator bleeding on the floor, it would be at least half an hour before Gabriel could be outfitted on a horse. With snow falling more heavily all the time, he might not find them by morning. By then, there would be no trail to follow.

He couldn't let himself think about Trina and what Blackburn might do to her.

The bartender peered tentatively over the bar.

"You, get a doctor. I'll take care of his wound. Every minute you wait means he's losing more blood. Go!"

Gabriel dropped to one knee, ripped the senator's shirt open and examined the wound. It wasn't bad. The bullet had grazed his belly, leaving a groove where flesh had torn away, making for a lot of blood but no serious damage. It probably hurt like hell.

"Hart?"

"Right here, Senator. You're going to be fine. You weren't hit bad." Gabriel took off his neckerchief, wadded it into a thick pad and pressed it into the wound. "Can you hold that in place? Good. The doctor—if they have one in this town—will be here soon."

Amos winced. "Are you sure? This puddle...I'm lying in...is my own blood."

"I'm sure. The bullet just grazed you."

"Thank God. If I could...just...get my breath."

"Mountain air. You oughta trim that gut some. Your lungs would be mighty grateful."

"I know. Trina's...always...railing at me...to cut down...on my...eating. Guess...she's...right...."

Gabriel didn't like the sound of his breathing at all. The pain and shock to his body made it harder to pull air into his lungs. He needed doctoring, and fast. The wound wouldn't kill him, but lack of air might. He didn't seem to know Trina had been kidnapped. Best he didn't know—until the doctor arrived, anyway.

"Don't talk anymore, Senator. Just lie still and try to breathe slow and easy."

McCabe nodded and did as Gabriel suggested. His chest rose and fell with the exertion of pulling air into his stressed lungs. Bleeding slacked off somewhat with the pressure. Gabriel wished like hell the bartender would show up and spell him on this job so he could make a stab at tracking Blackburn before the snow covered all signs and made it impossible to follow. He left the senator and went outside. Snowing hard now. Flakes the size of silver dollars, covering boot prints, horse tracks—everything.

"Damn you, Blackburn!" Gabriel shouted at the mountain. "If you hurt her..."

He ground his teeth, so angry he couldn't think. If Trina were here, he'd probably wring her neck. Foolish. That's what she was. Pouty. Temperamental.

Wanton. Sensuous. Desirable.

Damn.

Gabriel saw the doctor coming, carrying his little black bag. He called to McCabe. "The doc's coming, Senator. Lie still. You're going to be fine."

"Hart!" the senator wheezed. "Wait."

"What is it?"

"That miserable cur double-crossed me."

"You're surprised?"

"My son...Bo...set this up...with Blackburn. Don't kill him...when you go—" He gave in to a fit of coughing.

Gabriel shook his head. Wasn't it enough to have two fools in the McCabe family?

The coughing subsided. Amos spoke more quietly this time. "Got me mixed up, too. Bo's young. Got a temper. Blackburn still has...the deed." He started to cough again. The wheezing got worse.

"Don't talk, Senator. Bo's not my concern."

McCabe nodded. "Trina...?"

"She'll be back soon." He didn't dare say more.

A short, pudgy man in a heavy, fur-lined coat came puffing into the saloon.

"I'm Doc Stanley. What've we got?"

"Grazed his belly. I'll leave him to you, Doc."

The doctor didn't reply, just opened his bag and went to work on Amos McCabe. Gabriel pulled his collar up around his ears and left.

Snowflakes the size of ten-dollar gold pieces stung

his face and piled up around his feet as he trudged up the street toward the dry goods store, trying to penetrate the gloom with squinted eyes. Blackburn was long gone with Trina by now. Or he might have collapsed from his wounds, giving her a chance to escape. It was pitifully little to hope for, but all Gabriel had right now. Blackburn might not make it out of the mountains at all. Gabriel might never know what happened to him. Could he live with the uncertainty? He might have to. At least Blackburn was carrying two of Gabriel's bullets in him. There was a measure of satisfaction in that.

Trina tried to open her eyes, but the pounding in her skull made it impossible. Every other part of her body hurt, too. Back, shoulders, legs.

Moving. Swaying. Draped over a horse. Terror shot through her as memory returned. She stiffened.

"Lay still, woman." A hand twisted her arm painfully behind her.

Blackburn. She slumped, hoping to convince him she'd passed out again, even though her mind screamed for her to rebel and escape. Head down, arms and legs dangling, she surveyed their surroundings, trying to see something she might recognize.

Trees. Snow. Rocks and boulders, all banked with snow. More coming down all the time. Glancing behind, she saw only a few tracks left by the horse. Snow had obliterated most of them already. No way to track anyone or anything in this weather. She must have been out quite a while. Maybe one strong kick...

"I said, lay still!" He twisted her arm again. Pain shot through her shoulder, into her back. She had no choice but to obey.

Blackburn's voice had weakened from what she'd

heard at the Golden Eye. She struggled to remember. Wounded. She focused on his leg beside her head. Blood ran down his boot, dripped into the snow. He couldn't travel long, losing blood and strength.

The horse stopped, snorting steamy breath into icy wind. Blackburn slid down, pulling her after him. Did he mean to kill her? Using her as a shield to escape, he now had no further use for her. She'd become nothing but excess baggage. With difficulty, she stood, leaned against the horse, stretching cold, stiff muscles, eyes darting to seek some landmark, establish bearings.

Nothing. Snow and trees.

Panic tried to seize her again. She could outrun him—but not his bullet.

"Gotta stop," Blackburn wheezed, dragging her and the horse toward an outcropping of rock. Nestled among boulders and scrub brush, a black hole in the side of the cliff yawned ominous and frightening.

Snowflakes blowing hard into the mountain stung her face, melted into her eyes and on her lips. She licked at them hungrily, realizing how thirsty she was.

"Git on in." He shoved her hard toward the entrance.

"We can't go in there." If she went into that horrid black hole, she might never come out again. Gabriel would never know what had happened to her. Her throat constricted with fear. Tears stung her eyes. Her heart pounded until she felt faint.

"If we don't, we'll die. Git on, woman! Or—stay out here and freeze. I don't give a damn what you do."

"The horse—"

"Worried about Charlie, are you? He could freeze, for all I care, but I need him…to git outta here…come daylight. Move!" A fit of coughing doubled him over. Blood spattered onto the snow from his mouth.

Trina took the reins of the shivering animal and led him to the mouth of the tunnel. The horse shied, sniffing furiously to test stale air coming from the mine, then relaxed. Nothing there to spook him. Trusting his judgment more than Blackburn's, Trina led the horse into the tunnel, feeling along one side of the roughly dug passageway, willing her eyes to adjust to almost complete darkness. She heard a thud. Blackburn had dropped something. Saddlebags?

The sudden brilliance of a match, struck by Blackburn then held to the wick of a coal oil lamp hanging near the entrance, blinded Trina for a moment. Darkness retreated as they advanced. Her breathing evened. Inside the tunnel was noticeably warmer than outside. From the debris strewn about, Trina concluded Blackburn had been here before.

"Rest. Got to…rest." Blackburn dropped heavily against one wall, setting the lantern on a rock littered with dried beans and what appeared to be a bacon rind. Castoffs from a previous meal.

"You need a doctor," she offered, knowing he'd never allow her to take the horse and go for help, even if it meant dying in the dark.

"No doctors." He pointed to the bag he'd dropped near the entrance. "Git that bag. Bring it here."

She fetched it. No use angering him further by being uncooperative. She had to keep her wits about her. Learn what she could about where they were. Trying to find her way back to Silver Falls was out of the question. Unconscious most of the way, not seeing the way they'd come, she could wander in these trees for hours, die of exposure, and never be sure of going the right direction.

"Look in the left side. There's food—a little—and

more matches. We need somethin' hot in our bellies."
Coughing again, he held his arm over his mouth, wiped
blood on his sleeve when the spell subsided.

Trina's stomach roiled uncomfortably at the stench
Blackburn gave off. When the horse nickered softly, she
went to loosen his bridle, taking the bit from his mouth.
She might not have time to replace it if an opportunity
to run presented itself, but with the wind whistling past
the entrance and snow falling more heavily all the time,
there would be no opportunities until morning. There
was nothing to feed the horse. She checked the other
pouch. Full of grain.

She glanced at Blackburn. He must care something
for this animal; otherwise, it would be left to forage on
its own—and he never would have given it a name. At
home, her brothers didn't name a horse until they knew
it would be kept—and cared for. She emptied a handful
of grain onto a flat rock nearby. Charlie snuffled, liked
what he smelled, and sucked the kernels into his mouth,
munching contentedly.

"Now you've fed him, feed us." Blackburn propped
himself on the elbow of his good arm. The sight of his
face made Trina cringe.

"I'm coming. As you said, he has to be cared for so
you can get away later."

"Damn right."

She pulled out several strips of jerky and a couple of
shriveled yams, more suited to seed than to being
cooked in the small stewpot tucked into the bottom of
the bag. In a wad of brown paper she found a chunk of
salt—dirty, but usable.

"I have to have water for the yams. I'll bring some
snow to melt."

He didn't seem concerned about her trying to run

away. She knew as well as he did that she wouldn't get far. In fact, she figured he might welcome her escape. One less thing to think about.

Outside, snow blocked what little sunlight remained. Getting late. She scooped snow into the pot until level full, taking care to glean only fresh, clean snow from the rocks. At least that much would be clean. It wouldn't be wise to dwell on the rest. Then, desperate to leave some sign, in case Gabriel should be foolish enough to try to track them in this blizzard, she broke several branches near the entrance, bending them into what she hoped would be unnatural positions. Her hands were blue and throbbing when she went back inside.

"How long does it take?" Blackburn bellowed from within the tunnel.

"I'm coming." She hurried back. "I wanted clean snow."

"There's kindlin' lying around. See what you can scare up."

She searched and found twigs and small branches scattered about the tunnel. Blackburn arranged them into a pile, then used one of the matches to start a small fire. Trina welcomed additional light and the pitiful bit of warmth it produced. They'd be restricted to whatever fuel Blackburn had left here in the past. Everything outside was too wet to burn. She nested the pot in the center of the fire, mushing everything down until it burned all around the container, melting the snow quickly.

She knew she should still be scared spitless, but there didn't seem to be much use in cowering in fear. Blackburn had lost so much blood, she doubted he had the strength to hurt her. One stiff punch to his shoulder, as she'd done before, would be enough to incapacitate him long enough to run away. For a reason she couldn't understand or define, she almost felt sorry for him. All she had to do to banish those feelings was remember what he'd done to Gabriel's wife. She picked up one of the yams, shriveled and dirty.

"Your knife?" She held out one hand to Blackburn, who hesitated, then handed it over. It had a ten-inch blade, crusted with something Trina had no desire to identify. She took it outside, gasping at how hard the wind whipped, and plunged the blade into the ground a couple of times, using the grit of soil to scrub it, then into snow before wiping it on her skirt. This, too, would be clean.

Inside, Blackburn watched her with blatant curiosity. Finally he nodded.

"Damn purty woman, you are."

Revulsion oozed through her. She tried not to look directly at him. His ruined eye had caused that whole side of his face to contort into a nightmare of twisted flesh and sores.

"Women don't hanker after ugly men like me," he said softly.

"A wound like yours is hard to ignore."

"I didn't always look like this." He released a long breath that rattled in his chest, and struggled to get into a more comfortable position.

She took her time peeling and slicing the yams into the boiling water. Occasionally she glanced at him and found his features softening. The pain of his wounds, now clotted, had apparently eased. His eyelid drooped with exhaustion. With any encouragement, he would drift off to sleep.

Trina's mind whirled with possibilities. Nothing made sense with snow falling heavily and darkness imminent. No matter what plan she might concoct, she'd have to spend the night in this tunnel. With a killer. In the limited space, and with only that one small fire for warmth, she wouldn't be able to get far enough away to feel safe.

He roused, glared at her. "Whatcha lookin' at?"

"What happened to your eye?"

Blackburn laughed, rasping, coughing, choking on his own blood. "Hart. Clawed it out with his bare hands."

Trina shivered at the image in her mind. "After you killed his wife."

"An eye for an eye. A wife for a wife."

What did that mean? "Gabriel killed your wife?"

"Might as well have. He stuck me in that hellhole for somethin' I didn't do." He pinned her with his one, rummy eye. "Don't get me wrong. I wanted to kill that sorry bastard, but somebody beat me to it. Hart told the judge he saw me standing over the body. And I was. Kicking in his ribs, mad I didn't get to him first. Jury believed Hart. Since nobody saw me pull the trigger, they didn't hang me. Sent me up for ten years. Elvina lived alone after that. Rattlesnake got her."

Taken by another fit of coughing, he paused as his face turned bloodred with the effort. When he recovered, his lips were stained with blood.

"She dragged herself halfway to a neighbor's house afore she died, all swole up like a bloated fish." He ground his teeth. "If I'd've been there, she wouldn't have died."

Trina shuddered with another horrible image and squeezed her eyes shut, trying to blot it from her mind.

"Hart killed my wife. So I killed his."

"And his child."

Blackburn jerked his head around. "I never killed no child."

"Gabriel's wife was pregnant when you killed her."

Blackburn began to shake and shudder as though having a seizure. He screamed—animal-like, wrenching—until Trina covered her ears with her hands. Screams trailed off into wails of misery. Blackburn turned to face the wall.

The horse, spooked by Blackburn's wailing, danced around, wild-eyed. Trina went to calm him, appreciating the chance to soothe and comfort.

Gabriel didn't know about Blackburn's wife. And Blackburn hadn't known about the unborn baby. Tears streamed down her face, sobs shaking her as she buried her face in the horse's neck.

"Oh, God, why?" she pleaded. "Why?"

Chapter Eleven

Striding against a brisk wind, snowflakes crowding into his eyes, Gabriel went straight to the dry goods store. The shopkeeper wasn't anywhere to be found. Gabriel stormed around the counter, into the back room, and found a balding little man on a ladder, fetching a large box from a shelf.

"I need supplies—in a hurry."

"Just as soon as I get this box…"

Gabriel took the box from him and carried it to the front of the store. The man followed, cleaning his spectacles on his apron.

"Much obliged. Now, what can I get for you?"

"Jerky. Coffee. Got any biscuits already made?"

"A few. They're hardtack."

"Give me those, too." He'd have to pick up a bottle of whiskey before he left town. With all this snow, and the temperature dropping from icy to frigid in a hurry, a bottle of instant fire might be the most valuable thing in his pack.

The storekeeper wrapped everything in a bundle and tied it with string. Gabriel paid him and left.

Outside, he cursed again. Flakes swarmed from the

sky, reducing visibility to practically nothing. Any tracks made by Blackburn's horse would already be gone. Gabriel hurried to the saloon, came out carrying a bottle, then went to the livery for a horse. The liveryman was in the barn, pouring grain into a bin in front of a huge mare.

"I need a horse. Right now."

"In this weather? You gotta be crazy, mister."

Gabriel grabbed him by the front of his coat and hauled him almost off the ground. "Otis Blackburn kidnapped a woman about half an hour ago. Now, give me a horse."

His face, pale now, and sweaty, mirrored the horror Gabriel had seen in other faces after hearing Blackburn's name.

"If I could—"

"No excuses. A horse."

"I don't have one that'll last an hour. Not in the storm that's already here. Come morning, I'll give you Old Dobbin over there, but he's no good when he can't see. Going out in this blizzard is suicide—for you and the horse. I'm sorry. I can't let you have Dobbin till morning."

Gabriel set him back on the ground. "First light. Have him ready to go."

The liveryman nodded, swiping at his forehead with one sleeve. Gabriel headed back to the dry goods store. If he had to wait until morning, he might as well stock up on blankets and more food. It might take a while to find her, but he would.

His belly knotted painfully at the thought of Trina being with that miserable bastard. Never much for praying, he prayed now.

* * *

The yams weren't good, but better than nothing, and the jerky so tough, Trina thought she might yank out a tooth just trying to saw off a bite. Blackburn had settled into a fitful sleep after eating. He convulsed with pain, jerking himself awake again and again. His shoulder had started to bleed again. The bullet needed to come out.

Trina tried to pull Blackburn's coat back enough to see where the bullet had gone in. Blackburn grabbed her wrist and twisted her arm to one side.

"Whatta ya think you're doin'?"

"Trying...you're hurting me...trying to see how badly you're wounded." He released her. She rubbed her wrist, glaring at him. "Why I should care is beyond me. You're bleeding, though. The bullet—"

"Ain't too deep. It's gotta come out." He measured her with his eye. "You're gonna do it."

"Me? I've never removed a bullet in my life." Her heart pounded at the thought of cutting into someone's bloody flesh. "Don't be ridiculous. You need a doctor."

He pulled his gun from the holster and pointed it at her head. "Git that knife, stick it in the fire and cut out that bullet."

She tried to swallow, but her mouth was too dry to manage it. "I—I can't. The pain would be too much for you."

"You just better be careful you don't hurt me too bad. I'll have this gun aimed at your heart the whole time you're cuttin'. Git the knife!"

Trina trembled at the look on Blackburn's filthy face. What if he jerked from the pain and squeezed the trigger? Oh, God, how could she do this without fainting?

She picked up the knife and headed outside.

"Where are you goin'?" he demanded.

"To get it as clean as I can before I sterilize it in the fire. So you don't die of infection."

He grunted his approval and she went outside. The blizzard had intensified, making it impossible to see six feet in any direction. Trina plunged the knife into the soil several times, then into snow, wiped it on her skirt, and thought about the first time tonight she'd done this. To slice yams. This time she'd be slicing human flesh.

"Gabriel, where are you?" she pleaded. Icy wind captured her words and ripped them away.

Amos McCabe, bandaged until he could hardly move and medicated with something to ease his breathing and the pain, complained while the hotel owner's wife tucked in his covers and fluffed his pillows.

"Dammit, woman! Leave me alone! I'm not all that bad hurt and you know it. I can't stand being coddled like some sort of doddering old fool. Get out of here before I get up from this bed and—" He raised himself an inch and almost passed out from the pain.

She arranged the covers again, tucking and smoothing like a mother hen arranging the straw in a nest for newly hatched chicks. "Now, Mr. McCabe, quit acting like a child and stay put."

"A child! I'll show you...just who is a child...and who's the senator of the great state of Colorado...the minute I can...get up and...and..." He collapsed back onto the pillow in a heap, wheezing and straining to catch his breath. "My daughter! I want my daughter!"

The doctor, gathering up all his paraphernalia, shook his head. "He's going to be fine. I gave him some sleeping powders. He needs rest more than anything. This thin air almost did him in. Just let him get some sleep and I think you'll find him more amiable in the morning."

"Thank you, Doctor," she said, tucking a stray strand of gray hair into the bun on the back of her head. "I appreciate all you've done, even if this mule of a senator don't." She arranged the covers one last time and gave Amos a withering look, telling him clearly he'd better not muss them again.

"I'll be by in the morning to check on him."

"I'll be in the next room in case he needs anything during the night. I don't think I'll have any trouble hearing him."

"Before long, he'll be as good as new."

"'As good as new.' 'Needs rest.' Hogwash! What I need...is for everybody to clear out...and leave me alone!" McCabe hacked again and slammed his fist on the bed. "Trina! Where in tarnation are you?" A fit of coughing made him clutch at his side.

The hotel owner's wife followed the doctor out and down the stairs.

Gabriel came in about fifteen minutes later.

"He's in there." She pointed upstairs. "Second door. Yours is the third. If you want me to doctor him any more, it's going to cost you extra. That old goat—"

"Add it to my bill."

"Thought you was going after Blackburn."

News traveled fast in a town this size. "Blizzard. First light."

"Breakfast at five-thirty if you're of a mind to eat."

"Much obliged."

Gabriel peered into the senator's room. Snoring loud enough to shake the rafters. Good. He'd need rest before hearing about Trina.

Gabriel went on to the next room, closed the door behind him and stretched out on the bed.

If he weren't so keyed up over Trina being kidnapped by that madman, the mattress, lumpy as it was, might feel good to his stiff muscles and aching back.

Every time he closed his eyes, the only thing he could see was Blackburn's face—and Trina draped over that damn horse. Gabriel had managed to put two bullets into the sorry bastard. With any luck, he'd lose so much blood, he'd pass out, giving Trina a chance to escape. But to where? Into the blizzard? As hard as it was, Gabriel had to hope they'd found shelter from the storm. Without shelter against the snow and wind, they'd freeze solid before morning.

Gabriel tried to get up from the bed, but gave it up and collapsed back on the mattress again. Rest. He had to have rest.

How would Trina get through this? She'd shown some grit on the train, but would it be enough? It would take more than grit to stand up to Blackburn.

The knife was as clean as Trina could get it, using soil and snow. She'd have to heat it in the fire, and, if Blackburn had any whiskey in those saddlebags, pour some over the hot blade to kill anything else that might be there. Why she was taking such precautions for Blackburn's well-being she had no idea, and she didn't want to examine the reasons too closely. He was a human being, though a sorry one, to be sure, and deserved the best she could do for him. If he didn't maim or kill her, of course.

"Woman! Git back in here! Now!"

"Coming." Taking a slow breath of clear, cold air,

Trina closed her eyes, whispered a prayer asking for strength, and went back into the tunnel.

Blackburn had shucked off his shirt. His chest, sprinkled with wads of wiry black hair, appeared as filthy as the rest of him. She'd have to wash the area around the wound before cutting for the bullet. Her stomach twisted, sending bile into her throat. She'd have to have more water for washing.

"Stick that knife in the fire like I told you." Blackburn struggled to get the injured shoulder higher than the other. The hole was deceptively small. Clotted blood around the edges had blocked the entry to an extent. Fresh blood seeped from the center of the hole.

"I'll have to wash your shoulder first. I'll need more snow."

"Forget washing. Just dig it out. A little dirt never hurt nobody."

"But the infection—"

"Is already started. You ain't gonna stop it with snow water." He cocked the pistol and pointed it at her. "Put that knife in the fire. I ain't gonna tell you again."

Trina stooped and placed the blade in the flames. "Do you have whiskey in that bag?"

"Fresh out. I drank the last of it while you was outside."

That accounted for the new slur in his voice. His eyelid drooped more and more as they waited for the blade to heat. Trina turned the knife over. The tip glowed orange.

Another minute passed in silence. Trina took the knife from the flame. Smoke rose from the blade. She waited a moment, until the tip dulled to a smoky color, then wiped the soot on her skirt.

Blackburn pointed the gun at her. "Do it."

"If you keep that gun on me, my hands will shake. I give you my word, I'll do my best to get the bullet as quick as I can."

"Your word." He laughed, coughed, quieted.

"Unlike you, Mr. Blackburn, my word is good."

He glared at her, then holstered the gun. "Git on with it."

Trina laid the knife on a flat rock, the blade not touching anything but air, and tore several strips from her petticoats to use as bandages. Once she opened that wound, she'd need packing. She'd watched Tom treat a gash in Will's leg once. She hoped she remembered everything he'd done to stop the blood and bandage the wound.

Blackburn watched her without speaking. His lips sagged, his breath rasping, his eye almost closed.

Trina picked up the knife.

Gabriel woke with a start. Completely dark outside. He got up from the bed, stiff and sore, stretched his back muscles, then went to the window. He had no idea what time it was, other than the middle of the night. Even in daylight the heavy snow and wind would have blotted the sun into dusk. The windows, loose in their frames, rattled and shook, letting bitter cold air into the already frigid room. Gabriel shivered.

Trina. Where was she? Outside in this storm? Surely Blackburn had enough sense to build a shelter. If he could. Damn. Wounding him twice before he kidnapped Trina might mean he'd died and left her to freeze in the storm.

Gabriel went to his coat, pulled out his watch and peered at it, using the light from a guttering candle on the chiffonier. Just past midnight. A lifetime until dawn. He'd better get all the sleep he could.

He stretched out on the bed again, pulled blankets and counterpane over him and closed his eyes. Visions of Hannah, Trina and Blackburn tangled his mind. Then the images blended into a new face.

Corbett Hart. Lying facedown in the sludge of an alley. Blackburn standing over him, firing bullets into his father's corpse.

Blackburn had insisted Corbett was dead when he found him. That he was so angry at not being able to kill the lawman himself, he'd fired into the dead body and kicked his ribs from sheer frustration and fury. But Gabriel had had to testify to what he'd seen. Blackburn had gone to prison because of it.

If Blackburn hadn't killed Gabriel's father, the question remained: Who had?

Gabriel rubbed his eyes, wishing the memories would go away, but he knew, from hours of lying awake in the middle of the night, they would never go away— until Blackburn was dead.

Maybe not even then.

Chapter Twelve

"Please let me clean around the wound." Trina was stalling. Maybe Blackburn would allow this one last reprieve. The whiskey he'd consumed had left him limp.

"Yeah, sure, why not?" he mumbled.

Trina took the cooking pot and went back outside to fill it with snow again. She couldn't stay long, though. The blizzard raged with increased intensity every passing hour.

Her fingers blue and stiff, she went back inside. Adding more kindling, blowing to get the fire hotter, she placed the pot back in its nest in the flames and leaned back to wait for the snow to melt. In all too short a time, the water in the pot began to boil.

Blackburn snored noisily. Trina wished she could slip away, into the night, but the storm meant death for anyone exposed to the wind.

Gabriel would be worried sick. He had no way of knowing about the tunnel or the food in Blackburn's saddlebags. And no way of knowing she was uninjured and actually at little threat from the man Gabriel had sworn to kill.

She studied Blackburn in the light of the fire. As ugly as he was, he might once have been fairly decent looking. Never handsome, she couldn't say that. But not a nightmare the way he was now. What had happened to turn him into such a vile monster? She had a hard time, even now, thinking of him that way. He'd certainly treated her with a measure of respect. He'd barely threatened her at all, and even complimented her. Strange. He was nothing like she'd imagined. Yet he'd killed Gabriel's wife and child.

The water had cooled enough not to burn his skin now. She took one of the strips she'd torn from her petticoat, dipped it, then touched Blackburn's arm tentatively. It took several seconds for him to respond.

"I'm going to clean your shoulder now."

He nodded drunkenly and closed his eye again.

Trina left the rag sodden and squeezed warm water over the area around the wound. The bleeding had stopped, now that Blackburn had been still for a good while, and had crusted with clotted blood. She'd have to cut through all that to get to the bullet.

She dabbed his skin, removing layers of crud and dirt until clean skin remained. She noticed with a start that Blackburn was watching her as she worked.

"That feels real nice," he said softly, a different inflection in his voice than any she'd heard before.

"I'm afraid it won't once I start looking for that bullet."

"It don't matter. Worth it. To have you touch me so nice." He lapsed into unconsciousness.

Better to get it over with while he couldn't feel it. Trina's stomach threatened to rebel, but she scolded herself.

"You can do this, Katrina," she mumbled. "Just

think of it as cutting a piece of gristle from a roast.''
That image didn't help a lot. She picked up the knife.

Before she could reconsider, she plunged the tip into
the wound. Blackburn groaned, but didn't awaken. So
far, so good.

Blood gushed for a moment, then subsided. She
probed deeper.

Blackburn's eye came open in the midst of a scream.
Trina had to withdraw the knife from the wound to keep
from slicing into sound flesh.

A string of profanity made Trina's face burn with
embarrassment, but he soon hushed, taking deep
breaths.

''Mr. Blackburn, you're going to have to keep still if
I'm to do this.''

Shuddering, he nodded. ''Git on with it.'' He picked
up a rock lying near his right hand and gripped it until
his knuckles whitened.

Trina tried to ignore the pounding in her head, the
turmoil in her stomach, and raised the knife to the bullet
hole again.

Blackburn fought against the pain until it overwhelmed him. He passed out, slumping back against the
wall of the tunnel. Trina worked faster, trying to find
the lump of lead lodged in his shoulder, fighting revulsion and horror.

The tip of the knife touched something hard. There
was no way to get at the bullet. She'd have to widen
the hole. She took several deep breaths, trying to calm
her raging senses, cut an *X* over the wound to make the
hole bigger, and pushed one finger inside. She felt the
bullet, about the size of her little finger. Forcing her
thumb in beside her finger, she grasped the bullet, using
her fingernails to grip tighter, and pulled gently.

The bullet resisted, but gradually slipped from its resting place, down the passageway made by the knife, and out of Blackburn's shoulder. It made a sickening sound as it pulled free. Blood oozed from the wound, the flow increasing as Blackburn stirred. Alcohol had thinned his blood. She had to stop the bleeding.

She folded a strip of cloth into a pad and pressed it to the wound, followed by another, but the blood kept coming. Swallowing hard, she put the knife back into the fire, waited until it glowed red-hot, then, without giving it more thought than necessary, pressed it against the wound.

Blackburn's eye came open along with his mouth. He screamed. Trina pulled the knife away, smelling scorched skin and tissue, and cringed at the sounds of agony coming from him. Tears stung her eyes. Blackburn finally quieted, breathing hard. Then he lapsed into unconsciousness once more. She sighed with relief.

Blackburn was, thankfully, out cold, and might be for hours. If only the storm would subside, this might be her only chance for escape.

Charlie, the big roan, nickered softly. Hearing him, Trina felt better. Even if Blackburn died, she wouldn't be completely alone on this mountain.

She bandaged the shoulder as best she could, wishing Blackburn had saved some of the whiskey to disinfect the wound a little, but that might have been more pain than even he could bear. The whiskey had done its best work in Blackburn's belly, numbing his brain, relaxing him into a stupor.

She looked at his face. The lines around his mouth and across his forehead had eased somewhat. Hopefully, the worst was over.

Charlie shifted his powerful back legs, resting the

left, then the right. A reminder to Trina she needed rest, too.

Her skirt reeked of blood and gore. She was suddenly seized with the need to wash her face and hands. Another trip outside for more snow to melt. The wind had calmed somewhat. By morning the storm would have passed. She was too tired, too emotionally spent to think about what morning might bring.

With a sigh, she went back inside, melted the snow, then scrubbed her hands and face and her arms, as far as she could reach without removing any clothing.

Blackburn had curled into a tighter position now, his breathing easier, his snoring almost welcome. He'd survive. And so would she. Until morning.

She slumped against the side of the tunnel and immediately slept.

Gabriel woke before dawn, gathered his gear, stopped downstairs in the kitchen at five-thirty for breakfast—hotcakes, sausage and about a gallon of hot coffee—then headed for the livery. The storm had passed. Silver Falls looked almost beautiful under a fresh blanket of gleaming snow.

By the time the sun had risen enough to cast a pale light across the eastern sky, he was already into the trees.

Amos McCabe woke feeling sluggish and cranky. He'd slept through the night without waking—except for that one time when Mrs. Whoever-she-was had shaken him awake to ask if he was sleeping all right. How stupid could one woman be?

Where was Trina? He hadn't seen her since... His mouth dried up to cotton. Dammit. He hadn't seen her

since the Golden Eye. Fear settled into his belly like
hot lead. He'd been so woozy after getting wounded,
he hadn't had the sense to make sure she was all right.
He'd left that to Gabriel Hart.

"Hart!" No answer. "Anybody!"

The woman who had tended him the night before
appeared at the door. "Well, how are we feeling this
morning?" She came straight to the bed and plastered
one hand against his forehead.

Amos grabbed her wrist and pushed her away.
"Don't fuss over me like a hurt puppy! Where is my
daughter? And where is Sheriff Hart?"

"Mr. Hart left early this morning—before daylight. I
haven't seen your daughter. What's her name?"

"Katrina McCabe. Red hair. Feisty."

"Ain't nobody in this hotel like that. Now, why don't
you calm down while I go to the kitchen and bring you
something to eat? I still have some hotcakes and sausage—"

Amos's stomach contracted at the mention of food,
but he still hadn't gotten the answers he needed. "I
want to see Hart. Pronto! Understand?"

"Perfectly. When Mr. Hart returns, I'll tell him you
want to see him. In the meantime, he's paid me plenty
and extra to make sure you have everything you need.
The doctor will be by to see you in about an hour, so
why don't you—"

"Why don't you get the hell out of my bedroom and
bring me some breakfast? What do people have to do
around here to be fed?"

The ample woman bit her bottom lip and took a couple of deep breaths. "Breakfast will be here soon." She
turned toward the door, mumbling something Amos
didn't hear.

"What was that?"

"You don't want to know. If you beller at me again, breakfast will be delayed—no telling how long. Understand?"

Amos didn't answer. She closed the door behind her when she left. "Good riddance!" he yelled at the door.

Trina not in the hotel. Where in thunder was she, then? And where had Gabriel gone so early? He needed more information. There seemed to be no way to get it, except...

The diplomacy he'd learned, being a senator, kicked in. If he couldn't scare some answers out of that woman, he'd have to charm them out of her.

A few minutes later a heavy knock sounded at the door. She came in, carrying a tray. The aromas coming from the tray reminded Amos of home—Trina in the kitchen.

"I don't know your name," Amos said as civilly as he could manage. He tried to smile.

"Bertha. Bertha McNaught. *You* may call me Mrs. McNaught."

Still mad at him. To get any information out of her at all, he'd have to remedy that.

"Well, Mrs. McNaught, I must apologize for my previous behavior. Those hotcakes smell mighty good."

She eyed him suspiciously, then broke into a wide grin. "Them sausages are tasty, too."

"I'm sure. What kind of syrup is that? Smells like maple."

"Shore nuff is maple. Don't have a lot left, though. Enjoy it. Can't let you have any more."

"I'm sure this will be enough. Thank you very much."

"You're welcome, Mr. McCabe."

"Would you happen to know when Mr. Hart will be back to the hotel? It's really important for me to speak with him as soon as possible."

"He didn't say when he'd be back. Left before dawn. Rented a horse at the livery. Old Dobbin, if I heard right. I bundled up some leftover beef and a few boiled potatoes for him to take along with him. Talk in town would have it he's tracking that skunk, Blackburn. Believe he said something about it last night."

Amos's gut tightened. "My daughter was with us on the train. I can't imagine where she could be all this time."

"Heard tell a woman was kidnapped by Blackburn. Couldn't have been your daughter, though."

Amos tried to keep his racing emotions in check a moment longer. "Why is that?"

"'Cause your daughter wouldn't be caught dead at the Golden Eye Saloon, and that's where this woman was when Blackburn snatched her."

Amos buried his face in his hands. "Oh, dear God, what have I done?"

Chapter Thirteen

Not one blessed track remained in the snow from the Golden Eye to where Blackburn had disappeared. Gabriel scouted fifty yards in every direction from their entry into the forest. Nothing.

Trina woke up alone in the cave. Blackburn was gone. And so was Charlie. She scrambled up from where she'd spent the night and groaned at aches and pains that had settled into her joints. Places on her back stung where rocks had dug into her flesh. She could hardly straighten up, she was so stiff with cold.

At the mouth of the tunnel she squinted into the brilliance of sunshine reflecting off the diamond surface of new snow, covering everything, renewing the earth as nothing else could. Hoofprints led off to the east.

Half a dozen emotions scrambled in Trina's mind before she settled on elation. He'd left her here alone, but now she could get back to Silver Falls—and Gabriel. Without a second thought she rushed straight ahead, lost her footing and tumbled headlong into a drift, which covered her. Flailing her way to the surface, she struggled back to the tunnel and brushed furiously at snow and ice on her clothes.

"Foolish. What could I be thinking of?" Shivering, she gathered her coat around her and chose the only path possible—following Charlie's hoofprints.

Fifty feet from the tunnel the snow got deeper. Charlie obviously had had trouble plowing his way through the drifts. Trees were so dense here, she could hardly believe the big horse had found his way through them, but there was no sign of Blackburn or the horse anywhere, other than a gully in the snow where they'd pushed through, heading steadily east.

Was that the way to Silver Falls? She didn't believe for a minute Blackburn would go back there, not with Gabriel waiting to blow his head off.

The thought saddened her. Such a complicated situation. How would she ever be able to tell Gabriel what Blackburn had said? Gabriel would accuse him of lying, trying to win her sympathy, but she didn't believe it. Something about Blackburn told her he'd spoken the truth. Since Gabriel hadn't been there to hear it, she'd never be able to convey her feeling of intuition.

She stopped, gasping from the effort of following the horse's trail with nothing but thin mountain air to breathe. What would it be like to slog through on her own? She'd fall for sure. She might even start to roll and hit a tree without ever breaking the surface again. No one would ever know what had happened to her, until next spring....

Tarnation! What nonsense. She'd cut the bullet from a man's shoulder and survived to tell about it. She could handle a little snow. Correction. A lot of snow. She just had to handle it before the sun went down. She didn't want to think about having to spend the night on the mountain, alone and without shelter.

Silver Falls. Which direction should she go to reach it? If Blackburn had headed away from town, she ought to go west. Then it occurred to her she ought to be going down the mountain, no matter what direction it was. Silver Falls was in a valley, with high mountains all around.

Trying to remember what it looked like around the Golden Eye Saloon, she decided Blackburn had to have taken her up into the mountains from there, because there was no way to go down, other than the same way the train went down to Denver. Her logic might be completely skewed, but then again...

Movement off to the left.

"Gabriel!"

Her voice didn't carry two feet with all the snow to soak up the sound. She sighed. The sun was climbing higher in the sky with every passing minute. She had to make use of daylight.

Taking care to test the ground before applying full weight, she leaned into a three-foot drift and headed down the mountain.

Gabriel was having a hell of a time covering any ground. Three feet of fresh, powdery snow made progress slow at best and impossible at times. Another hour and it would be dark. Dobbin puffed huge clouds of steamy breath into the crisp air. The horse was already exhausted. Frustration built in Gabriel until he thought he'd explode.

He'd been calling Trina's name from time to time, but sound wasn't carrying the way it did without all this snow. He strained to see any sign of life.

Movement off to the right. He stood in the stirrups, trying to get a better view. Something tumbled down the slope, about seventy-five yards away. He couldn't tell from this distance what—or who—it might be.

A shriek, muffled yet clearly human, made Gabriel's heart pound until his ears roared with blood streaking through his veins.

"Trina!"

He spurred Dobbin in the direction of the shriek. The big dapple-gray gelding stomped through the drifts, straining to climb while clearing a path in front of him. Before long, he had to stop and rest.

Gabriel dropped into the snow, sinking up to his waist, and slogged toward the last glimpse he'd had of her.

"Trina! If that's you, yell!"

A sound. Muffled.

"Yell again!"

A branch cracked and broke. Farther ahead, off to the left.

With a rustle of feathers—an owl flapping its way to safer territory—Trina burst from the snow, coughing and spitting, digging ice from her eyes, trying to clear her nose so she could breathe.

"Gabriel! Help me!" Her feet slipped from beneath her and she disappeared beneath the surface of the drift.

In less than a minute Gabriel made it to where she'd gone under. Punching holes through the snow until he found her, he grabbed her skirts, heavy and sodden, and hauled her into the sunlight.

Gabriel wanted to kiss her, but he cleared her nose, mouth and eyes of snow first. Her lips were like ice.

"Gabriel, you found me. You found me."

"Damn right, woman." He gathered her close, felt

her shivering like aspen leaves in a brisk wind, opened his coat and pulled her inside. She was cold to the bone, and wet. He had to get her back to town.

When she finally was able to take a deep breath and turned her face, red and chapped, to his, he kissed her until she had to gasp for breath again.

"Can you stand to wait another hour to get back to town, or should I build a fire to warm you up now?" He dug in his pack, pulled out the bottle of whiskey and made her take a long swig. She coughed and sputtered.

"I don't care. As long as I'm with you, I'm all right." She buried her face in his flannel shirt and tightened her grip on his middle.

Gabriel took a long, slow, deep breath and closed his eyes. He breathed a prayer of thanks, pulled his coat tighter around her and held her until she stopped shivering. He had to ask her some hard questions.

"Trina, where did Blackburn take you?"

"To a mine tunnel. He'd been there before. We were out of the storm and reasonably warm." She looked into his eyes. "He didn't hurt me, Gabriel. In fact—"

Gabriel pulled her back against his chest. "Thank God."

Trina knew she'd have to tell Gabriel what Blackburn had said, but not now. Their first chore was to get back to Silver Falls.

"How far are we from town?"

Gabriel thought for a moment. "About an hour. We'd best get to it. The sun won't last much longer. It'll be cold on this mountain once it gets dark."

She grinned. "Not as long as we're together. We'll keep each other warm."

He kissed her again, then looked to see if they still

had a horse to ride. "Whoa, Dobbin." He caught the big dapple-gray, set Trina in the saddle, then led them down the mountain.

Amos McCabe sat in a chair by the window—against doctor's orders—watching for Gabriel. There could be no doubt now that he'd gone to find Blackburn—and Trina. Amos had hired the McNaughts' son to scout the town, asking about her. The report verified his worst fears. Trina hadn't been seen since the Golden Eye. The bartender said he'd been behind the bar when she left and hadn't seen exactly what had happened. After that, not one red hair had been seen in town.

Blackburn had her. And the storm had kept Gabriel from following. Trina had spent the night on the mountain with a killer.

It would be dark soon. Another night on the mountain?

Glancing from one street to another, Amos focused on the street leading past the Golden Eye and squinted at the figure of a man leading a horse. Slumped over the horse's neck...was a woman with red hair.

Amos forgot about being strong and stoic. Tears welled in his eyes and poured down his cheeks. His shoulders shook while he thanked God she was alive.

Mrs. McNaught barged into the room.

"They're back, Mr. McCabe! Frank saw 'em coming just now. Did you see?"

Amos ran one sleeve across his face and nodded, embarrassed to be caught crying. "I saw. Thank the Lord."

Behind him, she leaned over and peered out the window. When she turned back, she made a noise like "Aw," and handed him a lacy handkerchief from her sleeve. "It's all right, Amos," she said softly. "Your little girl is alive and, from the looks of it, not hurt bad. I'll see to it she and Mr. Hart get some hot stew in their bellies the minute they hit the hotel."

Suddenly he was dog-tired, and his side pained him again. How long had he been in this chair? Five hours? Six?

"You need your rest. I'll bring her up just as soon as she's eaten and washed up a little. She'll want to look pretty when she sees her pa." She helped him back to bed and tucked in the covers, all the way to his neck. "And you can call me Bertha, like most folks 'round here do."

"Thank you, Bertha. Tell...tell my daughter...I love her. Send her up...soon as you can." Amos drifted off even before she closed the door.

Gabriel helped Trina off the horse, then picked her up to carry her inside. The hotel keeper's wife met them at the door.

"Bless her heart. Is she gonna be all right? I have stew in the kitchen, and a bowl of warm water to wash her face." A catch in her voice showed relief and concern.

"She's all right. Just all in. How's the senator?"

"Better now his daughter's back and safe. He's been sittin' by that window most of the day. He's back to bed now. Wanted to wait to see her, but just couldn't stand the strain."

So McCabe knew Trina had been taken by Blackburn. And that she was back, safe.

Trina roused in his arms when he set her gently on one of the sofas in the parlor. She'd gone limp when he'd put her on the horse, and still felt as if she had no bones at all. Plumb worn-out. His throat tightened at the thought of what she'd been through. Pure hell. Nothing less.

"I'm going to the kitchen to get the stew. I'm Bertha, if you need me." She hurried off.

Trina opened her eyes. "Gabriel?"

"Rest now. We're at the hotel. Bertha is bringing us some stew."

"My father—"

"He's fine. Been worried about you, but he's sleeping, since he knows you're safe."

She touched his cheek with her fingertips. "You came for me, Gabriel. Thank you."

"Didn't have anyplace better to be at the moment, Miss McCabe." He kissed her lightly. Her eyes fluttered closed.

Bertha appeared at the door. "Stew's on the table. Come and get it."

Gabriel nudged Trina. "Want some stew?"

"You may have to feed it to me."

"With pleasure, ma'am."

After they ate stew and cornbread, Bertha helped put Trina to bed, leaving Gabriel in the hallway, dog-tired, needing to sleep for a week. Blackburn was still out there somewhere. Heading east, from what Trina had told him. He'd be holed up again tonight, in another mine tunnel, probably. No way he'd come back to Silver Falls.

They'd missed the noon train. There wouldn't be another into town for three days. For the best, Gabriel supposed. McCabe had to have time to heal. Trina needed rest and quiet. And Gabriel needed to be in Silver Falls for a couple more days, just in case Blackburn got desperate and decided to come back. Tonight, though...

He heard McCabe calling, and went to his door.

Amos tried to get out of bed, but fell back on the pillow, gasping for breath. Gabriel went into the room.

"Lie still, Senator. No need to get up."

"Katrina..."

"Sleeping. Full of stew. He didn't hurt her."

Amos squeezed his eyes shut. "Dear God, Gabriel, when I realized that scum had her..."

"I know the feeling. I'd put two slugs in him, though. Slowed him down. He made Trina cut one of them out of his shoulder."

Amos stared at Gabriel. "She cut out the bullet?"

"That's what she said. Blackburn downed a bottle of rotgut, passed out. She used his hunting knife."

Amos shook his head. "You think you know your children, then they do something to surprise the hell out of you. I never would have thought——"

"I know. It shocked me, too, and I haven't known her that long. She's tough, Senator. Gets that from you, I suspect."

"And her brothers. Raised in a houseful of men, I guess she had to be tough or take the hind teat. My sons would die for their sister."

Gabriel grinned. "I can see why."

Amos started to say more, but didn't. Gabriel decided not to ask.

"Get some rest, Senator. She's safe and we're stuck here until the next train—three days."

"Damn. I'll have to send a wire home. Could you..."

"Give it to me. I'll send it."

When Gabriel left McCabe's room he thought about trying to send the wire tonight, then decided it would be impossible in a town as small as Silver Falls. Morning would be soon enough.

In his room he didn't bother to take off his clothes. He fell into bed, pulled the covers over his head and sank into a deep, dreamless sleep.

Trina awoke at noon the next day, aching all over, stiff with cold and all she'd been through the past two days. She first thought of Gabriel. Then her father.

She dressed quickly and went straight downstairs to the front desk. A large woman with a bright smile greeted her.

"Up and around, are we? Bet you're starvin'. Dinner will be ready in about twenty minutes."

"Thank you. Where is my father, Senator Amos McCabe?"

"Senator? Didn't know he was a senator. He's in that room right next to yours. Took him his breakfast early this morning. He was shore glad to see you back to the hotel safe and sound last night. Wanted to see you, but he was plumb tuckered from sittin' at that winder all day. Lawsey, but he was worried 'bout you. We all were."

"Thank you," Trina said again, rather dumbfounded by all the talk. "I'll go and see him now."

"You do that. I'll be bringing his dinner to his room. How 'bout I bring yours, too?"

"That would be wonderful. Thank you." She hesitated. "Is Mr. Hart around somewhere? I want to thank him properly for rescuing me."

"He went to town early this morning. I'm expecting him back any minute— There he is now."

Gabriel came through the front door, grinned when

he saw her standing there. "Morning, Miss McCabe. Morning, Bertha."

"Mr. Hart." Trina warmed all over under his gaze. Bertha grinned more brightly than the sun.

"Your father asked me to wire your brothers about our delay. I sent word we'd be back in a couple of days. Your father is resting quietly, I assume?"

"Resting, perhaps, but I would bet he's anything but quiet. He does not take kindly to being ill in bed."

"Or to having his daughter kidnapped. I'm sure he'll be up and around in no time."

"I'm sure. Thank you again for rescuing me, Mr. Hart. It was most kind of you."

"My pleasure, ma'am."

Gabriel had to get away from the desk before he burst out laughing at all the pleasantry. If he couldn't kiss her pretty soon, he'd bust a gut.

Trina turned to Bertha. "Ma'am, do you have a bathtub in this hotel?"

"I reckon we do. Hot bath costs extra, though. Ten dollars."

"That's outrageous!"

"Not for a mining town, Miss McCabe. Water's a scarce commodity in the wintertime. Have to melt snow when the streams are all froze over. No baths tonight, 'cause I'm doin' laundry. Tomorrow. Take it or leave it."

Trina knew it was extreme, but she longed for a bath. "I'll take it. Would you please bring the tub and the hot water to my room tomorrow night, right after supper? I'll just have to make do with a spit bath tonight. In cold water."

"I'll send the tub with my boy, but you'll have to

haul the water yourself. I don't climb them stairs totin' water."

Gabriel intervened. "I'll be glad to carry the water for you, Miss McCabe. If you'd allow me, that is."

Trina felt the warmth of his nearness again and repressed the sudden need to fan her face with one hand.

"Why, thank you, Mr. Hart. That would be most kind. First door at the top of the stairs."

"I'll bring the tub to your room, as well, ma'am. You can have a bath just before retiring tomorrow evening." Gabriel tipped his hat at her again.

"Thank you kindly, Mr. Hart."

"Not at all, ma'am."

Trina bounced back up the stairs. Gabriel bringing her bath right before bedtime. My, my, what possibilities that suggested. She hadn't had someone to scrub her back in a month of Sundays. What she had in mind was scandalous, but she'd earned some pampering. She couldn't wait until tomorrow night.

First things first, though.

She pushed on her father's door. The hinges squeaked and woke him. He blinked several times, still groggy with sleep.

"Papa..."

"Trina?"

She went to the bed and straight into his arms.

"Thank God," he murmured. She heard tears in his voice, and shed a few of her own.

Chapter Fourteen

Would he come? Trina climbed into bed, as clean as
she could manage with only a pitcher of cold water, a
sliver of soap and a washing cloth from her bag. Shivering, she waited until the covers had warmed, then
shimmied out of her nightgown. If he came, she wanted
nothing between them. Nothing to separate his bare skin
from hers.

Dear God, please let him come....

Gabriel waited until almost midnight before slipping
into Trina's room. He detected the scent of soap and
felt his groin stir as he pictured her bathing before going
to bed.

He'd almost lost her. That realization forced him to
come to terms with how he felt about her. He wanted
her to know.

Her breathing, deep and steady, almost made him
change his mind. But then she turned over, stretched
and propped herself on one elbow.

"I've been waiting for you."

In three quick motions he dropped his boots, pants

and shirt on the floor and eased under the covers beside her.

Nestled close, Gabriel tried to tell himself he'd come only to make sure she was still all right and not suffering any ill effects of her captivity. It didn't take long, though, to abandon those thoughts in favor of the real reason he'd come.

Stroking her naked back, he nuzzled her ear, pulled the earlobe into his mouth and sucked until she moaned. His hands roamed over her firm little bottom, back up to her waist, then around and upward until he held her breast, squeezing the nipple in a steady rhythm.

Her kiss, intense and deep, invited him to continue.

He kissed his way to the pursed nipple and sucked. Switching to the other breast, he let his right hand wander down over her flat stomach. With his fingers he traced the line where the top of her bloomers usually rested, then lower.

Hair as soft as that on her head, concealing the essence of her womanhood, the center of sensation, the ultimate source of pleasure. Did she know it existed? Had she ever touched herself there? Or had she been so proper, so much a lady, she'd never considered such a thing?

Trina's body stiffened a bit when his hand covered that secret place between her thighs. She'd never known the wonders released by his lips, his tongue, on her mouth, her ears, her breasts. Could anything feel better than what she'd already experienced? Was it possible for…possible… Oh…dear…oh…

Gabriel teased her thighs apart and ran his fingers up and down the crease where those creamy thighs joined her body. With tenderness he'd forgotten he had, he tantalized her with feathery strokes, not touching anything with certainty, rubbing gently until she parted her legs voluntarily, her breathing ever deeper, slower, huskier. It was time to show Miss McCabe why he'd come to her bed tonight.

His fingers probed deeper.

A thin cry escaped her lips.

Wandering up and back, around, up and back again, he gave her pleasure, and found his own pleasure growing from the giving.

Trina's eyes filled with tears. Such ecstasy wasn't possible. Or so she'd believed. "Gabriel."

He lifted his lips from her breast. "Yes, Trina?"

"It's more than I ever dreamed it could be."

"There's more. Are you ready?"

"More? How could there...be...more...?"

He showed her with his fingers, so talented, so gentle, so educated, they surpassed her knowledge of her own body. Pleasure built steadily until she thought she couldn't bear it any longer.

"Gabriel...please..." She had no idea what she asked for. She only knew there was something... something coming...which might very well...drive her completely...out of her mind.

Gabriel took her all the way up. And held her when the moment came. He kissed her eyelids, lips and fingertips until the frenzy passed and she lay passive beneath him, breathing softly and regularly.

"Trina?"

Could she still speak? She didn't think so. Her throat felt numb. Her body warmly secure and fulfilled. Yet...

"There's more."

Her eyes fluttered open. "There couldn't be more."

"There is. But I hate to spoil what you're feeling right now."

"How could this feeling ever be spoiled? You've given me something I never knew to dream of. Such incredible feelings. Such pleasure. If only I could tell you…"

Gabriel knew making love would cause her pain, and he didn't want to do that, even though he ached for her.

He kissed her lips again and marveled at how beautiful she looked in the moonlight streaming through the window. The clouds must have cleared for the moon to shine through so brightly. The snow reflected, magnified and softened the moonlight, which bathed the room with a soft glow.

"I want it all. Now. Please."

"There would be pain. I don't think…"

"It doesn't matter. Please."

Gabriel needed her. "If you're sure."

She nodded and kissed him again, sweetly this time, without urgency, and waited for him to complete what they'd begun.

Gabriel stretched out beside her until they were side by side. Then he took her hand and guided her to him.

"Gabriel, I shouldn't—"

"Why not? You think it wouldn't be proper?"

She thought how ridiculous that sounded, considering what she'd allowed him to do. "I see your point." She closed her fingers around him and took a deep breath. Amazing. With all her curiosity and imaginings about what lay beneath a man's clothes, with all her spying and sneaking around, trying to catch one of her brothers naked, she'd never managed to do it. Her imagination had always filled in the blanks. Now she knew her imagination had been flimsy and pale compared to the real thing. She started to giggle.

"Trina?" Of all the reactions he'd expected, giggling wasn't one of them. "What's wrong?"

"Nothing. It has nothing to do with you. Really." She giggled again.

He propped himself on one elbow and traced her smiling lips with his finger. "A man doesn't take to having a woman laugh when she touches him. It isn't...flattering."

Trina had no idea what he was talking about, but she supposed he deserved a straight answer.

"Gabriel, you have to understand. I was raised with three older brothers. I always wondered..." Modesty stopped her for a minute, but then she plunged ahead. "I always wondered what—"

"All right. I understand. Why is it funny, now that you know?"

"I was imagining my brothers with— That is, built the way— Oh, dear, I'm not saying what I mean at all."

Gabriel laughed. Silly female. Picturing her brothers naked, now that she knew how a man was built.

"Trina, stop giggling."

"Yes, Gabriel."

"Touch me again."

"Yes, Gabriel."

He drew in a long breath.

"Now, let your fingers do whatever they want to do."

Did he mean... "I don't think I understand."

"Move them, Trina."

"Like this?"

He groaned.

"Did I hurt you?"

"God, no. I can't believe you never did this before. You're so good at it."

"I certainly have not done this before. I am a lady."

"Of course you are. I never said…" He groaned again. "I never said you weren't. Do that again, please."

"What? That?"

He buried his face in her left breast and sucked the nipple into his mouth. Never had a woman touched him in such a way. She knew exactly which spots made lightning flash through him. How could she be so lucky the first time? Damn, but it felt good. Had he been without a woman so long that any little touch would do this to him? He didn't think so. He also knew he couldn't last much longer at the rate she was going. Sliding those long, graceful fingers down over him, cupping him in her hand and squeezing—not hard enough to hurt, just enough to drive him crazy. If he let her go any further…

"That's enough, Trina."

"Don't you like it? It was rather fun. I thought I'd try—"

"It's time to finish up."

She stuck out her bottom lip again, disappointed the fun was almost over.

"That lip. Why do you have to stick out that lip?" Gabriel pulled it into his mouth and enjoyed kissing her again, while positioning himself above her.

"Don't scream, okay? We don't want to wake anyone at this hour."

"Scream? Why should I scream?"

"Just kiss me and shut up. I told you this is going to hurt, but it won't last long. Are you ready?"

"I'm ready." She wondered what he could be talking about.

He thrust hard into her. She screamed straight into his mouth, muffling the sound. He lay perfectly still for a moment, savoring the feel of a place so soft it couldn't really exist.

She didn't know whether to laugh or cry, scream or moan in pleasure. So many emotions, tangled in her mind, left her breathless.

"Does it hurt now?"

"No. Is it supposed to?"

"Maybe a little at first. I'm going to move now. It might be a little sore."

It was a lot sore! But Trina didn't make a sound. Instead, she felt that exotic thrill build inside her, just as it had before.

"Oh, Gabriel, it's incredible. Strange, but I love it. I never thought I would, listening to my stuffy old aunts talking about men having their way with women. But it's exquisite!"

"Damnedest woman I've ever met," he mumbled against her neck.

Gabriel began a slow, deliberate rhythm, which Trina learned and matched. Carefully he accelerated the pace, hoping he could hold out long enough to make it good for her, too, but he suspected it was a foregone conclusion, from the noises she made and the way she bit his neck and sucked on his ears.

Damnedest woman...

Higher, higher the sensations built. Faster and faster he catapulted to the top, then gathered her close, closer, until it was over.

"Gabriel? Did it hurt?"

When he could talk again, he whispered, "No, Trina. It was incredible."

"So, men feel such pleasure, too?"

"Sometimes. Not always." His head still swam, but

it would clear soon. "When everything is exactly right, then it's wonderful. Perfect."

"Then we must be perfect together?"

"Right." Gabriel didn't want to encourage her any further. In fact, he was already having second thoughts about making love to the virginal Miss McCabe practically under her father's nose. If the senator found out what they'd done tonight, there'd be no soothing his outrage. He doubted Trina would fess up and admit she'd come to him willingly. Then he thought about the young man back at the depot. Damn! Why hadn't Gabriel thought about him sooner? He rolled over and lay beside her.

"Trina, who was that man with you in Denver—the one who kissed your cheek before you got on the train?"

"My brother Tom. Why? I didn't realize you'd noticed me even before we boarded the train." The thought flushed her cheeks even more than they were already flushed.

"Never mind."

She had a lovely time running her hands over Gabriel's back, chest and stomach. She felt something rough on his rib cage, on the left side.

"Gabriel, what's this?" She tried to see, but it was too dark.

"An old scar. Nothing to worry about."

She pressed harder and he winced.

"It's still sore."

"I'd best be getting back to my own room."

He didn't want to talk about it. It had to be where Blackburn had shot him. Fighting tears, she continued to adore his body. There was another rough place on his right wrist. She didn't mention it. "Love me again, Mr. Hart?"

"With pleasure, Miss McCabe."

As Gabriel worked magic on her body, Trina savored every sensation, every sweet kiss and caress, as though they were completely new. They'd come so close to losing everything. To losing each other. She embraced him tightly as a sob escaped her.

"Trina? Are you all right?" Gabriel kissed her softly.

"Perfect. It's all so...perfect." She cried into his shoulder.

Gabriel laughed softly. He'd never understand why women cried when they were happy. Perhaps, though, he understood what she was feeling. They'd come too close to death, too close to losing everything that had grown between them during these short few days they'd spent together, to ever take any of it for granted again.

They still had each other. It meant more than either of them could possibly express.

Chapter Fifteen

"Papa, are you awake?"

Amos opened one eye, then clamped it shut again. "No."

She closed the door, set a bowl of oatmeal she'd brought from the kitchen on the table beside the bed, then pulled a chair close. "Supper. You have to eat so you can regain your strength."

"I'm strong enough." He wrinkled his nose. "What's that smell?"

"Oatmeal, with extra cream and sugar. Just the way you like it. You shouldn't have anything hard to digest until you're better."

"I don't like oatmeal."

"Of course you do. Don't be silly."

Both eyes opened at that. "Watch what you say to your father, young lady."

"After you've eaten, I'll bring a bucket of hot water and you can have a nice bath before going to sleep."

"Bath! You expect to give me a bath?"

"Who else? I doubt Gabriel would agree to do it, but I could ask."

"I'll do it myself." His nose twitched. "Extra sugar, did you say?"

"Mounds of it."

"I'll try one bite."

She spooned it into his mouth. "Good?"

"Tolerable. Yours is better."

Another spoonful. "Did you rest well this afternoon?"

"Hell, no, I didn't sleep well. My side hurts like hell."

"Watch your language, Papa. The doctor will come by again tomorrow, just as he did this morning."

He finished the oatmeal, then, refusing any help, turned onto his back, grunting and groaning.

"Let me fluff your pillows before I go."

"My pillows are fine. Leave them alone."

"Well, then, I'll be back with the hot water—"

"I don't feel like taking a bath tonight. Wait until tomorrow."

"Very well. Is there anything else I can do for you? I could read to you for a while."

"Katrina, you're worse than that excuse for a woman downstairs! You've done nothing but fuss over me the whole blessed day! Get out of here and let me rest!"

She kissed his forehead. "Mercy, but you can be a trial when you're sick," she told him, secretly pleased that her bout of mothering him had produced the desired result. Now she'd be free to plan her evening without having to include tending to her father.

Around eight, Gabriel gave up on hearing any new information about Blackburn's whereabouts and went to the kitchen to find Bertha.

She pointed him toward the shed out back, where he

found a washtub and two buckets. He piled the buckets into the tub, then went back to the kitchen, where Bertha had steaming kettles on the stove. While Bertha filled the buckets, he took the tub upstairs and tapped lightly on Trina's door, but left before she answered.

He took care not to slosh too much water while climbing the uneven steps the second time. He set the heavy buckets just outside Trina's door, then knocked lightly and waited.

"Who is it?"

"Water boy."

Trina opened the door just a crack. "How do I know it's really you?"

Gabriel picked up the buckets. "Water, see? For your bath. Want me to pour it into the tub for you, or shall I just pour it over your head right where you're standing?"

Would he actually do such a wasteful thing even in jest? She didn't dare test him. Bertha might not take kindly to heating more water. Trina opened the door wider, being careful to stay behind it so he couldn't see her. "By all means, come in, Mr. Hart."

Once he was inside, she closed the door and locked it.

Gabriel set the buckets down and turned around. She stood there naked, bold as brass.

"I'm ready for my bath."

"I guess you are." He took a step toward her, but she stopped him with one hand on his chest.

"Not yet. After I've had my bath. From the looks of it, you could stand one, too."

Gabriel looked down at his clothes. "Guess I could. It's a shame there's not room in that tub for both of us."

Trina's eyes twinkled with mischief. "I'll scrub your back if you'll scrub mine."

"Deal."

He poured the water into the tub, which was just big enough for a lady to sit down in if she were to pull her knees up under her chin, or hang her legs over the edge onto the floor.

"She calls this a bathtub?"

"Guess it's all they've got. It's better than nothing. Shall I go first?"

Gabriel unbuttoned his shirt. "You'd better. Once I get out, that water won't be fit for hogs."

"You aren't that dirty. Some of the men in this town are, but not you."

"Well, thanky, ma'am."

Trina giggled, then put one hand over her mouth. Whispering, she said, "We have to remember not to be too loud. My father is in the next room. He might hear us."

Gabriel couldn't wait any longer. He gathered her into his arms and pressed her firmly against his chest. "I don't think so. I looked in on him on the way to your room. He's snoring so loud, he wouldn't hear an avalanche if it crashed through his bedroom. He was glad to see you today."

"He actually had tears in his eyes when I came into his room yesterday. Hugged me harder than he has in years. We talked quite a while before I made him go back to sleep. Today I read to him, fluffed his pillow every twenty minutes, tried to feed him—"

"Is that why he yelled at you?"

"He told me to leave him alone the rest of the day. Are you disappointed we won't be visiting him this evening?"

"Terribly." Gabriel tweaked one nipple.

Trina smiled and nestled close to Gabriel. "Wash me head to toe?"

"It'd be my pleasure, ma'am."

Gabriel kissed her thoroughly, running his hands over her chilled skin, before helping her into the tub.

Trina sat down with her knees scarcely a foot from her chin and sighed at the velvety feel of warm water on bare skin. It had been too many days since she'd had the luxury of a full bath.

Gabriel found a bar of soap on the dresser, next to the pitcher and bowl, dipped it in the water and rubbed it in his hands to work up a lather. Then, taking his time, being careful to cover every inch, he washed Trina's back, the nape of her neck, her chest and then each breast.

"Umm. You're hired. I'll have a bath each morning when I get up, another after dinner, one each evening after supper and again before bedtime."

"Yes, m'lady." Gabriel asked her to stand, washed each foot as she held it up, then each leg, each thigh, then moved back to her breasts and worked his way down again.

"Oh, Gabriel, it feels heavenly. We'll have to hurry if this water's to be warm at all for your bath."

"Don't worry about me. I'll be warm enough."

He washed her stomach, then between her legs, while she cooed and mewed her approval.

He suddenly went to the door and opened it.

"Gabriel, you aren't leaving?" She shivered in the draft from the hall.

"Nope." He picked up two more buckets of water, which had been left outside in the hall by Bertha's husband—persuaded by Gabriel it was only right for charging ten dollars for the use of such a piddling little tub and that measly amount of hot water. He kicked the door closed and came back to the tub.

"We'll use half a bucket to rinse you off, then I'll add the rest to the tub. The second bucket will be to rinse me off. I have more to rinse than you do."

"Uh-huh." Trina picked at the buttons on his jeans. "When are you going to get rid of those?"

"Right after you're rinsed."

He poured half of one bucket over her head before she could protest.

Trina sputtered and gulped. "Gabriel! I wasn't ready!"

"Too bad. Out, woman. My turn to be washed."

She planted a kiss on his lips. "Well, I intended to soak a while, but I suppose—"

"Out!" He picked her up, letting her slip and slide against his naked chest, kissing her neck and her mouth as they came by, and almost changed his mind about the bath. But it looked too good to pass up. He set her on the rug, handed her a towel about the size of a man's hankie, then stepped into the tub himself.

He knew there was no way he could sit down with his feet inside the tub, unless he wanted to chew his own knees. That didn't appeal to him, so he sat down carefully with his knees over the edge and his feet on the floor making dark, wet ovals on the hardwood planks.

"If you weren't so tall, you could have a better bath." She lathered her hands and started at the top of his head, working her way down.

"You're hired, too. Twice a day should be sufficient, though."

Trina loved washing him. His skin was softer than

she'd ever imagined a man's skin could be, especially with soap making her hands slippery. His muscles lay hard beneath the surface, firm, yet relaxed. There was none of the cording she'd seen earlier when he was out to kill Blackburn. The thought gave her a chill.

"Cold?"

"A little. Warm me up later?"

Gabriel pulled her over to kiss her. Her wet hair in his hand felt like silk. Her breasts, hanging over the edge of the tub, begged to be caressed—or kissed. When he finished kissing her lips, he kissed each nipple.

Trina ran her tongue all around his ear while he was busy. "We're never going to get you clean if you keep doing that."

"Well, then—" he gave each nipple one last kiss "—I guess I'd better stop."

Trina groaned and went back to washing. She scrubbed his back, his chest and as far down on his stomach as the waterline.

"Stand up, please."

"Nope." He went back to work on her breasts.

"I can't wash the rest of you if you don't." Mercy, but it felt heavenly. Could anything possibly feel that good?

"Do my legs and work up." He switched to her ears.

"If you insist." She eased away and soaped his feet, between his toes, bringing a protest that he was ticklish, then each leg. There was so much hair on his legs, she found it fascinating to see what sort of designs she could make with the soap.

"Trina, what are you doing?"

"Playing."

"Play with me instead."

She looked up at him and he laughed. "What's so funny?"

"You have soap on your nose. Come here."

She leaned toward him. He carefully wiped the soap away, then gazed at her for a long moment.

"More soap?"

"Nope. I was just thinking about how pretty you are."

She blushed at that. "I'm glad you think so, Gabriel."

"I do. Wash!"

She reached into the tub and grasped him firmly.

He took a slow, deep breath.

"If you won't stand up, I'll just have to wash underwater."

"Be my guest."

His breathing quickened as she worked on him. Long, slow strokes, then quick, short ones. Then round and round, up and down.

"Trina..."

"Not clean yet, Gabriel."

"Clean enough. Get the water."

"Just one minute more, Gabriel."

"I won't last one minute more, woman."

"That's all right. You gave me such pleasure this way, I want to return the favor. Relax and enjoy. This is from me to you."

Gabriel smiled at her with such affection, she almost cried. Then he closed his eyes and let her work magic on him with her fingers. She used both hands, so it didn't take long before he reached the peak, groaning and breathing more and more. She stayed with him until it was over, then put her arms around him and held him as close as the tub would allow.

Gabriel felt dizzy and completely relaxed. "You're one talented lady."

"Thank you, kind sir."

"Now, hand me that bucket."

She gave it to him and stood back while he poured the water over his head and body. Water splashed all over the rug and spotted the frayed medallion print chair next to the bed. "Gabriel, Bertha will charge us extra for cleaning up all this water."

"Who cares? It was worth it. Hand me that other towel."

"I'm afraid it's almost useless. Not big enough to dry your face, much less all of you."

"Then we'll just have to use the sheets, won't we?"

Trina giggled a little. "Where will we sleep?"

"In my bed."

"But what if—"

"I paid Bertha's boy—can't remember his name—to sleep in the room across the hall from your father tonight. If he calls, the boy will knock on my door."

Trina wound her arms around him. "You've thought of everything."

"Almost. I forgot to light the stove in my room before I went for the water. It's going to be cold in there."

"Not for long. We'll warm it up soon enough."

The next morning Trina woke up smiling. She thought dreamily about making love to Gabriel the night before, after that luscious bath. Now that sunshine was beginning to peek through the dingy filet-crocheted curtains, she wished she could banish the sun behind the mountain. The train was due in about noon today. A day early. Couldn't the train have run on time? Loving Gabriel had become a habit she didn't want to break.

He lay prone beside her, one arm draped over her stomach. She eased her hand out and rubbed his back in long, slow strokes, softly, tenderly, lovingly.

"Umm," he groaned. "That feels good."

"It isn't time to get up yet."

He opened one eye and blinked several times, then watched her smile as she continued caressing. Beautiful. Even with her hair messy and the look of sleep just leaving her eyes, she was still the most beautiful creature he'd ever laid eyes on.

"Come here, woman."

"I'm already here."

"No, here." He pulled her mouth down on his and took his time kissing her.

Trina wound her arms around him and continued rubbing wherever she could reach.

Gabriel rolled back until he'd pulled her up on top of him, then let his hands wander from her neck to her cute little bottom and back again. She was soft as a kitten—to go with the kitten noises she made when he kissed her.

"Why did you get on the train in Denver?" He settled back onto the pillow, content to hold her and look at her.

"I came with Papa."

"Why?"

"I was concerned about his health. Why?"

He shook his head. "I don't know. I just can't believe you happened to be on the same train I was on, that's all."

She twirled her finger around his ear. "Are you glad I was?"

He stopped to think about it.

"Gabriel! If you have to think about it, then you must not be glad." She pouted.

He kissed her again, capturing that lower lip with no difficulty at all. "That's not it, Trina. When I got on that train, the last thing in the world I expected was to be kissing a certain redhead before we got to Silver Falls."

She pinked a bit at that.

"When Blackburn grabbed you..." The fear returned. He'd almost lost her. He tightened his arms around her. "I thought he was going to kill you, too."

"How long had you been married?"

"Two years."

Trina closed her eyes, but tears escaped anyway. "Gabriel, I'm so sorry."

For some reason, the usual anger didn't come. Gabriel pondered the absence for a moment, then let it go.

"When Blackburn grabbed me, it must have seemed as if it were happening all over again." She realized that what she'd said was terribly presumptuous. It implied Gabriel loved her just as he'd loved Hannah. She waited, wondering if she'd said too much.

Gabriel filtered her hair through his fingers. It tumbled over her back and down onto his shoulders. "Yes, it was much the same. That scum, holding the woman I—" What he'd almost said surprised him.

Trina froze.

Gabriel noticed the change. "Trina?"

"Yes, Gabriel."

"Look at me."

She did, terrified of what she might see in his eyes. Or not see. She twirled his hair around her fingers and caressed his ear with featherlight strokes.

God, but this woman knew exactly—

She switched to the other ear, then kissed one of his nipples. His chest rose faster as she sucked the flat bud and flicked her tongue over it until it was firm and wrinkled under her tongue.

He lost all thought for a minute. There seemed to be a direct line between...

She swallowed the lump in her throat and watched his eyes. All she saw was an intensity unlike anything she'd seen from him before, mixed with building desire.

"I love you, Gabriel. With all my heart."

For what seemed like a long, long time his expression didn't change. Then he smiled. Bigger and bigger, until he laughed and laughed, holding her, rocking her back and forth.

"Gabriel, what is it? Is something wrong?"

He swiped at tears. "There's nothing wrong."

She looked straight into his eyes. "Then what's so funny? Tell me!"

"I never would have guessed it could happen...." He touched his lips to hers, stalling, found one of her breasts under the covers and pinched the tip gently.

"What? Tell me this instant!"

"I love you, too."

All the laughter drained out of her. "You aren't just saying that?"

"I never say things I don't mean, Trina. I love you. How or why, I can't say. I just know I do."

Trina started to cry. She buried her face in his hairy chest and blubbered like a baby.

"Is it that bad?" He rubbed her back until she hushed, and felt warm and content for the first time in memory.

"I'm just so happy, I don't know what else to do."

"I'll show you."

She grinned and wiped her tears on the sheet, then disappeared under the covers with an impish grin on her face.

Gabriel closed his eyes and groaned with pleasure. He had to admit she'd been an apt pupil.

Kissing, caressing, touching, massaging, probing, teasing, exploring, they got to know each other all over again. It felt different this time. Something had changed.

Trina thought more about pleasuring Gabriel than about her own pleasure, and Gabriel used every skill he possessed to show her making love could be like going to heaven for a while.

She tried things on him she'd thought about since loving him only hours before, and he let her know with soft groans and ofttimes frantic kisses that he appreciated her creativity and ingenuity.

Gabriel took his time getting to know her in the daylight. Her soft skin and delicate curves all gave him immense pleasure.

"Gabriel, it's better every time."

Busy tasting the skin around her belly button, darting his tongue in and around until she gasped and giggled with the sensations, he mumbled agreement. "Uh-huh."

Gabriel pushed her thighs apart, knowing any other woman might consider him heathenish for wanting to kiss her most private parts. He suspected, though, Trina would welcome any new sensation, and had a feeling she'd love this particular one.

He started with the inside of each thigh, letting her get used to the idea before springing the finale on her.

Trina didn't mind his exploration. She only wished she could hold him closer, please him with her hands and mouth as he was pleasing her. Who would have dreamed her thighs would be so sensitive, the backs of her knees tingly where he touched them with his fingertips?

He inched upward gradually. Higher still. He curled his fingers in the downy hair between her legs and smiled when she moved her legs farther apart.

Trina lost all logical thought when his fingers worked their magic on her again. Never mind confessions. Right now she didn't want to think about anything else.

He kissed what his fingertips had primed for his tongue.

Trina drew in a long, slow breath and closed her eyes. She wondered if any woman had ever died of ecstasy or if she would be the first. Gabriel was doing something to her she would have considered animalistic before today. Barbaric. Decadent. But, oh, didn't it feel heavenly? No, that wasn't an adequate word.

Exquisite...immense...unbelievable...joyous...

Gabriel heard little kitten noises again and knew she was close to completion. This time, though, he wanted it to happen when he was deep inside her, kissing and holding her, making it all it could be. He stopped licking and sucked for a moment, felt her hips rise, her body tensed for release, then backed away.

Trina couldn't believe he'd stopped.

"Gabriel?"

He was above her now, and she realized it was time for the coupling.

He nodded and kissed her. "You got it, lady."

Yes, she had it. She had him. For these few wondrous moments he was completely, irrevocably hers. She intended to see to it he didn't mind one bit.

"I've got it." She reached for him, cupped him in her hands and massaged ever so gently until he slipped, eased, almost whispered into her. Wonderful. Marvelous. Incredible.

He began a slow, steady rhythm. She arched her hips until the sensation built gradually again. Before long, they moved together, tension growing, hands wandering, stroking, pleasuring, mouths tasting shoulders, ears, eyelids and lips.

Trina felt the explosion coming and gave herself to it completely. His tongue in her mouth intensified the release. She couldn't kiss him hard enough.

Amazement widened his eyes before he squeezed them tightly shut, lost in the power and strength of the climax when it came.

Lying still, breathing still rapid, bodies damp and warm, lips slack, they still sought another kiss.

Gabriel felt something he'd not felt in over a year. Contentment. Fulfillment. Love. For a woman he'd just met. A woman who'd found the empty place in his soul and filled it with herself. He didn't want that place to be empty ever again. He wanted Trina. From this day on.

"Gabriel?"

"Uhmm?"

"I love you."

Gabriel kissed the words away.

Chapter Sixteen

Amos McCabe tried to sit up, then grabbed his forehead and lay back on the pillow for a moment. Once the pain subsided, he got up slow and easy and swung his legs over the side of the bed.

He could barely move, thanks to the way the doctor had bandaged his middle, but he knew he had to send a second telegram this morning before they boarded the train at noon.

Damn that youngest son of his! Bo had been hard to handle since he was born, always into stuff he had no business being into, causing heaps of trouble when he should've been learning how to work.

That was Bo's biggest problem. He'd never learned how to enjoy working. He preferred gallivanting around, sowing wild oats, until it was a wonder the whole state of Colorado wasn't choked with them.

Once Amos got home, he intended to take care of Bo and his schemes once and for all. Why he'd let Bo get him involved with the likes of Blackburn, he couldn't explain to himself. This scheme could have gotten him—and Trina—killed.

Amos finally managed to stand, and cursed at the

pain shooting through his side. Waves of dizziness almost made him sink back onto the bed, but he steadied himself on the bedpost and waited until the spell passed.

His shirt. What had they done with it? Then he remembered. With a bullet hole in it and soaked with blood, it had probably been thrown away. So where were the rest of his clothes?

He spied his bag next to the door. After a couple of false starts he made his way over to it and picked it up.

Damn! Even that little bit of strain had set his wound to smarting. He found a shirt and managed to pull it on. The effort left him wheezing. He decided to sit down again until he could get his breath. Damn mountain towns, anyway. Why couldn't they have enough air for folks to breathe, like other places? Denver was bad enough. Silver Falls was downright torturous.

It took nearly ten minutes before he felt strong enough to walk again. Calling Trina occurred to him, but he knew she was probably sleeping late again this morning. After such a scare, she might be sick for a week. Good thing Gabriel had been there to bring her back safe.

Amos thought about Gabriel for a minute. Trina had really taken a shine to him, there was no doubt about that. But Gabriel had his mind set on one thing and one thing only. Blackburn. Why hadn't Amos been able to see it on the train? It had sure been easy enough to figure out in the Golden Eye. Whatever Blackburn had done to Gabriel, he intended to kill him for it. Probably would've, too, if Trina hadn't shown up when she did.

Foolish female! He'd told her to stay at the hotel. Amos shook his head. If only Melanie had lived to help raise her daughter, Trina might not be quite as headstrong as she'd turned out to be. But then, Trina was so much like her mother, there might not have been much difference.

Amos got up from the bed and walked slowly to the door. He opened it carefully, not wanting to wake Trina. He listened for a moment but heard nothing at her door. She must still be asleep. Gabriel, too. Well, that was probably best. The train wouldn't be pulling out for several hours yet. Plenty of time for Amos to do what he needed to do.

The stairs proved a real challenge. It took him what seemed like most of the day to get halfway down. Bertha saw him and came running.

"Senator McCabe! You shouldn't be up and walking already. Where's your daughter or Mr. Hart? I'll get—"

"Leave them be. I'm just fine. I need to send a wire to Denver."

"Telegraph office is down the street. Give me the message and I'll take it for you."

"Fine, fine. Get me some paper and something to write with."

McCabe collapsed into the nearest chair, a cane bottom that had more holes than cane. So much exertion had been a mistake. He could feel it. But he had to get word—

"Here go, Senator."

Amos took the paper and pencil, which needed sharpening badly, and scribbled the message. He handed it back to her. "Read that back to me. My penmanship isn't the best."

She read haltingly, as though she hadn't had much education. "'Meet train in Denver tomorrow. Bring Bo. Everyone fine.'"

"That's it. Can you get that out on the wire immediately?"

"You betcha. Now, you just let me help you back upstairs where you belong. That train won't pull out till almost noon."

Amos got up and put one hand over the wound, paining him something awful now. "Under the circumstances, I'd be obliged for your help, Bertha. And you *can* call me Amos. Let's see if we can get me back to my room."

"All right, Amos." She grinned, revealing two teeth missing, right in front.

Trina, wrapped in a patchwork quilt from the bed, opened the door and peeked into the hall to make sure no one was there, then gave Gabriel one last smile before returning to her room. He was pulling on his jeans and shirt. It was all she could do to look away again. She adjusted the quilt. It was so thin in places, light could shine right through. Not much to cover up with, but all she had since she'd come in last night wearing nothing but a wet sheet. Gooseflesh popped up on every inch of exposed skin.

"Better get back to your room before your father wakes up." Gabriel waved her into the hall, wishing at the same time she could stay the rest of the day. "And put some clothes on. It's cold in the mountains. You look like a plucked chicken."

Trina was tempted to tickle him silly for that, but voices on the stairs interrupted. She pulled Gabriel's door shut, then dashed to her own room. It was Bertha, coming upstairs with someone. Her father! What was he doing downstairs?

She hurried inside, closed the door quietly behind her, then gulped when she saw the mess they'd left the night before. She ought to clean it up, but there wasn't time. She rummaged through her bags for fresh clothes. She'd brought clean bloomers and a fresh camisole. They slipped on first. She shimmied into a long petticoat, then pulled on a blouse. The two-piece gray wool suit had been her first choice when packing for the trip because it didn't wrinkle too badly when folded. The blue wool she'd worn the first day would never have survived being cramped in a traveling bag. She pulled out the suit jacket and skirt, shook both hard a couple of times, then put them on, satisfied she'd look at least half-decent for the trip back to Denver.

Her hair was another matter. Right now it lay in ringlets over her forehead, shoulders and back. That would have to be remedied for sure. She'd have to do her best to get it brushed out.

Someone knocked at the door.

"Just a minute."

"Trina? Aren't you up yet?"

Her father had the constitution of a mule. How could he possibly be up and around so soon after his injury?

"Papa? Is that you?"

"Who else would it be? Oh, good morning, Mr. Hart."

Trina listened carefully, but heard only garbled voices. She had to get out there.

She wadded her hair on top of her head—it took three pins instead of the usual two—and prayed it looked decent. The mirror over the chiffonier was so cloudy, she couldn't tell. She was so flustered this morning....

Yes, her heart answered. Flustered. And completely, totally, irrevocably in love.

She opened the door, loving the surprise in Gabriel's eyes when he saw her.

"Good morning, Mr. Hart. I trust you slept well."

"I did indeed, Miss McCabe. You look mighty nice this morning."

Amos looked at both of them, then frowned. "Trina, I do believe we're going to have to have a talk when we get home."

Trina kissed him lightly on the cheek. "Why, Papa, I don't know what on earth about, but if you want to have a talk we certainly shall." She smiled a little too broadly and fussed with her skirts. Could her father possibly know she'd spent the night with Gabriel? They'd have to be more careful. Discovery would be disastrous.

Gabriel rescued her. "I think we ought to get our belongings together and down to the depot. The train will be leaving in a couple of hours." Gabriel could see the senator was standing there only because of iron will. "Why don't we see if this town has a decent place to get some breakfast? I'm starved after all that activity yesterday."

"Decent? Are you saying my breakfasts aren't decent? Well, I never..." Bertha stomped off down the stairs.

"Wouldn't want to put you to any trouble, ma'am, seeing as how we missed *your* wonderful breakfast," Gabriel called after her, but the damage was done. He'd have to apologize again later.

Trina smiled to herself, remembering the activities that no doubt had left Gabriel as ravenous as she. She figured he was probably hungry for food, as well. That set her to giggling.

"Trina, what in tarnation has gotten into you on this trip? I swear—"

"Don't swear, Papa. It isn't polite. Let's go to breakfast, shall we?"

Gabriel nodded to Trina to precede them down the

stairs, while he took the senator's arm and practically carried him down the steep steps.

"You're up early this morning, Senator. I didn't expect you to be recovered and moving around so soon."

Amos wheezed with the effort of so much walking, even if Gabriel was supporting his weight more than he would have liked. He had to admit he was grateful for the help, though. Without it, he'd be stuck in that bed, with Trina fluttering around him, poking medicine at him the way she had yesterday. Tarnation! How could he have gotten himself—and his daughter—into such a fix? He'd expected her to be sick after being kidnapped, but she seemed almost normal. Happier than usual. Nothing made any sense.

"Easy, Senator." Gabriel helped him out the door.

"With such a slight wound, I can't stay in bed any longer. I have business to tend to before leaving. Uh...I'd also be obliged if you'd help me take care of one other detail, Mr. Hart."

They followed Trina next door to the Spotted Horse Café. It was chock-full of people drinking hot, steaming coffee and eating grilled ham and eggs and fried potatoes. The tantalizing odors made Gabriel's stomach rumble.

The café had four long tables down the center of the room and several smaller tables around the edges. Gabriel guessed the place doubled as a boardinghouse, judging from the presence of big bowls of grits and gravy, platters of greasy sausage and biscuits, and jars of molasses strung out down the long tables. The men sitting there passed the bowls up and down until they'd been scraped clean, then handed them to a huge woman with an apron and wearing a sour expression on her flabby face. She returned to the kitchen for refills. Then the passing started all over again.

Patrons sitting at smaller tables seemed to be eating different foods. The sight of a sizzling, juicy steak made Gabriel's stomach rumble again. That's what he wanted.

They chose a small table as close to the door as possible. The senator had depended more and more on Gabriel the farther they went. Once they were seated, he bowed his head, wiped his face with a handkerchief from his pocket and struggled to breathe normally.

"Blasted...mountain air."

"Sit up straighter, Senator. Makes it easier on the lungs."

"Yes, Papa, sit up straighter. I think Gabriel is right." Trina felt a wave of embarrassment. She'd used Gabriel's given name in front of her father. If he'd noticed, he didn't show it.

"Smells good." Gabriel looked at Trina when he said it.

Gabriel motioned to a man wearing a greasy apron, who seemed to be tending the smaller tables, and ordered steak, scrambled eggs and fried potatoes for all three of them, along with plenty of hot coffee.

"So what is it, Senator?"

"Beg pardon?"

"Whatever you need me to clear up for you."

"Now, Papa, we've imposed enough on Mr. Hart."

"It's all right, Miss McCabe. I've finished with my business—for the moment."

A wave of chills ran down Trina's spine. He wasn't through with Blackburn yet. With all her heart she wished he'd killed the scoundrel so he could get on with his life—preferably with her in the middle of it. But that couldn't happen yet, thanks to her interference.

"First of all, you two can stop pretending and call each other by your given names. I'm not blind. With what you've been through together, it's understandable you'd get to know each other well enough to be more familiar."

"Yes, Papa."

Gabriel just grinned.

"I brought some trunks with me from Denver."

"Guns for Blackburn?"

Trina gasped. "Guns?"

The senator's eyebrows shot up. "What makes you say that?"

"I was at the Golden Eye, remember? I overheard your conversation."

McCabe hesitated. "Yes, those trunks contain guns." He closed his eyes for a moment and shook his head. "They were to be traded for the deed."

"Where are the trunks now?"

"At the hotel. I knew better than to take them to the Golden Eye. I need to make sure they're loaded back on the train. I don't want Blackburn's sidekicks getting their hands on them."

Their food arrived, greasy but delicious.

Amos forked a chunk of steak into his mouth, cutting off further conversation.

Gabriel exchanged glances with Trina. She frowned and shrugged, puzzled, no doubt, by her father's behavior and statements. She appeared to dismiss it for the moment, though, in favor of eating breakfast. Gabriel decided to do the same. There would be plenty of time later to get the rest of the story.

They made short work of it. Gabriel paid for everything, over the senator's protests, then they went back to the hotel to collect their things. Amos waited downstairs, agreeing he didn't need to climb the stairs again.

While Trina and Gabriel were upstairs, Amos went to the counter to talk to Bertha.

"Any answer to my wire?"

"As a matter of fact, there was. Came while you were next door." She fetched it from a cigar box under the counter and handed it over.

Amos read silently, then stuffed the telegram into his pocket. "Much obliged, Bertha. You got any children?"

"Just one son. We weren't blessed with a large family."

Amos sighed. "Sometimes they aren't such a blessing."

Chapter Seventeen

They boarded the train at twelve thirty-five and went straight to their Pullman quarters. Only three other passengers boarded, so they more or less had the train to themselves. Since the return trip would be mostly downhill, they'd be into Denver by ten o'clock the next morning.

Gabriel supervised the reloading of McCabe's trunks into the baggage car and settled things with the local law about the dead man they'd unloaded from the passenger car on arrival. He figured he'd just about paid his debt to McCabe, even though there hadn't been a debt to pay in the first place. Yet, seducing the senator's daughter—or had she seduced him?—made him feel obliged to do something for the old man.

McCabe had gotten weaker as the morning progressed, and Gabriel knew he'd been up and around much too soon for the wound he'd sustained, slight as it had been. A man of the senator's age and size and with his breathing difficulties had no business coming this far up in altitude, much less getting himself shot, then hauling himself up and down stairs before the scab had even started to form.

Trina seemed happy enough.

Gabriel had talked to Horace at the Red Devil Saloon and asked, loud enough for everybody to hear, to be notified if Blackburn showed up again in Silver Falls. The word should get back to Blackburn's men before the train left the station, giving Gabriel the advantage he needed.

In her Pullman quarters, after supper that evening, Trina spread her clothes on the bed in hopes they'd dry out a little before tomorrow. Land sakes, but they'd drawn damp in that cold, snowy little mining town. She wanted to look nice when they got back into Denver, but with wrinkles in the other skirt and jacket she'd brought, she might just have to wear this same suit again tomorrow. She'd packed for a three-day trip, not a week.

Now for the blouse in her other case. The case was nowhere in the compartment.

She went next door. Her father was already asleep, snoring like a rusty buzz saw. She tiptoed around, looking for the missing case. Not there, either.

She knew she'd brought it from the hotel. The only other place it could be was in the baggage car with the trunks. She'd just have to go get it.

Trina feared the case hadn't been put on the train at all. If she'd left it in Silver Falls, it would be a passel of trouble to get it back to Denver again.

The baggage car was empty and dark. Even though sunshine had actually penetrated the clouds today for a short while, it had retreated now. It took her eyes several minutes to adjust. The trunks were on the right side of the car. There, sitting next to them, was the missing case.

"Thank goodness!" She picked up the case and turned around. A hand clamped over her mouth from behind. The odor of rotten teeth made her want to gag. Trina tried to scream, and the hand tightened. A knife appeared in front of her. She stopped fighting and stood still.

"Now, missy, just forget about hollerin' again. 'Cause if you do, I'm gonna slit your throat, ear to ear. Hear me?"

Blackburn. Terrified, she nodded understanding.

He loosened his grip, hesitated, waiting to see if she would panic and scream in spite of the warning. When she didn't, he turned her loose completely.

Trina stood like a statue, afraid to move a muscle or say a word.

"Now, you just do like I tell you and we'll all git to Denver without any of your purty little blood soakin' into these old wooden floors."

"Wh-what do you want me to do?"

"Just keep your mouth shut. I'll be ridin' back here all the way to Denver. You're gonna go back up front and act like nothin's wrong. 'Cause if you tell somebody 'bout me bein' here, I promise—" He grabbed her again and placed the blade of the knife at the base of her throat. "You an' your paw, and that lawman, Hart, will all die. You understand?"

Trina nodded. "I understand."

"If anyone tries to flush me outta here before we get to Denver, you're all gonna be sorry. And when we git to Denver, I expect you to keep ever'body busy while I slip off the train. If you don't, I'll kill ever'body."

"I understand completely."

"Good." He let her go. "I could use some food. And water. Just leave them inside the door."

"I'll try. How is your shoulder?"

He didn't answer right away. "Healin'. You did a good job gettin' the bullet out. I'm much obliged to you for that."

"No one deserves to die, Mr. Blackburn. Death comes soon enough without us hurrying it along."

He didn't respond to that. If she could only convince him to leave them alone.

"Now, you just head right back to your fancy quarters and just let ol' Otis be. Ya hear?" He threatened her with the knife again, but it seemed a halfhearted gesture.

Fear subsided a little, allowing her to think rationally again. She'd go along with him now. "I hear you, Mr. Blackburn."

He pushed her toward the door. His shoulder oozed blood through his shirt. Using that arm had cost him dearly. She could see pain in his yellowed eye. She also saw he was far from finished. She stood erect and as poised as she could manage. "My case."

"What?"

"I came for my case."

He stepped back, allowed her to fetch it. "I'll bring you something to eat as soon as I can manage it without anyone seeing. I know you must be hungry." Kindness had tempered his cruelty before. Perhaps it would again.

"Much obliged," he said softly.

"And don't worry, Mr. Blackburn. I won't tell anyone you're here. I promise. My word is good, remember?"

He nodded. She left the car without speaking.

Back in her own quarters she sank onto the bed and gave in to terror. Sobbing, quaking like an aspen leaf, she wanted desperately to go to Gabriel, to tell him

Blackburn was on the train. But another part of her wanted Blackburn to escape, to run so far away Gabriel would never find him. If Gabriel thought Blackburn was gone for good, or dead, then he could put the past in the past and think about the future.

She washed her face at the water closet lavatory, then examined her eyes and nose to see if any signs remained to show she'd been crying. Her eyes were a bit puffy, but not too bad.

Before she talked to Gabriel, she would find some food for Blackburn. She had to keep him content to ride in the baggage car all the way to Denver.

Sounds of a door closing roused Gabriel from his after-supper siesta. He'd heard it twice in the past few minutes. He hadn't expected Trina to come out for a while. She'd said she had to tend to her clothes, and wanted to rest after supper.

He figured it was her way of telling Gabriel she'd come visiting as soon as she had her things in order, but she hadn't so far. If that was her running around the train, what was she doing? He decided to check on her.

When he knocked at her door, she came after a brief time and just stood there. An odd expression colored her features.

"What's wrong, Trina?"

"Nothing's wrong, Gabriel. I...I just had to go back to the baggage car to get my case, that's all. It got loaded with the trunks. I needed it here." She agonized over what to say next. How could she lie to him? She couldn't. But she didn't have to tell him the whole truth—not if it meant that he might be killed, along with her father.

Gabriel knew she was keeping something back. What could it be? "Is there anything else, Trina?"

"No! I—I just feel...tired. That's all. After all, we didn't get a full night's sleep last night." She looked away, embarrassed to be stalling after the honesty they'd shared. Oh, dear God, what should she do? Tears came unbidden and she had no choice but to give in and cry.

"It's all right, Trina. I told you—"

"Hold me, Gabriel. Please." She took his hand, led him into her quarters, then closed the door. Twining her arms around him, she cried into his flannel shirt until it was damp against her cheek.

"Trina, if you'll tell me what's wrong..."

"Just hold me." She tried to stop crying but couldn't. Before long, they sat on the bed, his arms around her.

"Talk to me."

Tarnation! Why couldn't she be stronger? "Blackburn." She reached into her sleeve and pulled out a hankie to blow her nose.

"Blackburn?"

"I guess...that is...being kidnapped—"

"Did he do something to you and you haven't told me?"

"No! I told you everything that happened. It just didn't...sink in...the danger I was in. I haven't felt really afraid...until now." It was mostly the truth. "The next time you find him, he might kill you. I couldn't stand it if anything happened to you, Gabriel. I love you. Promise me you'll quit trying to find him. He isn't worth killing. He was half-dead when I saw him the last time. He's probably dead on that mountain, frozen to death. He's dead, Gabriel. Can't you see that?"

He held her, stroking her hair, kissing the top of her

head. "Trina, there's no need to worry. Blackburn isn't going to do anything to me. If he's still alive, I'll find him in due time and take care of him for good."

"But Gabriel, he'll kill you! He'll kill all of us!"

"Trina, you've had a bad time. It's caught up to you, that's all. Just take it easy." He kissed her and tasted salty tears on her lips. "Everything's going to be all right."

The image of Blackburn killing Gabriel—or her father—was too easy to conjure up. She couldn't bear to live if either of them died because of her. And the memory of Blackburn's knife blade against her throat made her shudder. Even though she'd saved his life, she had no doubts he'd kill her if he thought he had to.

Gabriel kissed her again, long and deep, and stroked her back until she relaxed. The feelings he had for her got stronger and clearer all the time. Just as soon as Blackburn was out of the way, Gabriel would come back to Denver. Back to Trina.

Trina worked the buttons loose on Gabriel's shirt and ran her hands over his chest and rib cage. She wanted to feel his skin next to hers, to feel the security and comfort intimacy with him brought her. She needed, above all, to believe she was doing the right thing by not telling him about Blackburn. Maybe, before the train got to Denver, something would happen to make everything right. Blackburn might die, right there in the baggage car. If only he would…

In the meantime, she needed to be held and loved, and, judging from the way Gabriel had begun to work on her buttons, he needed that, too. He led her back to his quarters and locked the door.

At the McCabe ranch Bo McCabe picked up his gun from the bed and checked the chamber to be sure it was full. Hart's telegram had arrived first. It hadn't mentioned any trouble, just told them they'd catch the train later in the week. The second telegram from Paw had arrived this morning while Will was in town picking up some supplies. He'd sent a reply straight back, then come home to tell them the train would be in about ten. Will had been testy ever since. Bo didn't volunteer anything, and wouldn't until he knew what had happened in Silver Falls.

Paw hadn't mentioned trouble, either, but his mentioning Bo in the telegram could mean only one thing. Blackburn had double-crossed them. With any luck at all, his father had killed the son of a bitch and taken the deed off his quivering body. Relative or no relative, Blackburn had no right to make demands of the McCabe family, then double-cross them when they offered to meet him halfway.

Will came to the door. "Let's go, little brother."

Bo bit back his reply. Will hadn't called him "little brother" since he'd turned eighteen last fall. Why now?

"I'm ready. Big brother." He pushed past Will, standing in the bedroom door, and clumped down the stairs to where Tom waited. Bo had volunteered to go into Denver to meet the train by himself, but Tom said they'd all go. It would prove to be another opportunity to watch the youngest of the McCabe family get into trouble. Maybe, just maybe, Paw had managed to pull off the deal.

Will, tallest of the brothers, climbed into the carriage and reached for the reins. "Bo, if this is another of your harebrained schemes—"

"Well, now, it might be at that." Bo gritted his teeth and used all his willpower not to get riled up the way he usually did. In fact, when this day was over, he might be at the top of the heap, kicking rocks on two older brothers who'd never appreciated his talents.

"Let's ride." Tom spurred his horse. The others followed.

They had four miles to ride into Denver. It was clear to Bo that his brothers wanted to beat that train to Denver.

Gabriel woke up with hair in his face.

During the night Trina had rolled onto his shoulder, then tried to turn over, without much success. The result was a handful of red hair right across his mouth.

He brushed it aside, loving the feel of it between his fingers, then maneuvered Trina to face him again. She sighed at the interruption, then went back to sleep.

Gabriel thought about waking her up, but decided against it. They'd be into Denver soon. Better to ease away at this point. Until he'd dealt with Blackburn for good, he had no business thinking about a future with Trina. He could turn his thoughts that way after he was sure Blackburn was dead.

Trina's eyes fluttered open. She smiled and immediately rubbed his chest, his belly and lower. "Good morning."

"You never get enough, do you?" Gabriel closed his eyes and marveled again at her talented fingers.

"I'll never get enough of you. Even when I'm old and gray and toothless, I'll still want you."

Gabriel didn't comment.

Trina noticed his silence but chose to ignore it as early-morning sleepiness. She intensified her attentions and smiled when his mouth sought hers. What a delicious way to start the day.

* * *

Amos listened at Gabriel's door for a minute. "Humph." With one hand he swiped at what was left of his hair. Dammit. As if he didn't have enough problems, Trina had spent the night with Gabriel. Worse than that, he didn't know how he felt about it.

He should be outraged, pounding on the door, demanding Gabriel marry the girl, since he'd taken her virtue. The only problem was that Trina had obviously relinquished her virtue willingly. There had been no evidence to the contrary. The only facts missing were Gabriel's thoughts on the subject and his intentions toward Trina. Before they got to Denver, Amos had to know, clearly and without mistake, what those intentions were. Then he'd have to take the next step—whatever it turned out to be.

Amos thought about his sons. There was no reason they had to know about their sister's indiscretion on this little jaunt into the mountains. They'd insist Gabriel marry her for sure if they found out she and Gabriel had shared quarters during the trip.

It was a real hornet's nest, all right, and a complication Amos didn't need right now. He had his hands full with Blackburn. In the meantime, he'd play dumb and pretend he didn't know what was going on. Back home, he'd confront Trina and decide what to do after he'd heard what she had to say for herself.

Amos shook his head. Trina was so much like her mother—willful and determined. Once she set her mind on something, there was no changing it. Well, for better or worse, she'd decided she wanted Gabriel Hart. He didn't want to think about what would happen—what Amos himself would have to do—if Gabriel didn't want her. God help us all, he thought, if Gabriel tried to walk away from Trina when she was of a mind for him to stay.

Trina went back to her quarters in time to get ready for breakfast in the dining car. Her clothes had dried nicely, laid out by the baseboard heater and undisturbed, thanks to her spending the entire night in Gabriel's bed.

She giggled suddenly. If Papa knew, he'd be raving mad and probably have a stroke on the spot. She had to see to it he didn't find out.

Her next thought was sobering. In Denver, Gabriel would tip his hat, tell her how nice it had been to make her acquaintance, and disappear—on his way again to be sure Blackburn was dead. Gabriel wasn't the type of person to track a man for so many months, then, when he was on the verge of finding him, give up just because he'd bedded a redhead on the way. Her throat tightened, hoping that wasn't all it was.

She assumed Blackburn was still in the baggage car. She had put some bread, cheese and water inside the door last night. After breakfast she'd take him some biscuits and maybe a piece of leftover bacon or ham. If everything went according to plan, Blackburn would leave the train and Gabriel would never have to know she'd deceived him.

She checked her hair in the mirror, pinched her cheeks to pink them a little, then went to breakfast.

Blackburn would eventually go back to Silver Falls. Gabriel knew it, just as he also knew if he had stayed in Silver Falls, Blackburn would have sent his men to kill him in the middle of the night. When Blackburn found out Gabriel had left on the train, he'd relax, thinking himself safe for a while. What Blackburn didn't know was that Gabriel would be there—in Silver Falls—waiting for him when he came crawling back.

In Denver he planned to get right back on the next train and ride as far as the inner crest of Crenna's Peak. He'd leave the train and come into Silver Falls on foot, unnoticed by Blackburn or anyone else. Then Gabriel would catch him. He didn't intend to give Blackburn the same advantage he'd enjoyed at the Golden Eye.

Convincing Trina he had to leave would be tricky, but he could handle it. A few kisses and Miss McCabe would be agreeable to almost anything.

Damn. Having lived in the past for so many long months, the gentle tug of the future on his heart felt mighty good.

They met in the dining car. There hadn't been any mishaps at dinner the night before because Trina hadn't touched Gabriel's leg at all, anticipating their night together. Gabriel had done his best to keep conversation light and roughly meaningless, doing a little speculating on his own about what the night would bring.

This morning, though, Gabriel suspected Trina was feeling the strain of deception and guilt, and the dread of watching him walk away once they reached Denver. She didn't seem to be in the mood to make conversation just to be making it, and Gabriel felt the same. Amos also seemed quiet—maybe even bothered about something. Gabriel dismissed it as a symptom of his injury. If he suspected any goings-on between Gabriel and his daughter, he'd sure as hell say something.

Gabriel wasn't looking forward to goodbyes, especially since the senator would probably be there, listening to every word. He didn't want Trina to give away their intimacies of the past few days, so they'd have to say their goodbyes in private, before leaving the train.

Trina wasn't hungry. Her stomach just didn't want food this morning. She picked at grilled ham and poached eggs, didn't touch her coffee. It tasted bitter. The men said it tasted just fine. The bitterness came from knowing she had to tell Gabriel about Blackburn before the train stopped. He'd be waiting to escape the minute the train pulled in to the depot.

A thought skittered through her mind. If Gabriel got to Blackburn on the train and killed him, then Gabriel would be able to put the past away for good. An ache in her heart told her Blackburn deserved to die, yet he didn't. She had to focus on the hard truth. Blackburn had killed Gabriel's wife. There was no way Gabriel could walk away and leave Blackburn standing.

If only she'd told Gabriel about Blackburn yesterday, the whole thing could have been resolved and she and Gabriel could have been making plans for the future....

Trina forked the rest of her breakfast into her mouth at a lively pace. Even though the food had cooled to lukewarm, it had to be the most delicious breakfast she'd ever eaten.

"Whoa, there, girl!" The senator frowned. "Slow down, or you'll choke. What's gotten into you all of a sudden? When you sat down, you picked at those eggs like you were ailin'. Now you're wolfing food like you're starved."

Gabriel wondered about the change, too. He knew enough about Trina by now, though, not to try second-guessing her, because it wouldn't do a bit of good.

"Don't worry, Papa. I'm just happy, that's all." She grinned at Gabriel, still chewing, slurped from her cup—quite unlike her usual manners—then exclaimed that the coffee really was quite good after all.

Amos looked at Gabriel, then shrugged. "Females. Who knows what they're thinking."

Gabriel just smiled. He'd find out soon enough what was going on in that pretty little head.

Trina's hand on Gabriel's thigh made him jump just enough to slosh his coffee on the tablecloth.

Trina grinned. Gabriel apologized for his "clumsiness" and gave her a playful look of warning.

Amos looked at them, sputtered something about "mishaps" and went back to eating.

Back in his quarters, Gabriel rounded up his gear and waited for Trina to arrive, which she did about two minutes before he'd figured.

"Gabriel, I have to tell you something."

"I know."

Trina slipped her arms around him from behind and squeezed his middle. "How did you know?"

"You've gotten into the habit of, shall we say, teasing my leg when there's something on your mind. What earth-moving decision did you come to during breakfast?"

It was uncanny the way he could tell what she was thinking. "I can't believe you got all that from one little squeeze of your, shall we say, touchy spot. You do jump when I touch your leg in that little hollow just below—"

Gabriel kissed her into silence. Damn, but she tasted good. Like coffee and eggs and ham and biscuits. "Can you cook?"

Trina grinned and pecked at his lips like a pullet harvesting seeds. "Have you taken a good look at my father? Of course I can cook. I'm the only woman in a house full of men. Why do you ask?"

Why, indeed? Gabriel pulled her against him to stop the pecking and took his time having breakfast all over again. Someday he'd find out if Trina could fix a breakfast like the one they'd just had—day after day after day....

Trina knew she had to tell Gabriel about Blackburn. Time was running out. But he'd be angry with her for the delay and she couldn't stand the thought of him being angry. Yet, not telling him would mean adding months to Gabriel's quest.

"Gabriel, I have to tell you..."

"Tell me what?" He nuzzled her ear, thoroughly intoxicated by the fragrance of honeysuckle perfume, and wished she'd stop talking for once. This could be their last time together for a month of Sundays.

Now or never. "Blackburn."

Gabriel stopped kissing her and tensed. "What about him?"

"He's on this train."

Gabriel's eyes grew cold, and Trina could sense hatred in them. She gasped and wondered if she shouldn't have told him after all.

"Talk fast, Trina."

"I saw him...just before I came in here." Not a lie. She'd seen him when she took the biscuits left over from breakfast.

"Where?"

"In the baggage car."

Gabriel reached for his holster and strapped it on.

"Gabriel, please be careful." Trina suddenly realized Blackburn might be waiting for Gabriel, figuring she'd tell him before they got to Denver. She should have gone straight to Gabriel when she discovered Blackburn in the first place.

"You stay here. I don't want you hurt."

"But Gabriel—"

"I mean it, Trina. I don't need to worry about where you are when I go into that car."

"But don't you see? He'll be expecting you. He saw me when I spotted him. He knows I'm telling you. Please, Gabriel—"

Gabriel pushed past her. "Stay here."

Trina's tears started to run down her flushed cheeks. "Kiss me, Gabriel."

Gabriel turned around. His face, twisted with anger, was almost unrecognizable.

"What?"

"Kiss me before you go. I..."

Gabriel pushed the hatred down just long enough to take her in his arms. He sensed the same desperation in her that he felt in himself—only her desperation came from fear of losing him. God, but he wanted this woman. More than anything, he wished he could forget all about Blackburn and stay in her arms for the rest of their lives. But he couldn't. Nothing could ever be right in his life again as long as Blackburn still drew breath. Despite everything, he couldn't seem to stop kissing her, holding her, touching her....

Gabriel pulled the buttons loose on the front of Trina's blouse. Just as he closed his hand around her breast, the door slammed back.

Bo McCabe stormed into the room.

Chapter Eighteen

"What in hell—?" Bo stopped short.

Trina grappled with the buttons, trying to think what to do. How could she possibly explain?

Bo swung at Gabriel, but didn't land the blow. Gabriel saw it coming and blocked it with one arm.

"Let me explain!" Gabriel ducked to avoid the next swing.

Trina, rebuttoned but still frantic, stepped in front of Gabriel and put both hands in the middle of Bo's chest.

"Stop it! Stop it this instant!"

"But he was..." Bo looked deep into his sister's eyes, expecting to see tears of fright from being assaulted. What he saw instead puzzled him and took all the wind out of his attack.

Trina took advantage of Bo's hesitation and talked as fast as she could, praying he'd listen.

"Bo, it isn't what it looks like. Gabriel...that is, Mr. Hart..."

Amos McCabe pushed his way through his sons and came into the room. "I think I can straighten this whole thing out."

"Papa! You don't understand—"

"Oh, but I do, Trina. Now, just let your old father have his say and I think we can avoid a lot of unpleasantry." He turned to Bo and his other sons, trying to crowd into the small compartment to see whatever it was that had riled Bo so much. Amos knew they wouldn't take to being excluded, but he knew their hot tempers would do no good at all in this situation.

"Wait for me outside. I'll handle this."

"But Paw..." Tom started in.

"What's goin' on?" Will tried to muscle Bo out of the way, and got an elbow in the stomach for his trouble.

"I'll handle it! Do as I say." Amos set his jaw. They all knew what that meant.

Subdued but still angry, Bo pointed a finger at Gabriel. "If I find out you put more than your hand on my sister, you'll regret it, mister." He herded his brothers into the corridor.

Amos closed the door. "I was afraid something like this might happen."

"Senator, I have to leave. Right now."

"No one is going anywhere until we talk."

"Blackburn—"

"Not even Blackburn is more important that what I'm about to say to you."

"He's on this train."

"Not anymore."

"You've seen him?" Gabriel's face got redder and the pulse in his temple began to pound.

"No, but we've been stopped in this station for the better part of two minutes. If he was on this train, he's gone now."

"One more reason why I have to leave. I can't let him get away from me again."

Trina knew she had to do something to make everything right. But what? "Papa, he's telling the truth.
Please let him go."

Amos looked toward the door. "Think you can get
past my sons?"

Gabriel thought about it. Seconds clicked by. Even if
Blackburn had ridden the train all the way into the station after seeing Trina, he'd certainly have melted into
the depot crowd and into Denver by now. Damn! There
was no way those overgrown ruffians would let Gabriel
out of this room without a lengthy explanation. He let
out a long sigh.

"All right. What do you have to say that's so all-
fired important? I have to pick up Blackburn's trail before it turns stone cold."

"I'm afraid it's going to be colder than that before
you're able to follow it. You're going to be busy doing
one of two things."

"What in hell are you talking about, Senator?"

"I'd advise you to hold your tongue. After all, you
aren't in control here. I am. And right now I think you
ought to calm down and consider the predicament
you're in."

Gabriel ran one hand through his hair. He looked at
Trina and wished to hell he'd never laid eyes on her.
"All right. Spit it out."

"You have two choices from where I'm standing.
Face my sons and take whatever they decide to do to
you for robbing my daughter of her virtue—"

"Papa!"

"Do you think I'm completely dotty, Trina? I know
where you spent last night. I didn't mention it because,
frankly, I didn't know what to say to you. Your mother
would've known the words to use, but I'm not your

mother. I kept my mouth shut because I credit you with having a fair amount of horse sense, even though you can be every bit a twit when you feel like it.'' He sank into a chair and tried to catch his breath. The exertion of the past few minutes had been more than he was prepared for.

''Are you all right? Maybe I should get a doctor. Just sit still and—''

''Dammit, Trina, shut up. Quit tryin' to change the subject.''

The ploy hadn't worked. There was nothing else to do. ''So, you knew. Why didn't you say something? What did you—''

''What did I think? I didn't know what to think. Except that you'd found a man you obviously trusted enough to share everything with.''

Trina's cheeks burned with embarrassment. What on earth could she possibly say to that? It was true.

''Am I right, Trina?'' He motioned for her to sit on the edge of the bed, adjacent to him.

''Yes, Papa.''

Amos pulled her chin up and smiled, feeling a wondrous surge of love for the little girl he'd raised alone. ''Do you love him, Trina?''

Trina swallowed hard. ''With all my heart, Papa.''

Amos nodded. ''That's what I had to know.'' He looked at Gabriel.

''Well, Gabriel, you don't seem surprised to hear that my daughter loves you.''

Gabriel looked at Trina, then back at the senator. ''She told me in Silver Falls how she felt.''

Trina plowed ahead. Her father was being pretty reasonable about the whole thing. ''I suppose I should say

I'm sorry. But I'm not sorry. I'm glad. I love Gabriel. More than anything.''

Amos saw truth in his daughter's eyes and, earlier, he thought he'd seen something kin to it in Gabriel, too. Right now, though, Gabriel could probably walk out of here, as mad as he was, and never look back. For a while, at least.

"Now, Hart, tell me your intentions concerning my daughter.''

Gabriel thought long and hard before he spoke.

"I vowed to kill Blackburn. Until that's done, I've got no business making plans for the future.''

"Oh, but that's exactly what you're about to do right now.''

"But Papa—''

"Shut up, Trina! This is man's talk.''

"But you're discussing me. I have a right—''

"You have no rights whatsoever. You have tainted this family and my honor by allowing this man privileges with your body. As your father, my duty toward you stands clear.''

"But—''

"Not another word!''

Trina knew what her father was about to say next, and there was nothing she could do to stop him. What he was about to tell Gabriel might make him hate her. Oh, dear Lord, why did everything have to turn out this way?

"Gabriel, here are your two choices.''

Gabriel didn't like the sound of this. Not one bit.

"You can face my sons—who are, I'm guessing, of a mind to kill you on the spot by this time, now that Bo has had time to inform them of whatever he saw.''

Trina drew in a long breath.

"Or you can marry my daughter."

"Papa, no!" Trina grabbed her father's hands. "Not this way. It isn't right. Gabriel—"

"Gabriel knows I'm right, Trina. He's a man of honor. He would never leave you tainted. He *will* do the right thing."

Rage building in Gabriel dissipated as he digested the truth of the senator's words. It didn't help him to accept the situation any better, though. A wife had no place in his life right now.

Trina turned to Gabriel with tears streaming down her face. "Gabriel, I'm sorry. I never meant for this to happen. If I'd known, I never would have—"

Gabriel straightened his spine. "The fault is mine. Not yours." He faced Amos McCabe. "All right, Senator. We'll do this your way. But it changes nothing where Blackburn is concerned. I still aim to kill him, even if it means dying in the process."

Amos nodded. "I understand."

"But, Papa, don't you see—"

"Hush, Trina. This isn't what I wanted, either. But, thanks to both of you, this is what must be. Let's tell your brothers. You'd better wash your face first. If they see those tears, they're liable not to believe me when I break the happy news to them."

Trina wished Gabriel would give her a sign things would turn out all right—that being married to her wasn't a sentence, but a joy. His cold, hard expression reminded her Gabriel was being forced into the situation. Even if he'd had thoughts of asking for her hand before, they were gone now, shoved out by resentment and anger. Even if his anger wasn't directed toward her now, it would be soon enough. She went to wash her face.

Gabriel glared at Amos McCabe, hoping somehow he'd change his mind about forcing the marriage, but he knew it wouldn't happen. As her father, McCabe had specific obligations. In the same situation, Gabriel knew he would do what the senator had done. That didn't help the way he felt, though. When he killed Blackburn, he could be killed himself, leaving Trina a widow. Damn, but this train ride had complicated his life.

McCabe refused to look Gabriel straight in the eye. He knew what he was doing was wrong in a way. Trina's best interests were not being served by forcing the marriage, yet what else could he do? Nothing, that's what. Trina came out of the water closet looking a little better.

"Trina, I want to see you smile." He started to tell Gabriel the same thing, but changed his mind when he saw the look in Gabriel's eyes. He reached for the door-knob and braced himself for the chaos to come.

Bo got to the door first. "Stand aside, Paw. I mean to kill him."

"You'll do no such thing. Now back off and listen for a minute before you do something to break your sister's heart."

Bo looked puzzled, along with the others. Tom pushed past Will and came straight to Trina. "Are you all right?"

Gabriel recognized him as the "young man" he'd mistakenly assumed was Trina's beau. At least he wouldn't face an irate suitor in addition to three irate brothers.

Trina smiled as sweetly as she could manage. "Of course I'm all right, Tom." She looked at each of her brothers in turn and almost lost her tenuous smile when she saw the expressions on their faces—fury, indignation at what they assumed was the assault of their sister. Thank goodness Gabriel hadn't chosen to face them. "Lawsey, but you're all making such a fuss, I can't rightly believe it."

Gabriel couldn't believe the change in her. Just as he'd come to expect, she'd done exactly what the occasion demanded and taken control. Damnedest woman he'd ever met. In spite of the situation, he had to admit the idea of being her husband pleased him. Timing was all wrong, though. The image of Blackburn getting away scot-free obliterated any other feelings he might be having.

Bo elbowed his way through and took his sister by the arms. "What are you trying to tell us, Trina? Did this man—" He looked up at Gabriel with such venom that Trina shivered in his grasp. "Did he—"

"This man has not harmed or disgraced me in any way."

An audible sigh came from the group, and Trina saw her brothers relax, one by one.

She turned to Gabriel and slipped her arm around him. "This is Gabriel Hart. The man...I am going to marry."

"Marry! You can't be serious!"

Various exclamations followed, all of which Trina fended expertly, cutting them short before any mention of Geoffrey was made. She'd take care of that little loose end herself. There was no need to bother Gabriel with it at all.

"Oh, but I am serious. Yes, I know what I'm doing. No, it really isn't all that sudden. Tell them, Papa." She needed help. Gabriel was in no mood to give it, so her father—having precipitated this whole fiasco—would have to step in and help.

Amos gave her a look that said *Thanks a heap!* then approached his sons.

"What Trina says is true. Gabriel Hart is a former lawman. You've all heard of him, if you'll take time to cool off and remember. He saved my life in Silver Falls. Furthermore, I heartily approve of him as Trina's choice for a husband. I admit, it seemed rather quick to me, too...." He didn't dare look at Gabriel to see his reaction to that. "But quick or not, Trina has made her choice. In fact, they've decided...to be married immediately. As soon as preparations can be made and invitations delivered." Amos cringed at the flurry of protests. He listened for a moment, then raised his hands for attention. Pain from his wound made it hard to breathe. He needed to sit down—to lie down, to rest someplace quiet.

"There's nothing more...to be said. It's decided. Now, if you don't mind...I'd like to get off...this train."

Trina saw how pale her father was and realized what a strain the past few minutes had been. He wasn't a well man, and this hadn't helped one bit.

"Will, Tom, help me get him to the carriage." Her brothers rushed to comply.

Amos made his way down the corridor, outside onto the platform, down the steps with Tom and Will practically carrying him. His feet hardly touched the ground. Bo followed close behind.

Trina hung back, hoping to talk to Gabriel alone, but he gathered his things and headed toward the back door of the car.

"Gabriel..." Leaving. She couldn't blame him. Neither could she ask him not to go.

Gabriel looked back just long enough to see her wave

and blow a kiss. It made him feel terrible. "I'll be back, Trina. I promise."

She nodded, and wished with all her heart she could hold him once more. But that time was past.

Gabriel left the car and saw the McCabe clan gathered beside a stylish black carriage. Amos had been deposited inside. So far, so good. If only Gabriel could ease away unnoticed, then—

"Going somewhere?"

Gabriel felt the barrel of a revolver in his back.

"Turn around real slow." Bo McCabe stepped back, pointing the gun straight at Gabriel's chest.

"Something wrong?" Gabriel's mind whirled with alternatives. He didn't want to hurt Trina's brother, but if it came to that—

"I thought you were going to join the family."

"What makes you think I'm not?"

Bo grinned. His eyes, dark and round, penetrated straight to the heart of the matter. His beard and long curly hair, as dark as Trina's hair was red, couldn't conceal his youth. Bo McCabe thought he could handle Gabriel Hart.

Bo motioned with the gun for Gabriel to step away from the train. "Let's just say you looked a mite reluctant back there. Like maybe you weren't real happy about marrying my sister."

"What if you're wrong?"

"Then you wouldn't be trying to sneak off, would you?"

"I have some business to take care of in the baggage car. I believe your father's trunks are still back there. Aren't you interested in taking them home with you?"

Bo hesitated. "What trunks?"

Gabriel stepped down to the ground. "Don't you remember? The guns your father intended to deliver to Blackburn.''

''How do you know about that?''

''Let's just say I happened into the Golden Eye at the right time.''

''So Paw still has the trunks?''

''You didn't think I'd let Blackburn get away with them after double-crossing you and your father, did you?''

''So it really was a double-cross.''

Now Gabriel had him. Did he know about Trina being kidnapped? It wouldn't seem so. If he could keep Bo talking long enough, he might let go of everything Gabriel needed to know. He took one careful step backward.

''Knowing Blackburn, could you expect anything else?''

''What do you know about Blackburn?''

Gabriel laughed, but there was no mirth in the sound. ''I've known Blackburn for better than twelve years. In fact, I put him away. It's time someone put him away for good. That's exactly what I intend to do. In time.'' Gabriel chose his next words carefully. ''I'm surprised you don't feel the same after what he did to Trina.''

Anger grew in Bo like the flames of a prairie fire, catching the wind. ''Trina?''

''He shot your father, kidnapped your sister. He still has the deed. He intends to keep everything. You can't tell me you're surprised.''

Bo McCabe started to shake. ''Kidnapped? Nobody said nothing about kidnapping. That no-good son of a bitch—''

Gabriel slugged Bo and made a break for it. After

shaking his head, Bo bounded after him, yelling to the others to head Gabriel off.

Gabriel ducked between two cars on a side rail, dodged two men carrying large cases, slid under the car and rolled toward the far side. It might be enough of a diversion to give him time to get away.

When he rolled out the other side, two hammers clicked back. Will and Tom. Bo ran around the end of the car. There would be no escape.

Chapter Nineteen

Amos's breathing had become so labored, Trina feared he might stop breathing altogether if they didn't get him home and in bed immediately. She stepped down from the carriage and looked around. Her brothers had left abruptly, and with no explanation. It had to be Gabriel. What on earth could have— "Oh, no," she whispered. There was Gabriel, with Tom in the lead, Will and Bo behind.

"Don't worry, little sister." Bo punched Gabriel in the back with his pistol. "He tried to get away, but we caught him."

Trina decided, right then and there, to put a stop to the charade.

"Let him go."

"Just as soon as he's done right by you." Bo pushed Gabriel toward Trina.

Gabriel whirled around and swung at Bo, but Tom and Will caught his arms and held him firm.

"Stop it!" Trina pulled at Tom's arm until he and Will loosened their grip on Gabriel. "You're going to listen to me, and you're going to do what I say."

Amos tried to get up, but couldn't. So he mustered what strength he had and called, "Tom! Come here."

Trina, frightened for her father, as well as for Gabriel, gave Tom her most determined look. "See about him, Tom. I'm afraid for his life. Do you hear me?"

Tom gave a stiff nod and went to the carriage. He was back within a minute.

"Paw says to do whatever Trina tells us."

"You—he—can't be serious! Since when does Trina tell us anything?" Bo stuck out his chin in defiance.

Trina knew she'd have to handle Bo carefully. He'd always been the hotheaded, impulsive McCabe. If she could possibly get him on her side, she might have a chance of winning over the others.

"Bo, I need to speak to Gabriel alone. For just a minute."

"Trina, he'll bolt as sure as shootin'."

"No, he won't." She glanced up at Gabriel. "The only reason he tried to leave is because he has business to tend to. I knew he was leaving. I didn't try to stop him."

Bo scratched his head. "Trina, you're not making any sense at all. Paw said—"

"If you'll wait just a minute, you'll see the sense of it." She glanced around. "There's a bench over there. When Gabriel and I finish talking, I'll tell you exactly what's going to happen next." She stood on tiptoes and planted a kiss on her brother's hairy cheek. He smelled a little like soap and a little like his horse. She counted on this kiss to soften him up, as it usually did.

"All right. But don't be long. Paw says you and Hart are gettin' hitched. Time's a-wastin'."

"We won't be long."

Trina linked her arm in Gabriel's and led him to a

bench missing one back leg, leaning against the wall of the depot for support. They sat down with almost a foot of space between them. Trina slid over closer to Gabriel, took a deep breath and plunged in before she could lose her nerve.

"Gabriel, I won't marry you."

Gabriel stared at her. "What?" It was the last thing in the world he'd expected her to say.

"I said, I won't marry you. Not this way. I don't care what my brothers or my father say about it. I won't trap you into a marriage you don't want."

Gabriel swallowed hard and tried to decide what to say. If he told her how relieved he was, she'd be mad for sure and feel rejected.

Trina saw his astonishment—and indecision. "I want to tell you something before I tell my brothers to let you go where you please."

Gabriel suddenly felt sad, and it surprised him. She reached for his hand and squeezed it. A surge of affection made him want to kiss her, right there. "What is it, Trina?"

"I love you more than anything. I'd be proud to marry you, be your wife and bear your children. I'd do everything in my power to ease the hurt you've suffered and love you until you couldn't remember anything bad from the past at all. But I won't marry you until you ask me." She squirmed. "That is, if you ever decide to ask me."

Gabriel glanced at the McCabes, watching every move they made. They couldn't hear what Trina had said, but they could sure as hell see what he was about to do. "Come here, woman."

She met him halfway.

Gabriel took his time kissing her.

Trina clung to him, tasting her own tears in his mouth as they flowed freely down her cheeks. If she lived to be a hundred, she'd never find a man she loved more.

"I'll be back. It's then I'll have a question for you."

Gabriel felt three sets of eyes on them. He touched Trina's lips lightly with his thumb, turned to the McCabes and tipped his hat. Without another word, he strode down the street toward the livery.

Trina went to where her brothers stood with their mouths open and their hands poised on their guns, and wiped away her tears. "Let him go."

Bo's jaw quivered with tension. "Trina, he's—"

"Coming back—someday." She watched Gabriel walk down the street and tried to swallow the lump in her throat. "When he does, we'll be married. Not before."

"Well, I'll be—"

"Let's get Papa home." Trina gathered her skirts and headed for the carriage. "I have a feeling he's sicker than any of us realize."

Will took the reins. Trina and Amos sat together on the second seat. Tom and Bo swung into their saddles and headed toward the ranch.

Amos had slumped into the corner and fallen asleep. Trina wanted to look back, to see Gabriel one last time. But she knew she shouldn't. She'd done the right thing. From this moment on she would pray to God every minute to keep Gabriel safe and send him back to her.

Once they were past the rail yard, Bo fell behind the others, then headed back toward the livery.

Hoofbeats behind him. Gabriel quickened his pace, then decided it was time to stop running. He turned around and faced Bo McCabe squarely.

"Take it easy," Bo said with an easy drawl. He stopped about six feet away and stepped down from his pinto. "Trina's told us how it is. We need to talk."

Gabriel focused on why Bo McCabe would want to talk to him if Trina had explained things. "All right." He nodded toward a saloon two doors down on the right. "How about a drink?"

"Suits me fine."

They went to the bar without speaking at all. Gabriel knew he could knock Bo out with one sharp punch and make his escape, but this whippersnapper might have information to make capturing Blackburn quicker. Bo was nothing but a kid. It shouldn't take long to pry information out of him.

Gabriel ordered a beer and took it to a table near the back wall, away from other patrons. Bo followed with a mug in his hand, sloshing beer over the sides onto the rough floorboards.

Bo took a long swig, wiped foam from his mustache. "I'm going with you."

To the point. Gabriel admired that. "Where are we going?"

"To find Blackburn."

"You want to find Blackburn?"

"He double-crossed me and shot my father. I intend to make him pay for it."

"Why do you need me?"

"I don't. But I know you're after Blackburn, too. If we work together, we'll find him sooner, and we won't get in each other's way. The way I see it, we both want Blackburn on the wrong end of a rope. Am I right?"

"Hanging is too good for him. I don't intend to take any rope."

Bo grinned. "I knew we could work together."

"I didn't say that." Gabriel leaned forward. "Just remember, when we find him, Blackburn is mine."

Bo nodded and offered his hand to Gabriel. "Agreed."

They shook hands. Gabriel wondered about this upstart and questioned how he could do business with a man one minute and want to kill him the next. If it could happen with Blackburn, it could happen with anybody else—even the man his sister loved. Gabriel knew he shouldn't trust Bo McCabe any farther than he could spit and step on it, but with a kid, you never knew.

"You know where to start?"

Bo nodded, finished his beer, dragged his sleeve across his mouth, then studied Gabriel with a curious glint in his eye.

"Why don't you just spit it out?"

"I'll bet you didn't know Blackburn is our kin."

"Kin?" Gabriel's skin crawled with the notion of Trina being related to Blackburn.

"Through marriage."

Gabriel relaxed somewhat. "I'm listening."

"You heard Paw talk about Cobb's land."

"So?"

"So Cobb was Ma's cousin. And Cobb's sister was married to Blackburn."

Gabriel said nothing. His mind whirled with implications.

"Cobb knew Blackburn was no good and wanted his sister, Elvina, to have something after Blackburn left her or got killed. When Elvina died, Blackburn thought he ought to inherit the land Cobb was planning on leaving to her. But Cobb backed off, didn't want Blackburn to have it. We all knew Blackburn wouldn't live much longer after he got out of prison."

"What does all this have to do with me?"

"Nothing, I suppose. I figured you'd want to know how Paw got mixed up in this deal with Blackburn, that's all."

"I wondered."

Bo nodded, swigged beer, wiped his mustache. "Cobb sent word to Paw that Blackburn stole the deed and wanted guns in exchange. Paw told Cobb if he'd donate the land to the state, the guns would be brought to Silver Falls and the deal struck with Blackburn."

"He did this because your mother—"

"Was Cobb's cousin. Ma always had a soft spot for him. She never would've wanted Blackburn to have that land. Elvina was a good woman. Decent. We never could understand how she got hooked up with scum like Blackburn."

"You said she died?"

"While Blackburn was in prison. Rattlesnake. No one to help her. Blackburn went crazy when he found out. Killed a prison guard with his bare hands. We wouldn't have thought he cared that much for anyone but himself."

Gabriel's mind roiled. After he got out of prison Blackburn had come straight to Gabriel's place and killed Hannah. Both wives dead...

"So," Bo said, finishing the beer. "What's your connection to Blackburn?"

"He killed my wife."

Bo winced. "I'm sorry. I didn't know...."

"Let's get out of here. Where would Blackburn go from Denver?"

"Half a dozen places. I'll put out the word we're looking for him. We should hear something in a week or two."

"Two weeks? You think it'll take that long?"

Bo nodded. "Blackburn is good at two things. Killing and hiding. The minute we hear something, we'll be on his back like ticks on a hound dog."

At the McCabe ranch Tom helped Amos down from the carriage, with Trina on the other side, and they took him into the house. Will took care of the horses and carriage.

Amos squirmed and shook free once they were inside. "I'm not feeble. I just had to catch my breath." He leaned against the banister. When he was ready, Tom helped him up the stairs with one hand on his arm. Trina followed all the way to the bedroom.

"I can put myself to bed, thank you very much." Amos sat down on the side of the bed and glared at both of them.

"Well, then, Papa, do it. I'll bring you some supper after a while." Trina wanted to hug him and sit on his lap just as she had as a little girl. But she knew she couldn't. Maybe not ever again.

"Just leave me be, child. Leave me be."

Trina closed the door, leaving Tom to help him out of his clothes, and swiped at a tear. Her father wasn't as strong as she'd always imagined. The wound had weakened him. As soon as it healed, he'd be as good as new again. It made her feel better to think so. Tom came out and they went downstairs.

Before long, Tom and Will got into a heated discussion in the study, which served as office for the ranch.

"What's the matter? You'll wake Papa if you don't keep your voices down." She looked around. "Where's Bo?"

"That's the matter." Tom dropped into the big

leather chair behind the desk and propped one ankle over his knee. Will sat on the sofa and propped his boots on the heavy oak table.

"Didn't he come in with us?"

"Nope. He must have turned back before we ever got out of Denver. I didn't realize he was gone until it was too late to go back." He glanced at Will. "He went after Hart, didn't he?"

Will pulled his feet up onto the sofa and stretched out. "I reckon."

Fear knotted Trina's stomach. "We have to go after him. If he finds Gabriel—"

"Hart can take care of himself, Trina." Tom got up from the desk, slapped Will on the shoulder and headed out the door. Will followed with a groan and a creaking of leather when he pushed up from the sofa.

"You're going after him?"

"Nope. Got work to do. Wasted a whole morning as it is. Don't know why all of us had to traipse off into town just to bring Paw home. And I'd like to know why Paw mentioned Bo specifically in his telegram. Never had a chance to ask him about that."

Trina perked up. "Paw sent a telegram?"

Will straightened his vest and reached for his hat on the hook by the front door. "Yep. Too bad we didn't have time to ask Paw what little brother's been up to this time. Must've been a doozy."

"Did he…that is…did he mention me in the telegram?"

"Nope. What'd you do?"

Will guffawed at that. "Making eyes at some miner, were you, Trina?"

So. They didn't know she'd been kidnapped. Well,

tonight after supper she'd have the pleasure of seeing her brothers speechless for once in their ornery lives.

Tom opened the front door. "It'll have to wait until Paw feels like talking or Bo gets home. I don't have time to chase after him all over Colorado. Trina, we'll be back at dark. If Paw gets worse, send one of the hands to get us. We'll be in the south pasture. You can tell us later why you thought Paw ought to mention you in that wire."

"After supper. Don't be too late."

Trina watched them go. Somehow she had to get back to Denver and find Bo before he found Gabriel. But how? She slumped into the big, overstuffed chair next to the door in the study, heard the air whooshing out of the cushion, felt coolness from the leather against her back. It was no use. Too much time had already passed. She'd have to wait, and pray Bo wouldn't kill Gabriel on sight. Would he do such a thing? She didn't think so. But then, lately a lot of things had happened that had surprised her. Her once serene, dull little life had taken on a passel of new troubles all at once, and the biggest ache of all was Gabriel—gone from her life as quickly as he'd come into it.

Trina got up wearily from the chair and went to start supper.

Gabriel girthed the saddle down tight on the big red roan, then dropped the stirrup into place. He tossed some coins to the hosteler. "Thanks for taking care of him. He looks good."

The man pocketed the coins and stroked the sleek animal's neck. "Fine animal. Whatta ya call him?"

"Clancy."

"Funny name. Fits him, though."

"I always thought so. Much obliged." He reined
Clancy around and out of the stable and pulled up next
to Bo.

"How far is this ranch of yours?"

"Four miles, give or take a little. We'll be there in
time for supper. I'm sure glad Trina's home again.
Tom's cooking never won no prizes."

They headed out of Denver at an easy lope.

As they headed southwest, Gabriel organized everything he knew about Blackburn. This new information,
about Blackburn's wife and being kin to the McCabes,
answered some questions and brought others to mind.
Coupled with what Gabriel knew about Blackburn, prior
to Corbett Hart's death, it started to make sense for the
first time.

It all added up to something Gabriel would just as
soon not know.

Chapter Twenty

Trina couldn't believe her eyes. Gabriel! And Bo, riding beside him, as big as life. What on earth had her impetuous brother done now? If he'd dragged Gabriel here to marry her... She ran onto the porch, ready to do battle.

"Bo, I told you—"

"Cool off, Trina." Bo stepped down from his horse. "Gabriel is here of his own free will."

That took all the wind out of her. "He is? Then..." Could she dare hope he'd changed his mind about going after Blackburn?

Gabriel saw Trina's eyes light up and knew it had been a mistake to come here. She thought he'd come to marry her. Damn. Why hadn't he realized it would be her first reaction to seeing him again so soon? He stepped down from Clancy slow and easy, trying to figure out the best way to explain.

"I'll take care of the horses. You two go on inside." Bo led the horses to the barn.

Trina couldn't believe it. Bo had called Gabriel by his given name and offered to take care of his horse, as polite as if they'd suddenly become best friends.

Gabriel stopped at the edge of the porch. "It isn't what you think, Trina."

"Right now I'm not thinking anything, except maybe my brother took a dose of happy pills or something." She let her emotions rise to the surface. "Why have you come, Gabriel? If it isn't what I think, what is it?"

"Your brother…well, maybe I'd better let him tell it. We're going after Blackburn. Together."

She couldn't have been more astounded if he'd knelt and proposed, right then and there. "Together? You and Bo? But—"

"He'll explain everything, I'm sure. Your other brothers are going to want to hear it, too, I expect."

"You're right about that. Well, come on in the house. There's no one here right now except Papa, and he's asleep upstairs. I'm fixin' supper. Come to the kitchen for a cup of coffee." She wanted to kiss him, but decided this wasn't the time or place. Later, for sure.

"Coffee? I'd like that fine." Gabriel started to reach for her but changed his mind. Maybe it would be best if he kept his distance. At least for a while.

They went into the house. Gabriel took a quick look at the front room of the spacious ranch house. Heavy oak furniture with a definite male slant dominated the front room. Braided rugs cushioned the floor. The curtains weren't frilly, yet they still lent a slight woman's touch. It was obvious the four men who lived in this house overruled the single woman when it came to furniture. Yet he saw Trina's presence in little things. A basket of sewing waited on the floor beside a rocking chair near the massive stone fireplace. Dainty pillows, trimmed in crocheted lace, had been scattered across a massive leather couch. The room was a curious, homey mixture.

"Gabriel?" Trina smiled with amusement.

"You have a nice home here, Trina. Mighty nice."

Trina saw wistfulness in his eyes. His home must have been nice once, too. She wondered what it looked like, then and now. Had he been back there since his wife's death?

They went into the kitchen, and Gabriel experienced a different reaction. This room was, without question, Trina's domain. Copper pots, shiny and scrubbed within an inch of their lives, hung from hooks in the ceiling. The black iron cookstove gleamed. Across the room a huge oak table, in front of a bank of windows framed with sunny yellow curtains, had chairs for six. He could imagine an arrangement of flowers in the center during the summer. Now that winter was almost here, Trina had decorated it with bowls of apples and pears. They filled the room with a spicy, delicious smell mingling with mouth-watering odors coming from something cooking on the stove. Beef stew? He took a long breath. Cornbread in the oven. His stomach growled with anticipation. Hannah always made the best cornbread....

He closed his eyes, clenched his fists, struggling for control. His heart swelled with grief. Curtains. Braided rugs made with her own hands. Stew on the stove. Stirring up cornbread with flour floating in the air like pollen from a thicket of beebrush.

Trina touched his arm.

Gabriel gathered her close, burying his face in her hair. With deep breaths he tried to swallow grief rising from the depths of his being.

"I know," she whispered, and held him tighter. Damn that Blackburn! Given the chance, she'd choke the life out of him herself for hurting Gabriel the way he had. She could've killed him in that tunnel. Should have.

When he came into the house Bo stopped and listened for a minute to see where Gabriel and Trina were. There was no sound at all. He eased through the front room to the kitchen door and saw them standing there, holding each other. Bo's throat tightened. His sister really loved this man. And, from the looks of it, Gabriel might just love her, too. Once Blackburn was dead, Bo figured Gabriel would become part of the family without any coaxing. The thought didn't bother him at all. From what Paw had told them, Gabriel was a fine, decent man. When word came, telling where Blackburn was, Bo would have to make sure Gabriel stayed alive and well and able to marry his sister—by taking care of Blackburn himself.

Gabriel sipped hot coffee and marveled at how good it tasted. For months he'd had nothing but coffee boiled in a tin pot. How a woman could make coffee taste so good was a puzzle to him, but a real pleasure.

"You're a good cook, Trina."

"How do you know? You haven't tasted anything I've cooked."

Gabriel pointed at the empty cup in his hand. "Proof's in the coffee. When a woman can make coffee this good, the rest of her cooking is bound to be good, too."

Trina smiled at that. Her brothers thought she was a good cook, but they were just brothers.

She doubled a dish towel in her hand, opened the oven door and took out four pans of cornbread. With a cold north wind assaulting the house, worming its way into the kitchen around window panes and under doors, heat from the stove felt good. Trina always made sure the kitchen was warm when Tom and the others came in from some cold job. And her coffeepot was always full.

Gabriel's belly button was trying to hook onto his backbone. The smell of hot cornbread made it hard to sit still.

Trina sliced the bread, lifted out a huge chunk, slit it with a knife, spooned in a generous amount of creamy white butter then handed it to Gabriel. "I can hear your belly rumbling from here. Eat this. It'll tide you over till supper."

Gabriel grinned and bit into the crisp-on-top, tender-in-the-middle cornbread. Butter oozed over his lips, but he didn't care. He'd never tasted anything so good in his life. "I was wrong. You're not a good cook."

"Gabriel!"

"You're the best cook in the world."

Trina swatted him on the arm with her dish towel, then, on impulse, kissed the butter from his lips.

"Jelly couldn't be any sweeter," Gabriel mumbled between kisses. When she went back to the stove, he finished the cornbread and wished for another chunk. Reaching for one, though, got his hand slapped.

"It won't be long now. Why don't you check on the fireplace?"

"Work for my supper?"

"Absolutely. I have some last-minute things to do before we eat. So, make yourself scarce. But not too scarce, Mr. Hart."

"Yes, Miss McCabe." Smiling, he left the kitchen.

Trina watched him go. *I'd much rather be Mrs. Hart.* That thought made her giggle like a schoolgirl with a bad crush.

Gabriel met Bo when he left the kitchen. Delicious cooking smells filled the house. "Ready for supper, Bo?" Gabriel selected a couple more logs for the fireplace from the stack near the hearth and pitched them onto the mound of flaming wood.

"Uh...just about. I have a little more to do in the barn."

Gabriel perked up. "What is it, Bo?"

He gave Gabriel a blank look. "I don't know what you mean."

"I think you do. There's no use trying to pull anything on me. It won't work. Why don't you just spill it?"

"There's nothing to spill. See you at supper." He stalked off down the hall toward the back of the house. Damn! Gabriel had seen right through him. Well, he could still pull it off if—

Tom and Will came in the front door.

"Bo! Where are you?" Tom piled his coat on top of Will's, hung his hat on a peg, then came to warm his hands at the fire. His eyes on Gabriel were cold. "I didn't expect to see you here, Hart. Change your mind about Blackburn?"

"Nope. Waiting for news of where he's hiding out."

Tom's eyebrows went up at that. "So you'll be staying the night here?"

He nodded once. "Bo and I are going together. He'll explain."

"Damn right he will. Trina!"

Will went to wash up.

Trina appeared at the door, cheeks flushed from the heat of the stove.

Gabriel thought she looked especially beautiful with a smudge of flour on her chin.

"What is it? Supper's just about ready. Have you washed?"

"Did you know Gabriel was coming here tonight?"

"No. But I'm glad Bo decided to bring him. We'll talk about it later. Come on, now, before it all gets cold." Her eyes lingered on Gabriel a moment before she hurried back to the kitchen.

Tom shook his head. "I don't know what Bo is up to this time, but it looks like he's trying to rope you into whatever it is."

"Bo thinks he can find out where Blackburn may be holed up. I'm not too proud to use any method available to find him."

Tom nodded. "What did Blackburn do to warrant this level of hate from you?"

Gabriel stiffened. "He killed my wife."

Tom's expression hardened. "You have every right to want him dead." He hesitated. "What about Trina?"

"When it's done."

Trina yelled from the kitchen, "Come and get it or I'll throw it to the hogs!"

Gabriel took the opportunity to relax a little. "I'd hate to see her throw that cornbread to a hog."

Tom grinned. "I'd be right there beside that old sow with my mouth wide open."

They laughed together, and Gabriel knew Tom McCabe was a reasonable man. Trina was lucky to have such a man for a brother. They went to the kitchen where Will was already seated. Steaming bowls of stew, china plates for the bread, spoons, knives and mugs of coffee, steaming and fragrant, covered the table.

"Where's Bo?" Trina untied her apron and brought the last dish to the table—a bowl of turnips.

Will buttered a chunk of cornbread. "His horse was still saddled, tied up outside, when I came in. Guess he's puttin' him away for the night."

Gabriel tensed. "He put our horses away when we got here."

Tom looked at Gabriel. "You don't think—"

Gabriel ran for the front door, the others following.

Bo had just stepped into the saddle. When he saw everyone rushing onto the porch, he stood his ground and waited.

Gabriel grabbed the reins. "Going somewhere, Bo?" Chief tried to pull away, but Gabriel's grip was too tight.

"You don't have to go. Stay here with Trina. I'll kill Blackburn for you."

Gabriel pulled him off the horse. Chief bolted and ran toward the open barn door. Hauling Bo up by his coat lapels, Gabriel glared straight into his eyes.

Bo, angry at being hauled down like some sort of kid, cringed at what he saw in Gabriel's face. Anger beyond comprehension. Hatred, venomous and deadly.

The words came in bitter growls. "He slit her throat. While I lay bleeding." Gabriel hauled him in closer, his knuckles blanched white with the strain. "She was carrying our child."

Bo shivered with revulsion and horror. He gulped hard, said nothing.

Gabriel, trembling with rage, dropped Bo and staggered backward a couple of steps. The grief, hatred, would consume him if he didn't get it all pushed back down again.

Disbelief shone in Bo's eyes. "Gabriel, I—"

"I have to be the one to kill him. No one—" he grabbed him again "—no one is going to do it for me."

Chapter Twenty-One

Amos stepped onto the porch. A loose board creaked beneath his feet, alerting the others to his presence.

"All of you get in the house."

Trina swiped at her tears. "Papa! You should be in bed." She went to help him, but he waved her away.

"Gabriel, Bo—I intend to speak to both of you. Right now. The rest of you go back to the kitchen. Trina's supper is gettin' cold."

"But, Papa—"

"Do as I say, Katrina!" He would tolerate no nonsense from her. Not this time.

"All right." She glanced at Gabriel and saw he had calmed down. She herded Tom and Will toward the door.

Tom stopped short. "Paw, if you need us, just holler."

Amos waved him inside. "I will, I will. Somebody needs to put some more wood on the fire. This old man's bones are turnin' blue and startin' to crack."

Gabriel took the cue and volunteered to bring in more wood from the cord stacked beside the porch. Bo jumped in to help, glad for the delay.

Five minutes later, with the fire roaring, Amos McCabe stopped poking embers and rearranging logs and sat down in his favorite tan calfskin chair. The arms, ragged from years of Amos's elbows, had been covered with lacy crocheted antimacassars.

Gabriel sat opposite in an overstuffed chair with more doilies, while Bo sank onto the couch and leaned forward, elbows on knees. No one said anything, waiting for the elder McCabe to speak.

Amos took his time, staring at the fire.

"Eighteen years ago I lost my wife."

Gabriel took a deep breath. Bo seemed impatient, too.

Amos went on, still staring into the flames. "She died giving birth to Trina. I thought my life was over." He looked at Gabriel. "But it wasn't. I had three sons and a newborn baby daughter to remind me that Melanie had given me everything she could give—her love, our children, everything."

"Paw, what does this—"

"Shut up, Bo. You never have learned to listen instead of jawin' all the time."

Gabriel thought he knew what the senator was up to, but until he decided to come to the point, there was no use rushing him. "You were lucky, Senator, to have those children."

"Yes, I was. Whether or not you believe me, I think I know how it felt when you lost your wife, Gabriel."

Gabriel shook his head. No one could know.

"I didn't lose her to a lowlife, and I had my children to love me through the loss. I can't say I fully understand how you felt, but I think I can come close. When you lose someone you love, it's like having a piece of your soul ripped away. It leaves an empty place you think will never be filled, no matter what you do."

Trina tiptoed up to the door, careful not to be seen by the men. She didn't want to intrude, so she stayed just outside and listened. Tears in her eyes, love burning in her heart, she remembered Gabriel's description of how his wife had died. Her father, though, surprisingly enough, seemed to be talking about her mother, Melanie. Trina listened more closely.

Amos opened a humidor on the table next to his chair, filled a pipe and tamped it down. Then he broke off a twig from a log in the pile, stuck it in the flames until it caught, then lit his pipe. Aromatic smoke swirled around his head.

"But then, Gabriel, there comes a time to fill that emptiness with work, with a purpose. And, even though it doesn't seem possible at first, with someone else."

Now Gabriel knew where he was headed. "I think I—"

"Hear me out. I don't know for sure how you feel about my daughter. I doubt you could love her after so short a time."

Gabriel couldn't argue with him. Yet there was something between him and Trina he couldn't explain with anything else but love.

"Of course, Trina's probably the first woman you've...shall we say...gotten to know...since the death of your wife. Is that an accurate statement?"

Gabriel nodded.

"That could be clouding your judgment, although men don't usually fall in love with every woman they...well, you get the drift of what I'm saying."

Bo sat up straighter. "You mean he—"

"Shut up, Bo. I won't tell you again." Amos glared at his youngest son. Bo hushed.

"Spit it out, Senator. There are other things to discuss."

"Yes, there are. But this one is first on the list—on my list, anyway. If you don't intend to come back for Trina once you've killed Blackburn, I want to know it now."

Gabriel didn't have to think long. "I'll be back."

Trina almost gave herself away when she heard that. She whispered a prayer of thanks and kept listening.

"I'm glad to hear it." Amos got up and poked at the fire. "Now, let's talk about Blackburn."

"There's nothing to discuss, Senator. I mean to kill him. Bo knows where he might be. Once I know, too, I'll be on my way."

Bo finally worked up the nerve to say something. "I'm going with him, Paw."

Amos looked at his youngest son. "Oh, you are, are you? What makes you think I'll let you go?"

Bo worked his mouth in anger. Then he reminded himself to settle down. "I'm a man, Paw. If I choose to go, I'll go."

Amos smiled. "That's what I wanted to hear."

"It is?" Bo looked at Gabriel, but got no response one way or another.

"Paw, I thought you were gonna want to thrash me after what happened with Blackburn."

"Would you have let me do it?" Amos's eyes twinkled in the shadowed room.

Bo thought about it. "No, sir."

Amos nodded, smiled, went to the couch and offered his hand to Bo, who shook it, puzzled.

"Now that's settled, let's talk about what's going to happen next."

Bo leaned back, thoroughly confused. "You've lost

me, Paw. Gabriel and I are going after Blackburn. What more is there?"

"Plenty. Blackburn's men. You don't think they're going to forget what was supposed to take place in Silver Falls, do you?"

Bo sat up straight again. "Wait a minute. What exactly was supposed to happen? I thought—"

"You thought we were trading guns to Blackburn in exchange for the deed to Cobb's land. Right?"

"Right."

"Well, you were only half right. I owe you an apology, son."

"What for?"

"For not confiding in you. I knew Blackburn would double-cross both of us. That's why I hired a couple of his men away from him. Yes, Gabriel, I knew about Wilson. I did it to see things went the way I'd planned. They almost did."

Bo was completely baffled by this time. "But Paw, you hadn't planned on bein' shot. And you didn't get the deed."

Gabriel waited. It was all falling into place now.

"No, I didn't. But I will. The part of it I hadn't planned on was Trina getting in the way and being kidnapped by that heathen."

Trina sneezed. Hell's bells! Paw would have a conniption for sure to catch her spying.

"Come on in, Trina. I'm sure you've heard enough by now to know that all is not as it seems."

Bo looked from Gabriel to Trina to his father. "I'm lost."

Gabriel stood up. "Your father is trying to tell you the trunks he had on the train weren't full of guns for Blackburn."

Amos's eyes gleamed. "Give the man a cigar."

"Papa! What on earth—"

Bo jumped up from the couch. "Now, wait a minute…"

Tom and Will came into the room, apparently having overheard part of the conversation, and demanded to know what was going on.

Gabriel sat quietly, waiting for the furor to subside. Amos didn't seem to be the least bit inclined to give out any further information. In fact, he appeared to be gloating. Crafty old bastard. Gabriel had to admire him, but not much. He'd almost gotten himself and his daughter killed with his little game. Gabriel knew playing games with Blackburn was like trying to pet a rattlesnake.

Amos could see his children weren't about to shut up on their own, so he took a deep breath and yelled, "Quiet!" Then he made them wait before he spoke again, just to let them know who was still boss around this ranch.

"I'll answer your questions one at a time. First, it's none of your business what I put in those trunks. Second, I'm hungry. Trina, is there any of that stew left?"

Startled beyond belief, Trina nodded.

"Good. Gabriel, would you care to join me? Trina's stew is famous around here. You have to be hungry after your long trip today. I sure as hell am. I'm sure Bo, Tom and Will have work to do somewhere."

Tom shifted weight to his other leg. "Paw, nobody ever said anything about Trina being kidnapped until now. What happened?"

"Later. I'm sure she's dying to tell you all about it. But not until my belly is full." He headed for the kitchen, leaving his sons to pinch their mouths shut and wait.

Gabriel glanced at Trina on his way to the kitchen. All three of the McCabe brothers muttered something under their breaths as they left the room.

Gabriel didn't answer Amos's continuing prattle about Trina's stew and how tired he was until they got to the kitchen.

"What was all that about, Senator?"

Amos settled himself in the chair at the head of the table and took a deep breath. "Family. That's what it's about. How 'bout some stew?" He picked up a bowl half-full of stew. "I'm guessing this one's yours, Gabriel. Fill it up, Trina."

She refilled the bowl with fragrant, steaming chunks of lean beef and vegetables, added an extra dipper of broth, then handed it back, along with several chunks of cornbread. She filled Amos's bowl, and they commenced eating.

Trina left the kitchen when Amos shooed her away, and Gabriel was glad. He needed some answers from McCabe, and he wasn't likely to get them with Trina sitting at the table, interrupting every other breath.

Amos dabbed at his mouth with a napkin and sat back. "Cobb was my wife's second cousin."

"Bo told me the family connections. The trunks were meant for him?"

"No, for Blackburn."

Gabriel frowned.

"Cobb never was worth spit. A black sheep all his life. Never could understand why Melanie coddled him the way she did. After disappearing for twenty years, he came whinin' to her, beggin' for money, equipment, even food. The man was a waste of—"

"I get the idea. What was in the trunks?"

"Guns. But all of them had the firing pins removed and the barrels scored. Nothing but a pile of junk."

"Worthless to a skunk like Blackburn. You took a mighty big chance tryin' to swindle a swindler. Once Blackburn found out—"

"I'd have been on the train to Denver." Amos pushed his bowl back, wiped his mouth with the napkin again and rubbed his eyes tiredly. "I knew I shouldn't do it. But I had to have that deed from Blackburn and I sure as hell didn't want to trade good guns for it. He didn't deserve that land. It was meant for his wife, God rest her soul."

"How did Blackburn get the deed in the first place?" Gabriel went to the stove and ladled more stew into his bowl. Damn, but it tasted good. He grabbed another chunk of cornbread to go with it.

Amos shook his head. "Took it from Cobb at gunpoint. Cobb drank himself into a stupor before confronting Blackburn, demanding the deed. Blackburn laughed in his face and shot him without a second thought."

"Dead?"

"As a doornail. That's when Cobb's sons came to me. They said the mine was worthless, so they were heading for California. Promised the land to the state if I could get the deed from Blackburn."

"So how did Bo get mixed up with Blackburn?"

"Bo was here when they came to the house. He thought he could get Blackburn to give up the deed in exchange for guns and ammunition. He left here without telling me where he was going or what he was up to." Amos shook his head sadly. "He set up the deal, intending to do it all himself. I told him how stupid he'd been and that *I'd* take care of it—not him. I had no choice but to meet Blackburn in Silver Falls. But I didn't have to give him the guns."

Gabriel finished the stew and pushed back from the table, too full, but loving the feeling. "So why were Cobb's men trying to kill you on the train?"

"They weren't Cobb's men."

"Blackburn's?"

"Exactly. Used Cobb's name to throw off suspicion. I guess Blackburn never mentioned the family relationship between him, Cobb and this family."

Gabriel remembered grilling Wilson on the train. The bastard had lied to him. If he was still running with Blackburn when Gabriel caught up with them...

"So, now what, Senator?"

"I don't want Bo going after Blackburn. You don't need him along, and I don't want him caught in a cross fire when bullets start to fly."

Gabriel nodded. "If I find Blackburn and he survives, he'll be yours to deal with as you see fit."

Amos scraped his chair back. "Fair enough. Let's find out from Bo where Blackburn is hiding—if he knows. Just because he was lighting out doesn't mean he knows anything. If that's the case, I'd be pleased to have you stay with us until you get word where Blackburn's gone. If you want our help tracking him, you've got it."

The look on Amos's face told him Amos wanted Trina to have Gabriel around a while longer. He had to admit the thought had crossed his mind. And it didn't make sense to look for Blackburn until he had a pretty firm idea of where to start looking.

"I appreciate your hospitality, Senator."

Trina peeked around the door frame to see what was happening in the kitchen. Gabriel and her father were chatting at the table like old friends. This day had been absolutely baffling from beginning to end. Exasperating. Frustrating. Yet she wouldn't have missed it for the world. Any day with Gabriel was a wonderful day. And any night with Gabriel—

Tom touched her elbow and she jumped about a mile. "Sorry. Didn't mean to spook you, but you have a visitor."

"Who?"

"Geoffrey."

She sighed.

"He's dressed fit to kill and has some sort of little box he's clingin' to like it might try to run off if he lets up on it even a little." Tom peered into her eyes. "A ring?"

Trina sighed again. "I'm afraid so."

"Can your big brother give you some advice without being hit or cussed?"

Trina smiled at that. "I've never cussed at you, Tom, and you know it."

"Not to my face, anyway."

"Tom…" She waggled a finger at him.

"Tell him the truth. Don't let him keep on thinking you might change your mind and marry him someday when you know that's never going to happen."

Was she that transparent? Could Tom see in her eyes that Gabriel was the only man she could ever truly love? On impulse, Trina wound her arms around her big brother's neck and hugged him for a long time. His arms around her felt good and safe and brotherly.

"Thank you, Tom."

"He's in the front room. Will and Bo and I have some work to do in the barn."

Trina kissed him on the cheek. Tom rounded up his brothers from the front room and herded them outside.

When Trina came into the room, Geoffrey was standing by the fireplace, shifting his weight from one foot to the other as though he needed to visit the outhouse.

"Why, Geoffrey. What a surprise to see you."

"I told you I'd meet you at the depot, but nobody let me know when your train got in. I—I thought…well, it doesn't matter now." He stuck the box out toward her. "This is for you, Trina."

Swallowing hard, Trina took the box and opened it. A ring lay there, giving none of the pleasure intended. It had a huge red stone in the center with three green stones surrounded by gold filigree. It was so gaudy, Trina had to remind herself to smile. "Why, Geoffrey, wherever did you find such a…an unusual ring? I've never seen one quite like it before."

"You don't like it." Geoffrey slapped his hat hard against his leg. "I knew I should've let you pick it out yourself."

She had to do something quickly. "Geoffrey, it isn't that I don't like the ring. It's…lovely. I just can't accept it, that's all."

Geoffrey's face blanched until Trina thought he might faint.

"Can't accept it! It's your engagement ring. We talked about it before you left for Silver Falls. If you don't like it, I'll take it back. You can go with me and pick out the one you—"

"Geoffrey, stop!"

He closed his mouth and stared dumbly at her. Trina marveled at the fact she could have considered marrying him at all. He lacked the conviction a man needed to be the right husband for her. He also lacked the common sense and ability to see exactly what her needs were and how to meet them.

He wasn't Gabriel.

"Geoffrey, I know this will be painful for you to hear, but it's best said straight out. I can't marry you. Because I love someone else."

Geoffrey started to say something, but the words died on his lips.

Trina babbled on, unsure of just what to say next. "You don't know him. I met him only recently. He isn't from around here."

He fussed with his vest, put his hat on his head, took it back off, shifted from one foot to the other, then finally sank into a chair and slouched there, miserable as a dog left out in the rain.

Trina felt so sorry for him, she didn't know what to do. Maybe Tom had been wrong. Maybe she should have avoided Geoffrey for the next few weeks until he finally got the idea on his own.

Geoffrey kept staring at his feet. "His name?"

"Gabriel Hart."

"Where is he from?"

"Texas."

"Where did you meet him?"

Trina drew in a long breath. "On the train to Silver Falls." She braced herself for the outburst to come. But he didn't say anything. Not a word! "I know it seems sudden—"

"Sudden? It's downright indecent."

Trina's blood began to boil. "You're calling me indecent?"

"Well, what would you call it? Have you let him kiss you?"

Trina straightened her spine. "That, Mr. Monroe, is

none of your business. I think it's time for you to go now.''

"You've got that right." Geoffrey stormed toward the front door.

Trina straightened her spine and called after him, "I never meant for things to get ugly. I decided to be honest and straightforward with you because I felt you deserved respectful treatment." This wasn't going at all the way she'd hoped.

To his credit, Geoffrey nodded, straightened his coat, bowed slightly, then smiled. "I wish you all the happiness in the world, Trina. Mr. Hart is a lucky man."

"Thank you. I appreciate your understanding."

Geoffrey nodded once, curtly, then left, still clutching the ring box.

Trina went to her chair beside the fireplace and picked up her crocheting.

Gabriel, standing at the door to the kitchen, watched Geoffrey depart. When Tom came into the hall, Gabriel pointed toward the front door. "Was that someone I should know about?"

Tom shook his head. "Old news. Nothing to concern yourself about. I'm going to check on the horses. Your room's second on the left. Why don't you see if it suits you?"

Gabriel nodded and went down the hall.

Tom took a deep breath and went into the front room. "Gabriel went to check on his room."

"You wouldn't believe how they're talking and visiting—just like Gabriel had been coming to supper for years."

Tom shook his head. He'd expected to find his sister in tears. Instead, she seemed almost serene. "These past few days have brought a lot that's hard to believe. You really love him, don't you?''

Trina smiled. ''More than anything.''

Tom hugged her again. ''I just hope everything turns out the way you want. And, later, I expect every detail of your…kidnapping. Was Paw kidding about that? Bo said—''

''I'll tell you everything.''

Gabriel came walking down the hall. The young man who'd left had been riled about something. Gabriel didn't know if he wanted to know the details or not. He would just let Trina bring up the subject in her own time, in her own way. She'd never mentioned a beau—something else he didn't know about her. It would have been absurd to think she didn't have beaus, though.

Amos bellowed from the kitchen. ''Trina! We're ready for dessert.''

Tom squeezed her affectionately. ''Save some for us?''

''Of course. I made enough for an army.''

Tom went to get Will and Bo. Trina straightened her hair and her skirts, smiled at Gabriel, then went flying into the kitchen, trying to put on an ''all is as it should be'' face.

''Peach cobbler. In the oven. I assume you both want a big bowl with cream over the top?''

As full as Gabriel was, he wouldn't pass up peach cobbler and cream. He couldn't remember the last time he'd had such a treat. He sat down at the table again.

When she set the steaming bowls in front of them Trina warned them to be careful. The rest of the McCabes poured through the door and sat down. By the time they'd all been served, there was just enough for

Trina to have a taste, and an entire pitcher of cream was gone.

After the cobbler had disappeared and every man at the table had groaned his appreciation and lumbered off to sit by the fire, Trina gathered the dirty dishes and plunked them in the sink, poured in hot water from the kettle on the stove, added soap shavings and swished the water around to make some suds. For some reason, washing dishes soothed her, provided time to reflect on life in general. After straightening the table, she tackled the dishes with enough vigor to send soap bubbles floating about the room.

When she heard the kitchen door open, she didn't turn around, figuring it was one of her brothers looking for something else to eat.

When she felt two strong hands slide around her waist, two soft lips against her neck and the brushy softness of Gabriel's beard on her cheek, she stopped washing the bowl in her hands and closed her eyes, surrendering to sensations darting all through her. She sighed and longed to hold him.

She set the bowl down in the sink, pulled her hands from the soapy water and dried them on her apron.

His hands inched upward to enclose her breasts.

She pivoted within the circle of his arms and laced her fingers through his hair while kissing his lips softly.

Gabriel ran his hands up and down her spine and smiled when he realized she wasn't wearing a corset.

Trina had a fleeting thought one of her brothers might come in unexpectedly, but decided she didn't care. Let them come. Let them see how much she loved this man.

"Gabriel, tonight—"

"Better not. It's too soon."

She knew what he meant. If her brothers found him in her room, they'd hit the ceiling for sure.

Gabriel wound his fingers through her hair and tipped her head back. "Have you changed your mind about me?"

Did he have to ask? Surely her fingers roaming over his scalp, her tongue darting in and out of his mouth, her body pressed against him until she could feel the hardness of him told him she had no doubts. She took a long, shuddering breath.

He left her trembling.

Chapter Twenty-Two

Gabriel went to find Amos McCabe. He sat out back, staring at the mountains across a huge vegetable garden, a sprig of sweet grass in one corner of his mouth. "Pull up a chair, Gabriel."

"I need some information, Senator."

"I'll tell you what I know. What about?"

"Blackburn. Before he went to prison."

Amos nodded, leaned forward in his chair. "Otis Blackburn lived with his ma and pa, one brother and a sister until he was fifteen. Back then, he was as ordinary as any kid you'd ever meet."

"What happened to change it?"

"Three no-accounts showed up one day to water their horses. Otis was out hunting. Before they left, they'd burned the house, raped and killed his mother and little sister, killed his father and brother. He came home just in time to see the men leave. Saw their faces."

Gabriel felt sorry for Blackburn—a foreign feeling. "That's mighty rough."

"Yep. After he buried the bodies, he went to find the sheriff. Gave him a full description of the three men. Was told they'd be hunted and made to pay."

Gabriel knew what he was going to say next. "But nothing got done."

"Nope. The sheriff—"

"Sheriff Corbett Hart."

Amos looked at Gabriel for the first time since he'd sat down, nodded, continued. "Sheriff Hart went looking for them. Came back with folding money instead."

A story Gabriel knew too well.

"After that, Blackburn set out to kill those three himself. Killed the men he found them with, too. Made a reputation for himself. Folks started to see him as ruthless and coldhearted."

"Seems he had good reason." The words were bitter, but no less true.

"I'd say so. He never found the third man. Then he went after the man he hated as much as the men who had killed his family."

"My father."

"Yep."

"Swore he didn't kill him, though."

"That's what I heard." Amos leaned back farther in his chair.

"Said he wanted to kill him, but someone beat him to it."

"Yep."

"But I saw him shooting…" Gabriel buried his face in his hands.

"He went to prison for a crime he said he didn't commit. Blackburn was guilty of murder, several times over…." Amos glanced at Gabriel.

"But not that murder."

Amos took a long, deep breath. "It doesn't really matter now. What's done is done."

Gabriel sat back in the cane-bottom chair, balancing on the back legs. "It's time to stop."

Amos raised his eyebrows. "Stop what?"

Gabriel shook his head. "Never mind. Thanks, Senator."

"Amos. In the family, everybody calls me Amos."

Gabriel nodded.

Amos sat there for a long time after Gabriel left. Time to stop. Lord, yes.

In the front room Gabriel found Trina standing in front of her seated brothers, acting out every detail of being kidnapped. Gabriel listened and grinned in spite of the topic of her speech. She actually enjoyed horrifying her brothers with being dragged on the back of a horse into the mountains, kept in a tunnel with a killer, forced to dig a bullet from his shoulder.

"He passed out cold from the pain—and from all the whiskey he'd consumed. I never knew whiskey could keep a man knocked out during such suffering. The three of you ought to consider that the next time you—"

"Trina, just get on with it." Bo shifted in his chair. "We know how to drink."

Tom gave him a wry look. "Oh, we do, do we, little brother?"

"I told you to quit the 'little brother' crap, Tom."

"Whoa, now," Will said, "with the bad language. Your sister is present."

Gabriel laughed out loud. Coming to meet him, Trina gave him a smile to melt his heart.

"Where have you been? You just about missed the best part." She rose on tiptoes to kiss him. Over her shoulder Gabriel watched all three brothers gawk at the sight.

"Get on with your story, woman. Your stalling is enough to make a man run for cover."

She led Gabriel to the couch. He sat on the far end from Will. The quiet McCabe.

"Now, where was I?"

"About to cut out the bullet." Bo shook his head. "I still can't believe you did such a thing. You've never even watched when we slaughter cattle."

"Watching you kill defenseless cattle will never be my choice, Bo. It wasn't my choice to dig a bullet from a man's flesh, either."

Tom gave an impatient gesture for her to continue, followed by a long sigh.

"All right. I'm getting there. Blackburn had drunk so much, he couldn't keep his eye open."

Gabriel had heard this story, only through tears instead of smiles. Damnedest woman...

Bo shot up from the chair. "Wait a minute. You pulled the bullet out? With what?"

"My fingers, of course."

All three brothers talked at once.

"Aw, Trina, come on..."

"You're making this up..."

"Do you expect us to believe..."

Gabriel said nothing, waiting to see how she'd handle it. To her credit, she didn't whine or pout, just waited until they calmed down.

"I reached into that bloody hole until I felt that bullet, worked my fingers around it and pulled it out. It made a sucking sound when it pulled free that almost turned my stomach."

Gabriel nodded. She couldn't have made that up.

All talking again. Gabriel eased to the door and went out. Trina waved to him. "Then I cauterized the wound."

Gabriel laughed to himself. She wasn't about to end this little performance until she'd wrung the last bit of shock and surprise from three brothers who, up until now, obviously had considered her too delicate to have endured being kidnapped and performing field surgery on a wounded man.

In his room Gabriel washed his face again, needing the shock of cold water to help settle tangled emotions warring inside him. He lay on the bed—the feather mattress felt heavenly to his back—and stared at the ceiling with his arms crossed behind his head.

"Blackburn was a decent man...."

That statement didn't fit Gabriel's idea of Blackburn at all. Yet Corbett Hart had been a decent man once, too. A good husband to Mariah, and a good father to his children, Gabriel, Michael and Angel. Until the townspeople offered him the sheriff's job. The power he felt, enforcing the law, and the opportunities to make money in addition to his pitiful salary corrupted him totally. After only a few years Sheriff Hart became as notorious as the outlaws who chose to hole up where decent citizens once lived.

Mariah Hart kept her children at home, where she could keep them safe. Gabriel became the man of the family, for all practical purposes, at the age of twelve. When Corbett didn't come home for days at a time, Gabriel saw to it the family was fed and protected, stock cared for and chores done by Michael and little Angel, only five then.

When Gabriel was seventeen Mariah declared she'd had enough. She bought tickets on the stage for all of them. "Back east, we'll be safe. You can go to school and be respected for the fine people you are."

Six years later Gabriel kissed his family goodbye and headed west. Somehow, he had to make amends for his father. He set out to be a lawman.

Trina knocked lightly at the open door. Gabriel sat up, calmed by his thoughts, needing…her.

"Come here, woman." He stood.

She required no other urging, and ran straight into his arms, her mouth pressed to his, breasts firm against his chest. Gabriel let some of the emotion he'd been feeling flow into the woman he'd met on a train.

"What were you thinking? I watched from the hall for a minute before I came in."

"About my family. How different it was from yours."

"What do you envision for our family, Gabriel?"

The thought rocked him. "I never got that far into the future, I guess." He frowned. "Hard to let myself hope—"

"You can always hope. When a man stops hoping and dreaming, he stops living. It's time you got back to living again."

He nodded. "Might be, at that."

"Can you dance?"

"What?"

"I'm guessing you know how to dance. You can prove it to me tomorrow night."

"What's happening tomorrow night?"

"Barn dance at the Pickards', four miles east. We've been looking forward to going for a month or more. I can't wait to dance with you…show you off."

The person he held in his arms now sounded like a

little girl instead of the passionate woman he'd made love to the past few days. "Trina, I don't dance anymore."

"Why, of course you do. Everybody dances."

He eased her away. "Not everybody. Only people with time to spare."

She touched his arm. "And people who are happy."

Happy. Such a foreign thought. Yet one he'd been toying with, after a fashion, since he'd met this spitfire on the train.

"You haven't been happy in a long time, but you're going to be happy again. With me. Starting tomorrow night."

"Trina, I—"

"I don't want to hear another word about it. Besides, everyone and his great-aunt Maudie will be there. You can meet the influential men in this area. Papa will introduce you."

She prattled about food and fun, but Gabriel's thoughts wandered a different path. There might be someone at the dance who knew where Blackburn had gone from Denver. News traveled fast when it concerned a man with one eye and an evil reputation.

"All right. I'll think about it."

"You will? I knew I could convince you."

"I only said I'd think about it." He kissed the tip of her nose. "Now, woman, can you stop talking for one solid minute?"

"Why? What's going to happen during that minute?"

She knew. And met him halfway.

Chapter Twenty-Three

The Pickard place lay four miles or so to the east of the McCabe ranch, their only close neighbor. The ranch extended miles farther in every other direction, keeping other neighbors hours away at best. Amos, Tom, Will, Bo, Trina and Gabriel arrived at the Pickard house just before sunset. Fiddle music could be heard from the barn, along with clapping, shouting and general gaiety.

Gabriel tied Clancy to a hitching post, then helped Trina down from the carriage. She looked good enough to eat tonight, in an emerald green gown made of shiny material that practically squeaked when she moved. Lace and ruffles at the neck, wrists and in tiers down the skirt reminded Gabriel of lush fields of well-watered grass, swaying in the breeze. Her red hair, brushed until it shone like polished copper, was gathered into a green bow at the crown of her head, then cascaded down her back, all the way to her tiny waist. Gabriel could tell she'd worn that confounded corset. Her walk was stiff as a poker and she took short, shallow breaths.

Last night Trina had invited him to her room, but he'd thought it best not to challenge the hospitality of the McCabe household. He hadn't slept worth a damn. Tonight he might just have to help her out of that corset.

Trina disappeared into a swarm of young ladies dressed in every color of the rainbow and then some. The chattering coming from the wad of lovelies reminded Gabriel of a gaggle of geese, pecking at corn. More than once he caught one of the ladies peering in his direction with a glint in her eyes and a blatantly flirtatious grin. He shook his head. He'd been daft to agree to this shindig.

Taking in the expanse of the barn, he tried to see through dancing couples to the far side where several men clustered, paying little attention to dance activities. Gabriel made his way around the edge of the barn, past ladies and gentlemen sitting or standing beside bales of hay covered with quilts and blankets to provide seating. He listened to the men's conversation from the perimeter for a few minutes.

They discussed the price of cattle, grain—farming and ranching matters, for the most part. Then Gabriel heard the name Blackburn and listened more closely.

"I heard tell he was dead."

"Not unless they killed him yesterday. He came into town for ammunition and general supplies. Headed back toward the Wilson home place. He's holed up there before. Interesting thing was, he bought enough supplies for a dozen men. Wilson has lived alone the past two years."

Gabriel moved closer. "Excuse me, gentlemen. I couldn't help overhearing. Is this James Wilson you're talking about?"

"It is. Who might you be, sir?" inquired a large man with a bushy mustache.

"Gabriel Hart. I met James Wilson on the train to

Silver Falls about a week ago. He was going to meet a man I've been tracking for more than a year. Otis Blackburn.''

No doubt every man listening knew of Blackburn. Their expressions portrayed distaste, outright fear and anger.

Gabriel watched carefully to analyze their reactions. ''I wounded Blackburn at the Golden Eye in Silver Falls. He escaped into the mountains, doubled back to the train, got away in Denver. Have any of you heard where he might have gone from there?''

No one spoke for a moment. The man with the mustache responded first.

''I wish I could help you, Mr. Hart.'' He squinted, thinking. ''Would you be Sheriff Hart, from Texas?''

''Retired.''

He nodded. ''I'm Stephen Collinswood. Blackburn stole some cattle from me a while back. Never seen the bastard in person. Mind my asking why you're tracking him?''

Gabriel took a deep breath. ''He killed my wife.''

Every man there shook his head sympathetically.

Collinswood glanced around the circle. ''Wright, tell Hart what you heard about Wilson.''

''I was in the store just after Wilson left. The owner's a friend of mine. He'd heard Wilson had gotten mixed up with Blackburn a few months back. Seems Blackburn had been in the store a few days before.''

Gabriel nodded. ''After he left the train.''

''Sounds like it. Then Wilson came in a couple of days later. Could be they're holed up at the Wilson place.''

This was exactly what Gabriel had hoped to hear. ''Where is that?''

* * *

Trina watched Gabriel from across the room. He'd made a beeline for that group of men right after they'd arrived.

Tarnation! This corset was cutting her in half. You'd think she'd gained five pounds from not wearing it four or five days. But what heavenly days.

She stopped to answer the same question, from yet another friend just joining the group.

"Gabriel Hart. We met on the train to Silver Falls." She could have guessed the next question. "Yes, he did. Saved my life after I was kidnapped." Another pause. "Otis Blackburn." What had been fun to relate fifteen minutes ago had become tedious on the fourth telling. "I know. I'm lucky to be alive. If it weren't for Gabriel—"

He broke from the group and headed across the room.

"Excuse me. Gabriel is coming this way." She lifted her hankie and waved at him daintily. He grinned, so she knew he'd seen her. In less than a minute he'd wound his way through the dancers and stood in front of her.

"May I have this dance, Miss McCabe?"

"You certainly may, Mr. Hart." She turned to her girlfriends. "Excuse us, won't you?"

She could swear they sighed collectively as she took Gabriel's arm and walked with him to the center of the room. The fiddler ended a reel and started a waltz. Trina placed her hand in Gabriel's, the other hand on his shoulder. His warm hand on her waist made her tingle with anticipation.

They danced at arm's length for a few minutes. Trina found it terribly frustrating.

"Why don't you hold me closer, Mr. Hart?"

"Are you looking to start a scandal, Miss McCabe?"

She glanced at the girls watching their every move. "Why not?" She took a step closer. His arm slipped farther around her until she was close enough to be kissed if he should lean down with her face turned upward.

As they turned, she noted a flurry of discussion going on, and grinned. Then she saw Geoffrey standing alone behind them. Smiling at her. Another turn, and she focused only on Gabriel.

"I knew it."

"Knew what?"

"You're an excellent dancer."

"Thank you, ma'am."

Her breathing quickened when he pulled her hand to his chest and gathered her another inch closer. She smelled soap and shaving cologne—Bo's, if she wasn't mistaken—and the heady male scent he gave off when they made love. She knew without a doubt what he was thinking.

"Tonight, Miss McCabe...? Midnight?"

"Perfect. My room or yours?"

"Best be mine."

She nodded. The dance ended.

Gabriel stepped back. "Thank you, Miss McCabe. I trust I'll see more of you later?"

"You can count on it, Mr. Hart."

He escorted her to the table where Mrs. Pickard was serving punch and cookies and various other treats the ladies had brought. Trina saw that her dish of cookies was already empty, and smiled, pleased with herself. Her cookies always disappeared in a hurry at these dances.

Geoffrey appeared at her elbow. "May I have this dance, Trina?"

Trina glanced at Gabriel, gave him a tiny smile she hoped he'd understand, then replied, "Thank you, Geoffrey."

They danced stiffly, at arm's length.

"I see you haven't changed your mind about Mr. Hart."

"No, I haven't."

"Very well. I wanted to be the first to tell you…"

She looked up sharply into his dull brown eyes. "Tell me what?"

"Katie Bell Crump has agreed to marry me."

Trina stopped stone still. "Katie Bell?"

He smiled with an odd expression. "Why not? She's as pretty as you are…if not prettier."

Trina clinched her jaw. So. Trying to pick a fight, was he? She hated to disappoint him. "I think you're right, Geoffrey. I've always thought Katie Bell was lovely."

He hesitated. "And she appreciates my qualities, whereas you never seemed to. I think I deserve a wife who won't feel she…settled for less." He gazed across the room.

Trina spotted Katie watching them dance with daggers in her eyes.

It all made sense now. Geoffrey had given in far too easily when they had discussed this earlier. He'd no doubt been seeing Katie before Trina ended their relationship. Sneaking around behind her back. Did he think she'd cry and pitch a fit—and decide to come back to him? Poor Geoffrey.

"I wish you and Katie Bell all the best. In fact, I

think you and she are perfect for each other. More than any two people I know, in fact."

Geoffrey looked down at her sharply. "You mean you aren't angry?"

Trina smiled. "Of course not. Thank you for the dance. And be sure to invite us all to the wedding. We wouldn't miss it for the world."

She dropped Geoffrey's hand and left him standing in the center of the room. She never looked back, even though curiosity burned holes in her to see his expression—and Katie Bell's. After a minute or two she allowed herself to find him again, dancing with Katie, a wimpy little thing who would spend the rest of her life saying, "Oh, Geoffrey, you're so wonderful."

Speaking of wonderful…she glanced around, searching for Gabriel, but didn't find him. Bo saw her, and came by on his way across the room, probably intending to ask another girl to dance. He pointed toward the front doors.

"He went outside for some air. I'm betting you need a little, too." He kissed her cheek, then headed straight for Eliza Matthews, who beamed like the morning star when he asked her to dance.

Someday, Trina knew, Bo would find one special girl. Until then, his goal in life seemed to be to keep every girl happy within a fifty-mile radius.

At the doors she spotted Gabriel standing beside an apple tree, just on the edge of the lantern light illuminating the front of the barn. She came up beside him quietly. He was frowning, deep in thought. "Gabriel?"

The frown melted into a smile as she melted into his arms. His mouth found hers before she could even rise on tiptoes to meet him. Still kissing, he eased her around the tree until they were concealed from prying eyes.

"Mercy, woman, will this dance ever end?"

He ran his hands over her breasts and waist, then sighed with frustration. "What have I told you about corsets?"

"I had to wear it tonight, Gabriel. All the other girls would wag their tongues about me for years if I came without it." She nibbled at his lips playfully. "Help me loosen it when we get home?"

"How about now?" He ran his hands up and down her spine, leaving her with a tingle she knew would last until the corset was a memory and his hands had soothed the skin beneath.

"Not now. Soon, I promise. I'd better get back inside. They're already whispering about us. This will only make things worse."

He released her reluctantly and followed her back to the door, but didn't go inside.

"Dance with me again, Gabriel, please?"

Dancing was the last thing on his mind. He'd be riding toward the Wilson place at first light, after spending what could be his last night with Trina. But he couldn't disappoint her. Not with his future being as iffy as it now stood. He took her hand and obliged her until the musicians played, "Good Night, Ladies," at midnight.

Well past midnight. Trina checked the hall to make sure all was quiet in the house, then tiptoed to Gabriel's room. They'd have to be perfectly quiet. No giggles, moans or sighs could be risked, for fear of being caught by her brothers.

He'd left the door ajar. She smiled to herself. Less

noise if she didn't have to turn the knob. Gabriel had obviously been thinking along the same lines.

Dark in the room. The barest sliver of luminous moonlight slanted through the curtains. She knew exactly where the bed was, and that's where she headed, one tenuous step at a time, just in case Gabriel had left his boots in the middle of the floor.

Gabriel watched as she picked her way across the room. The fragrance of sweet-smelling soap preceded her. She'd taken a bath. Too bad he couldn't have been there. His hunger for her grew with each step she took. At the edge of the bed he saw her nightgown whisper to the floor.

Gabriel pulled her down beside him in one smooth motion, his mouth on hers, hands sliding over her bare arms and back.

Trina kissed him, caressed him, held him closer— then started to cry.

"Trina, what's wrong? Did I hurt you somehow?"

Desperation seized her. "You didn't hurt me, Gabriel." She was crying because she didn't know what else to do.

"Then what is it? I don't understand." Gabriel kissed her trembling lips and held her closer.

Trina clung to him, unable to get close enough.

Gabriel felt helpless. "Trina, tell me how to fix whatever it is that's troubling you."

How could she tell him? How could she ask him not to kill Otis Blackburn after what he'd done? Yet how could she live without Gabriel if Blackburn killed him? The reality of what he'd be trying to do had overwhelmed her as abruptly as rain clouds gathering in the mountains. The nightmare of losing him threatened every bit of happiness she'd come to expect.

"Dammit, Trina, talk to me. If you've changed your mind—"

"Don't go! Stay here where you'll be safe. If he kills you—" She broke down again, unable to stop the fear breaking her heart. Her body shook with heavy sobs.

So that was it. Gabriel took a long, deep breath and kissed her again. Instead of trying to come up with the right words, he just kept on kissing her until she started to kiss back.

Trina's fear suddenly turned into fierce passion. She knew he'd be leaving eventually—maybe even tomorrow—but tonight he belonged to her. She intended to make this the most intensely memorable night of their lives. A night to bring Gabriel running back to her the minute Blackburn hit the ground.

"Love me, Gabriel. Love me."

He didn't hesitate.

"I love you with all my heart. Don't ever forget." She kissed him again and again, unable to taste enough of him.

Gabriel matched her passion with his own. He wanted to be free to love Trina this way every night for the rest of their lives. Soon...

Bo stood outside Gabriel's door and listened. The sounds he heard were soft, yet revealing. They were together. Trina was crying.

Bo's first thought was to break down the door and beat Gabriel senseless for taking liberties with his sister.

But then he heard Trina say, "I love you," and it took all the heat out of his anger. They were saying goodbye. That's why she was crying. His sister had made her choice and Bo had no right to interfere with it as long as her indiscretion could be kept within the

family. There'd be no disgrace for her as long as she
and Gabriel were married. If Blackburn got lucky,
though, and fired the first shot, his sister...

Bo set his jaw and nodded once to emphasize the
decision he'd just made. He knew he had to be the one
to find Blackburn. He couldn't take the chance on
Blackburn killing Gabriel and leaving his sister disgraced, without a husband, and—the thought suddenly
occurred to him—possibly carrying a child.

Bo knew what he had to do—find Blackburn and kill
him. By the time Gabriel found out where he was and
caught up, it would be over. He'd be angry, but he'd
be free to marry Trina, as was his duty.

Bo went to pack his gear.

The first rays of sunlight had not yet meandered
around the distant mountains when Gabriel eased out of
bed, careful not to wake Trina. There'd be a ruckus
when her brothers discovered her in his room later on,
but she'd be able to handle it. Hell, Trina could handle
anything. Even Gabriel Hart.

Trina sighed and turned over, exposing one breast in
the morning light.

Through the night, Gabriel had realized Trina had
become more important to him than anything else in his
life. More important than Blackburn. That scum had
dominated his every waking thought for the past fifteen
months, but Gabriel had wasted enough time on Blackburn. It was time to get on with life—with Trina. Damn,
but he'd love to crawl back in beside her, stretch his
body next to hers and caress every inch of creamy skin
she owned.

But he couldn't right now. He had to tell Bo he'd
changed his mind. Blackburn wasn't worth risking both

their lives. He could keep running forever, looking over one shoulder for the rest of his life.

Gabriel pulled the blankets up to Trina's chin. She latched on to them and snuggled down into the soft folds, making noises like a contented cat. Damnedest woman...

He carefully pulled the door around behind him, but didn't dare close it completely for fear of waking her. She'd make a fuss until he could tell her his decision not to pursue Blackburn, and might wake the other McCabes. It would take some convincing to persuade Bo to give up on Blackburn, too, but Gabriel could be persuasive when he put his mind to it.

Bo's room was at the end of the hall, just at the head of the stairs. Gabriel approached the door, slightly ajar. Leaning left just a mite, he saw the bed—empty.

Damn.

Gabriel pushed the door open. The counterpane hadn't even been turned down. Bo had left sometime last night, no doubt intending to find Blackburn and kill him before Gabriel got to the hideout.

Anger coursed through Gabriel like hot lead. He had no choice now. Bo added a dangerous element that might very well cost both of them their lives.

Gabriel took a long, shuddering breath and hurried down the stairs and outside. In less than five minutes he had Clancy saddled and ready.

Before leaving the yard, Gabriel took one last look at the McCabe house. Trina stood at the window of the bedroom they'd shared last night. She pressed her hand against the windowpane in a silent farewell.

Gabriel raised his hand in reply, then kicked Clancy into an easy lope. Bo had several hours' head start. Gabriel would have to push hard to catch him.

Trina watched until Gabriel disappeared into the pale opalescence of imminent sunrise. Tears streamed down her face and her heart swelled until it felt as if it would shatter into a thousand pieces inside her.

"God be with you, Gabriel," she whispered.

Chapter Twenty-Four

"Trina? Are you in there?" Pounding at the door.

"Just a minute." She pulled her gown over her head to cover her nakedness then peered into the mirror over the chifforobe. Red, puffy eyes and cheeks. Dreadful. Well, there would be no concealing the fact she'd been crying. Might as well get it over with. She went to the door—realizing too late she was in Gabriel's room, dressed only in her nightgown. The look on her father's face told her he understood the situation exactly.

"Trina, I swear—"

"Don't lecture me, Papa. What I've done is by my own choice."

Amos McCabe started to say something else, but changed his mind. He touched her cheek. "Come here, child." She came gratefully into his arms, shedding new tears.

"Oh, Papa, what if he dies? What will I do?" Trina clung to him until she remembered his wound and loosened her hold. "Did I hurt you? I'm so sorry, Papa. I wasn't thinking. I—"

"You didn't hurt me. Now, stop bawling and listen." He wanted to rub the sore spot she'd mashed but he didn't want her to feel any worse than she already did. Damn, but he hated being injured.

She snuffled a couple of times and asked for his hankie.

Amos pulled a handkerchief from his pocket and handed it to her. "Now, listen to me, child. Are you sure about this man?"

Trina looked up at him while she dabbed at her nose. "Sure that I love him? More than anything in the whole world."

The words were a bit hard for Amos to take. After all, he'd been the most important man in Trina's life since the day she'd been born. Now he'd been replaced. The hurt wasn't a bad one, though. In fact, his throat tightened with emotion, his eyes moist. If only Melanie had lived to see this day. Their little Katrina in love with a man who had happened into their lives on a train. A man who was headed for what could prove to be his death.

What would that do to Trina, to lose Gabriel now? She might never find another man she could love. Amos smiled. He'd never found another woman he loved the way he'd loved Melanie. It was time to do something about getting Gabriel back here alive, with no regrets, nothing to distract him from his duty to this woman.

"And you are a woman, aren't you, Trina?"

Trina frowned. "What?"

"You aren't a little girl anymore."

"No, Papa. I'm not." What on earth was he thinking about?

"I expect Gabriel will be back before long. Bo's been gone too long to catch him now."

"Catch him? I don't understand. Bo is gone?"

"Left last night sometime. Gabriel went to find him.

He talked to Tom just before he headed for Denver. Bo had no business butting in on what Gabriel has been over a year trying to do. Bo will be scouting Denver, trying to pick up a lead on where Blackburn went from the train. If Bo finds him, Blackburn might decide to kill him, just for the hell of it. Excuse my language. We have to hope Gabriel gets there in time to save your brother from his own stupidity. Tom is going to Denver now, to see if he can find one or both of them.''

"I'll go with him."

"Are you daft, girl? You'll stay right here, out of harm's way. Tracking an outlaw is no place for a woman."

Trina knew there would be no use arguing with her father. She'd just have to let him think he'd convinced her.

"I hope Tom will be careful."

"He will. Now get dressed and come downstairs. Your brothers left some breakfast for you in the kitchen. You should have heard me trying to explain where you were." He kissed her tenderly on the forehead. "We'll try to bring Gabriel back to you, darlin'. That's all I can promise."

Different tears came this time, affection for her father dominating all other emotions for the moment. "I'll pray for all of them, every minute they're gone."

"See that you do. Now git!" He shoved her gently down the hall, then entered Gabriel's room for a minute.

The bedclothes were wrinkled, and the scent of Trina's toilet water still fragranced the room. His baby had grown up, all right, right under his nose and more quickly than he might have liked.

A twinge of pain jerked him back to the present. Blood seeped through his shirt. The wound had opened up again. He'd have to bind it tighter. No way he'd go back to bed. Even if it killed him, he was determined to do whatever was necessary to bring Gabriel home to his daughter.

Gabriel inched forward on his belly through a patch of needlegrass, taking care not to disturb a twig or leaf that might give away his position. He'd ridden fifteen miles to find this place—a cabin supposedly owned by the Wilson family, according to a bartender in Denver. He knew Bo was heading this way, because he'd talked to the same bartender a couple of hours before Gabriel got there.

Peering over the outcropping of rocks on the edge of the ravine, Gabriel could see that the cabin lay in a state of general disrepair, apparently abandoned months ago. The front porch had a dozen holes in it, and the roof didn't look much better.

Movement behind him. The snap of a twig, nothing more, yet threatening, all the same. Gabriel rolled and aimed, ready to shoot the instant he saw who was stalking him.

"Whoa! It's me! Don't shoot!" Bo held up both hands, his face twisted with fear.

Gabriel let out a long breath. "Damn fool kid," he mumbled.

Bo eased beside him and glanced around nervously. "This is it. Wilson's home place. I met with Blackburn here a couple of months ago to strike the deal. Bartender in Denver said Blackburn had mentioned this place last time he saw him."

Stupid kid, Gabriel thought. He'd had no idea whatsoever the kind of vermin he'd gotten mixed up with.

Since they were already here, he might as well finish what he'd set out to do.

No smoke curled from the chimney, and there were no horses anywhere they could see. No signs of life at all.

"Maybe they didn't come back here after all. Let's go down and see if they've been here. Maybe we just missed 'em." Bo stood and headed toward the cabin. "You comin'?"

"Yeah." Gabriel followed him down the ridge, gun drawn and ready, in case things weren't what they appeared.

Bo didn't share Gabriel's caution. He went straight to the door and was about to open it when Gabriel stopped him.

"What do you think you're doing?"

"Goin' inside. Why? You see somethin'?"

Gabriel shook his head with disbelief, pushed Bo off to the far side of the door, then stood on the other side. With one swift kick, he slammed the door back into the cabin. Gabriel pressed back against the wall.

A shotgun blast peppered the space where the door had been.

Bo hit the porch like a sack of cement. "Damn! Who's in there?"

Gabriel shook his head again. How Bo had managed to stay alive until now was a puzzle. "Just stay back. I'll take care of this."

Bo nodded, apparently glad to be excluded.

Gabriel eased over to the edge of the door frame. "Throw out that shotgun! Now!"

Another blast. "Come in and get me!"

"If that's what you want." He heard two more shells being loaded into the gun.

"Aren't you gonna—?" Bo insisted.

"Quiet."

"Come on in!" came the voice, weaker this time. "I'm ready for ya!" He blasted again.

Gabriel didn't move a muscle.

"Are ya comin' or not?" A fourth blast.

Gabriel threw himself through the door, sizing up the room as he rolled.

One man on the bed. Reloading. With his left hand.

Gabriel took aim and shot him through the left shoulder.

The scream brought Bo to life. He ran through the door, ready to shoot.

"Stop!" Gabriel got up, lifted the shotgun off the coverlet. "I want him alive and able to talk."

Bo stared in awe. Gabriel had incapacitated the sniper with one shot, on the roll.

"Damn, Gabriel. I never…"

Gabriel figured that Bo had realized for the first time how dangerous it had been to try to do business with Otis Blackburn. Bo started to shake as if he had malaria.

Gabriel moved closer to the bed. James Wilson. His eye twitched until it was useless. "All right, now, let's have a talk."

"I got nothin' to say." Wilson's blood slowly soaked into the mattress beneath his shoulder.

"If you don't want to bleed to death, I think you do." He'd been wounded before they arrived. His leg was bandaged just above the ankle and his foot blazed with infection. The stench of illness permeated the room.

"I don't know nothin' 'bout nothin'." Wilson flopped back on the bed, in such pain he almost passed out.

Gabriel nudged his leg with the gun barrel. Wilson

groaned pitifully. "I wouldn't want to hurt this leg, so start talking. How long ago did Blackburn leave?" Gabriel knew this scum would die soon. He'd have to work fast. With one swift motion Gabriel jabbed the barrel of his gun against Wilson's bandaged leg again.

Wilson screamed and tried to get to Gabriel, but the pain in his shoulder proved too much to endure. He fell back, panting and groaning, his face knotted into an agonizing grimace.

Gabriel's gut tightened. This was the kind of thing Blackburn would do. It didn't set at all well with him that he'd stooped to the outlaw's level.

"Tell me when Blackburn took off and which way he went. He left you here to die. You don't owe him anything."

Wilson, crazy with pain, hesitated. "All right...I'll tell you everything. On one condition."

"Keep talking."

"Get me to a doctor."

"Agreed."

He'd never make it to a doctor. "Bo, tear up something—anything—to make another bandage."

Bo searched the cabin. Nothing. "It's going to have to be the sheet he's lying on, Gabriel. This place is so bare—"

"Get to it, then. He's bleeding pretty bad."

Bo tore the bottom off the sheet. "It's awfully dirty."

"It won't matter. I need something to pack the wound." He took the strip of cloth from Bo, folded it into a tight square, pressed it into Wilson's shoulder. He cried out in misery.

Gabriel winced, remembering his own pain from Blackburn's bullet, and regretted causing Wilson the same pain, even if the bastard had lied to him.

"This is the man with the twitch you mentioned back at the ranch?" Bo dropped to one knee beside the bed.

"Yep. We rode the train together. Come on, Wilson, wake up." Gabriel slapped Wilson's face a couple of times.

His eyes fluttered open. "No! Don't shoot! Don't…"

Delirious. Gabriel would have to work fast.

"Tell me where Blackburn went."

A milky glaze had formed on Wilson's eyes, preventing them from focusing. "Blackburn? He's here? Don't let him shoot me again."

Gabriel's gut tightened more. There was no telling why Blackburn had shot Wilson, but more than likely it had been for sport. It gave Gabriel something to use. "Tell me where Blackburn went, Wilson. So I can kill him for you."

The words burned into Wilson's mind. "Yeah. Kill the bastard for me."

"Just tell me where—"

"West. He went west."

"We just came from the west. Are you sure?"

"West. Seen 'em leave. Heard you was at the McCabes'. Left me here…"

Wilson's eyes closed. His shoulders slumped into the filthy mattress. Gabriel covered Wilson's face with the sheet, then stood.

"Bo, we have to get back."

"Did he say Blackburn was headed for our ranch? We'll never catch him in time—"

Gabriel was already out the door.

Waiting was worse than being in the middle of trouble. Trina remembered the Golden Eye, her father lying on the floor, shot by Blackburn. Being thrown over the horse, forced into the tunnel. As frightened as she'd been, she hadn't felt anxiety and dread like this.

Trina closed her eyes. Tears spilled down her cheeks as she thought about Gabriel—his smile, his eyes, his mouth. She tried to remember how it felt when his lips touched hers. A memory could never replace the real thing.

She sat on the edge of the bed, feeling helpless and afraid.

"Trina?"

She pulled a hankie from her sleeve and dried her eyes before turning to face her father.

Amos saw her red eyes and wet cheeks. "Come here, child."

Trina went into his arms exactly as she had as a little girl, being careful this time not to touch his wound. "Oh, Papa, I'm so afraid. What if Gabriel doesn't come back? What if—"

"Now, you hush that business right now, you hear me? Gabriel is not a man to die easily. If he were, he would've died over a year ago, when Blackburn shot him." He tipped her chin upward. The pain in her eyes made him want to choke the life out of Blackburn himself. "Now, you listen to me, Katrina McCabe."

She nodded and tried not to cry, but tears continued to pour, anyway.

"Gabriel Hart is not just any man. I know it, and you know it, too. He's not about to let Blackburn get the drop on him again. The best thing you can do right now is wait patiently for his return."

"But Papa—"

"No buts, Trina. When Gabriel comes back to you—and he will come back—he'll need to know you were strong, that you supported what he did, and agreed a man like Blackburn has no business killing and terrorizing good people. It takes a man like Gabriel to put an end to Blackburn's brand of terror. And it takes a woman like you, Trina, to make him feel whole again after it's done.''

The tears slowed. Trina, kneeling beside the bed, held her father's hands and listened carefully.

''He's been after Blackburn for a lot of months now. His wounds may have healed physically, but when he faces Blackburn again, all the pain of losing his wife is going to come back. After it's done, there'll be a huge void in him.''

''Even if he feels relieved and satisfied to have taken his revenge?''

He nodded. ''You have to remember he's been living on hatred. It's consumed him—like fire—for a long time. Once Blackburn is dead, the fire will die, leaving an empty place where all that hate was before.''

''You mean he might feel his purpose for living is gone. Is that what you're saying, Papa?''

Amos smiled and nodded. ''Exactly. But it won't be gone, because he has you to come home to. Your love for each other will fill that space in him with something good and positive. Because of you, Trina, Gabriel will learn to live again.''

It gave her such a warm feeling to think she could be that important to Gabriel. ''Thank you, Papa. I'll try to be more patient.''

Amos's eyes shone with tears. ''You're so much like your mother. So much.''

Bo and Gabriel rode as fast as their horses could manage. Gabriel knew he was pushing Clancy to the limit. But if Blackburn got there before they did—

Bo pulled up alongside. "Gabriel, we have to rest the horses. They'll die under us if we keep up this pace. They've been going hard all day."

Gabriel knew he was right. A dead horse wouldn't do them any good at all.

"We'll stop for a few minutes. No more."

Could they spare the time? The way Clancy was puffing and blowing, Gabriel knew they'd have to, or end up walking the last mile.

"Quarter of an hour."

The McCabe house lay quiet and peaceful. Tom and Will were working in the barn. Supper simmered on the stove. All in all, things had settled to a quiet hum.

Trina sat rocking and crocheting by the fireplace. Amos sat on the divan, reading a newspaper for the third time. Every few minutes he studied his watch as though he hadn't checked the time in hours.

Instead of being jumpy and cross, Trina had become almost serene. She felt her father's eyes on her as she rocked and stitched. Her fear had settled into the core of her, quiet now, yet very real and extremely dangerous. The possibility of Gabriel never coming back loomed like a nightmare.

From time to time she spoke to Amos about crops or livestock—trivial subjects—and he'd answer with no enthusiasm for the topic. All the while, she murmured prayers asking God to bring Gabriel and Bo home safe and sound.

Amos shot up from the divan without warning.

"Dammit, this has gone on long enough. I'm taking Tom and Will. We're going after them."

Trina caught him before he got to the door and put

one hand on his cheek so he'd face her squarely. "Papa, listen to me."

"Make it quick. Time's a-wasting."

"You told me I had to be strong. So I'm being strong. Now it's your turn to be strong, but not this way. If you ride again too soon, you'll start to bleed, and we may not be able to stop it this time. Tom and Will have to stay here, in case Gabriel and Bo come back and need help. You have to find the strength to be patient. Isn't that what you told me before?"

"Looks like I taught you more than I thought." He pondered. "All right, Trina. I'll be patient if you will."

Trina smiled, helped him to the divan, then resumed her rocking and crocheting.

Amos was secretly glad to be sitting again. The wound pained him almost as much as it had that first day. Tom and Will came in from the barn. Amos called them into the front room.

"Tom, I want you to follow Gabriel and Bo."

"But Paw—"

"Not now. In the morning. If they don't come back tonight. Gabriel's going to need more help than Bo can give him if he's to kill Blackburn and come out of it alive." He glanced at Trina to gauge her reaction to his words. She never even blinked. Damn, but he wished Melanie had lived to see the woman her daughter had become.

"All right, Paw. We'll talk about it in the morning."

Amos knew when he was being patronized, and he didn't like it one bit. "Tom, when I tell you something—"

Trina stepped in. "Papa, it's time to rest. Tom, go on to the kitchen. Chicken and dumplings will be ready in about five minutes. Why don't you and Will bring in some wood for the fire?''

Tom headed outside to the wood box.

Amos winked at his daughter. "Now you've got Tom obeying your orders, along with every other young man who happens to show up. Makes me wonder who'll be next."

"You, that's who! Now get yourself to the kitchen, and don't let me hear a peep out of you until every last dumpling is gone."

"Yes, ma'am." Amos couldn't wipe the smile off his lips.

Gabriel and Bo took advantage of the time the horses were resting and had a quick supper. Hard biscuits with beef jerky from the bottom of Gabriel's saddlebags were a far cry from Trina's cooking, but it filled them up. Strong, hot coffee washed it down.

"Bo, tell me about the man who danced with Trina—the only one other than me."

"Name's Geoffrey Monroe." Bo pitched the dregs from his coffee into the fire, making the flames dance and hiss. "He used to be Trina's beau."

"Used to be...or is?"

"She dropped him like a hot spud after meeting you."

Gabriel didn't know how to take this little piece of news. "How long had she been seeing him?"

"About six months, more or less. I gave up trying to keep up with Trina's beaus. Too confusin'. Then she managed to snare Geoffrey. Every girl in Denver had her eye on him. Took on around him like he was something really special. I never could see it, myself. When he chose Trina, the other girls stopped talking to her for days. Their curiosity got the best of them, though. Pelted her with questions all the time. Trina loved being the center of attention.''

"She loved him, then?"

"Trina loved the attention, but she never loved him. It was like winning a prize at the fair. She won him, then didn't really want him. Geoffrey did everything Trina told him to do. No backbone. Didn't really surprise me when she put off accepting a ring from him. She thought she was being real careful, not to let us know she was stalling him, but I saw right through her.'' Bo shifted and poked at the fire with a stick. "As far as I know, he never talked to Paw about asking for her hand. Like I said, Trina dropped him—"

"Yeah, I know what you said." It bothered him. If Trina had been so flighty that she'd hop from one beau to another, then maybe she'd just hopped from Geoffrey to Gabriel. A new challenge. He shook his head. Couldn't be. Trina had given herself to him body and soul. There'd been no doubt she was a virgin when they made love the first time. In fact, the more Gabriel thought about it, the more it seemed Bo was talking about an entirely different woman than the Trina McCabe Gabriel knew.

"Bo, does your sister seem, well, different since she met me?"

"You'd better believe it. I've never seen her so determined and…" He paused, thinking. "I guess I'd have to say Trina seems more like a woman now, instead of a little girl." He grinned slyly.

"You think she's over Geoffrey, then?"

"I don't think she ever gave a whit for Geoffrey." He grinned. "I think she loves you, Gabriel. What's more, I think you love her, too."

No doubt about that. "Let's get going."

"I'm right behind you." Bo stood up, grinning like a possum.

Gabriel went to saddle Clancy.

Tom soaked up the last bit of gravy from his plate with a piece of cornbread, then got up from the table. "Mighty good, Trina. Glad you're home."

"Thank you, Tom."

Will perked up from his third helping of dumplings. "Someone's coming."

Tom listened. "Are you sure?"

The sound of horses snorting, pawing the ground, came through the quiet. Could it be Gabriel and Bo coming back? Maybe they hadn't found Blackburn. Maybe— Trina ran toward the front door.

"Trina, wait!" Tom was right behind her.

Amos stood at the window in the front room, holding the curtains back just enough to see the front yard.

"Three men. Never seen 'em before. No, wait. One of them...is Blackburn."

Chapter Twenty-Five

Tom went to the window where Amos watched the unexpected visitors. With waning light, it was hard to make out features on any of their faces.

"Better get the guns, Tom."

He went straight to a gun case and fetched a rifle, a shotgun and a pistol. After rummaging in a drawer for ammunition, he loaded all three weapons.

"Hello the house!" one of the men called. A flurry of raucous laughter followed.

"They're drunk." Tom handed the shotgun to Amos. "Trina, get on upstairs."

"But, Tom—"

"Do as I say!"

Trina hurried to the kitchen, but no farther, and pulled the door around but didn't close it completely. She had to know what was happening.

"Damn, but it's hard to see." Amos rubbed the glass with the palm of his hand, but it didn't help visibility.

"Hello the house!" the man outside called again. More laughter echoed through the twilight. The man turned sideways to look at his companions.

Amos saw the ruined eye clearly. "It's him, all right. Blackburn."

"Are you sure?" Tom tried to see, but all three men stood in silhouette against the sunset.

"I'm sure. We're going to have to kill him. If we don't— Blackburn!"

"Paw, don't—"

Blackburn slapped one of his buddies on the back and laughed until he started to cough and choke. "Send Hart out, Senator. With the guns. Time to settle accounts."

"Keep riding, Blackburn. You're not welcome here." Amos knew he'd never leave without a fight— or the guns he'd been promised.

Blackburn came toward the porch. The other men disappeared around the corners of the house.

Gabriel and Bo reached the McCabe ranch at dusk. Gabriel reined in his exhausted horse. "We'll have to approach carefully, Bo. Tie the horses. Be quiet about it."

"But—"

"Blackburn could be waiting for us, just like Wilson."

Bo tied the horses, then squatted next to Gabriel. "How about if we split up? I'll go around the back while you—"

"Stay close until I tell you otherwise. We have to see if Blackburn's there."

Light from the window flickered. Gabriel tensed. It could be that someone had walked in front of it, either inside the house—or outside. "Watch that window. Tell me what you see."

"Why? Did you spot someone?" He strained to see. In a few minutes it would be completely dark.

Laughter, followed by shouting, pierced the silence.

Gabriel took a deep breath. "They're there, all right, but still outside." Thank God. "All right, Bo, here's what we're going to do."

Blackburn stopped just shy of the porch. "All we want is what you promised. Tell me where the guns are. We'll be gone before you can spit three times."

Amos cocked the rifle and smashed one of the windowpanes to facilitate clear shooting. "The deal's off. No guns. Get back on your horse, round up your men and head out."

Amos could see Blackburn's face better now. The man was uglier than sin and filthy, as though he hadn't seen water in months. The socket where Gabriel had gouged out his eye was sunken and festered. Amos knew he'd suffered two other gunshot wounds at the Golden Eye, but there was no evidence of it now. How the man managed to stay alive was a mystery.

"Get out, Blackburn! Or die right where you're standing!"

Blackburn laughed until he doubled over, then straightened so suddenly it made Amos jump. He'd drawn his gun, aiming at the window where Amos stood.

"I have somethin' fer ya, Senator. Come on out and git it!" He fired at the window.

Amos pulled away in time to avoid being hit by broken glass. There could be no easy end to this thing.

"Tom!"

From another window in the front room. "Yeah, Paw?"

"See any of the others?"

"Nope. They're layin' low. Waiting."

"If you get a chance, shoot to kill. It's the only way we're gettin' out of this alive."

Tom disappeared into the back of the house.

Trina appeared at the door. "I think I should help—"

Without warning, Blackburn's men attacked the house, yelling and shooting until it sounded as if hell had opened up all around them.

"Get down!" Amos fired two shots out the front window and dropped to the floor.

Will fired at Blackburn, then jerked backward with a sharp cry. Blood gushed from his arm. Trina ran to tend the wound.

Tom rushed into the front room. "They're comin' around front!"

A huge man smashed through a window, fired, grabbed Trina by the throat and pointed his gun at Amos.

"Hold it right there, or she dies. Drop your guns." He pointed the gun at her head.

Tom dropped his gun and raised his hands. "Let her go. She's no threat to you."

He laughed raucously. "A threat? Not hardly. But fun?" He pulled Trina's face over closer to his. "Give old Jute a kiss, whatta ya say?" She tried desperately to pull away, but his hold on her was too much to break. "Yeah, you're gonna be lots of fun, aren't ya?"

She whimpered, terrified.

"Trina—" Amos took one step toward her.

"Shut up! Git away from the window." He dragged Trina along with him, glanced outside, then yelled, "Come on in! I've got 'em."

Blackburn was through the front door in two breaths.

Amos took a step toward him, then retreated, searching his mind frantically for a plan—any plan.

"Papa, please don't! Give him the guns. Give him whatever he wants." Otis Blackburn had to be the ugliest, foulest, most contemptible human being she'd ever encountered. His stench filled the room. His face mirrored more evil than the devil himself. Yet she'd seen another side of this man. And she'd saved his life.

"Well, now." Blackburn surveyed the situation. "Looks like you shoulda just let us in for some grub and a warm place by the fire, now, don't it? But since you didn't, I guess we're gonna have to teach you a lesson in hospitality."

"I saved your life." Trina spoke quietly and as calmly as she could manage.

Blackburn stared at her, stunned by the statement.

"That you did, missy."

"You owe me a life."

Blackburn didn't react immediately, but finally nodded. "Right again." Blackburn came toward her, signaled to Jute to release her.

She rubbed her arms, straightened her spine, faced Blackburn without flinching.

"I'm here for Hart. He won't quit until one of us is dead. It's time to settle the score."

"I ask you for his life."

Blackburn shook his head. "Won't work, missy. Hart's the one intent on vengeance."

"He didn't know about Elvina before. He does now. He's ready to stop the killing, just as you are."

Blackburn stepped closer, reached to touch Trina's cheek.

"Please..." she begged.

Without warning, Tom threw himself between Trina

and Blackburn, grabbed his arm just as he fired. The bullet went wild. Tom slammed him into the door frame.

"Stop, Tom! Leave him alone!" Trina clutched at Tom's back, trying to pull him off Blackburn.

"Let him go, Tom." Gabriel stepped into the room. Bo appeared from the back of the house.

Blackburn staggered backward, pale as a ghost.

Gabriel took a step forward. "The time's come, Blackburn, to pay for what you did to my wife."

Blackburn's jaundiced eye darted around the room, from Gabriel to Bo, Amos, Tom, back to Gabriel.

"I killed your wife. Just as you killed mine."

Something snapped inside Gabriel. He quaked with anger flooding from the depths, as festered and putrified, malignant and vile, as Blackburn himself.

"She was carrying our child when you slit her throat, you bastard."

Blackburn's face lost all color. Drenched in the foul sweat of fear, his body shook as though he had malaria. He went straight for Trina.

Trina turned to run, but her feet tangled in her skirts. She stumbled. Blackburn grabbed her around the throat, tightened his hold, choked off her scream. From a scabbard on his thigh he pulled the knife Trina had used on his shoulder. Grinning like a demon, Blackburn pressed the blade against her throat. A trickle of blood oozed down her neck to stain her collar crimson.

Gabriel felt as though time had turned back fifteen months. He raised his gun, cocked the hammer, aimed at Blackburn's ruined eye.

"No, Gabriel!" Trina pleaded. "He's suffered enough. Both of you have suffered enough."

Gabriel stared at her, then lowered his gun. Anger

drained out of him suddenly, completely. Hatred withered and died. The love he felt for this woman flooded in, filling every inch of space in his soul.

Gabriel heard the hammer of a gun click back across the room. Jute pointed his gun at Gabriel.

Blackburn shoved Trina toward Gabriel, raised his gun—and shot Jute through the head. Before Jute collapsed, he shot Blackburn in the chest.

Blackburn sagged to the floor.

Epilogue

Gabriel spied the house when he crested the hill. There was no sign of Trina anywhere. He frowned. Trina usually heard him coming and came to meet him after he'd been to town.

He grinned. Now that the baby was so close, she was probably napping, or sewing more baby clothes, or just sitting, rocking, smiling, as she tended to do a lot these days.

He unsaddled and put Clancy in the corral. At the well Gabriel reached for the bucket, lowered it until it sank into the cool water, then pulled it up and took a long drink.

Trina ran from the cabin. "Gabriel, you're home! What did you bring me?"

Gabriel laughed. Just like a kid. "Nothing. Not a thing."

Trina stuck out her lower lip, knowing the result it would have on her husband.

Gabriel gathered his wife—and her round belly—into his arms and pulled that pouty lower lip into his mouth. Damn, but she tasted good. In fact, she tasted better every day.

"Now, show me what you brought. Did you get the flannel? And the thread? The baby will need clothes and blankets and—"

"Yes, I know what the baby will need." Love tugged at Gabriel's heart the way it always did when she talked about the baby.

Trina was already into the bundle he'd brought from Fort Worth. She squealed with delight at the bolt of white flannel, and pink and blue yarn he'd brought for her to crochet little dainties for their baby.

"Oh, Gabriel, how could I be any happier?"

"Well, would a letter from your father help?"

"You're so mean! Why didn't you tell me sooner you had a letter?"

He pulled the envelope from his pocket and handed it to her. "Your father sends his love. Bo thinks he's in love again. Tom bought a new bull he thinks is going to improve their stock. Will has a new horse. They want to come for a visit after the baby's born. That's pretty much it."

"We'll read it aloud after supper. Are you hungry?" She turned toward the house, but Gabriel maneuvered her into his arms, kissed her until she could hardly breathe. Her tongue in his mouth proved pregnancy hadn't cooled her hunger for him. Of course, they had to be careful of the baby when they made love, but Trina never seemed to run out of ideas or new ways for them to pleasure each other.

Damnedest woman he'd ever known.

His love for her had become so full, so expansive, he couldn't hold it all. It had to be lavished on her at every opportunity.

Trina ran her fingers over Gabriel's scalp while she kissed him and marveled again at how they fit together, even with her belly round and full. He picked her up and carried her into the house, straight to the bedroom.

"What have you dreamed up for us to do today, Mrs. Hart?"

Trina grinned impishly. "Have you ever had your toes kissed, Mr. Hart?"

"My toes? Can't say I have. How about you?"

"Never. Shall we give it a try? Right after we've had a bath, of course. I'll help with the scrubbing if you will."

Gabriel kissed his wife, his lover, his best friend. "Haven't had someone to scrub my back—"

"In at least two days."

Damnedest woman...

* * * * *

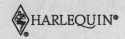
 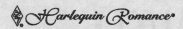

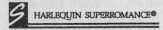

Available in March
from *New York Times* bestselling author

ELIZABETH LOWELL

Carlson Raven had no choice but to rescue Janna Morgan—
the beautiful, courageous woman who struggled against the
stormy sea. When he pulled her from the choppy waters and
revived her with the heat of his body, his yearning was as
unexpected as it was enduring.

But Carlson was as untamed and enigmatic as the sea he
loved. Would Janna be the woman to capture his wild and
lonely heart?

LOVE SONG FOR A RAVEN

Available in March 1998
wherever books are sold.

MIRA BOOKS **The Brightest Stars in Women's Fiction.™**

DEBBIE MACOMBER

invites you to the

HEART OF TEXAS

Join Debbie Macomber as she brings you the lives
and loves of the folks in the ranching community
of Promise, Texas.

If you loved Midnight Sons—don't miss
Heart of Texas! A brand-new six-book series
from Debbie Macomber.

Available in February 1998
at your favorite retail store.

Heart of Texas by Debbie Macomber

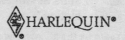

HARLEQUIN®

HPHRT1

New York Times bestselling author

LINDA LAEL MILLER

Nathan McKendrick—world famous, devastatingly
handsome, undeniably passionate… Was it any
wonder half of America was in love with him? And
Mallory O'Connor McKendrick was just as successful in
her own right. Their storybook marriage had defied
the odds…as well as the rumors.

They believed that they were different, that their love was
something special. But suddenly, inexplicably, the marriage
was crumbling. What could destroy such a strong bond and
what could they do to save it?

SNOWFLAKES ON THE SEA

Available in March 1998 wherever books are sold.

Welcome to *Love Inspired*™

A brand-new series of contemporary inspirational love stories.

Join men and women as they learn valuable lessons about facing the challenges of today's world and about life, love and faith.

**Look for the following March 1998
Love Inspired™ titles:**

CHILD OF HER HEART
by Irene Brand

A FATHER'S LOVE
by Cheryl Wolverton

WITH BABY IN MIND
by Arlene James

Available in retail outlets in February 1998.

LIFT YOUR SPIRITS AND GLADDEN YOUR HEART
with *Love Inspired!*™

Steeple
Hill™

LI398

Look for these titles—
available at your favorite retail outlet!

January 1998
Renegade Son by Lisa Jackson
Danielle Summers had problems: a rebellious child
and unscrupulous enemies. In addition, her Montana
ranch was slowly being sabotaged. And then there was
Chase McEnroe—who admired her land and desired her
body. But Danielle feared he would invade more than just
her property—he'd trespass on her heart.

February 1998
The Heart's Yearning by Ginna Gray
Fourteen years ago Laura gave her baby up for adoption,
and not one day had passed that she didn't think about
him and agonize over her choice—so she finally followed
her heart to Texas to see her child. But the plan to watch
her son from afar doesn't quite happen that way, once the
boy's sexy—*single*—father takes a decided interest in *her.*

March 1998
First Things Last by Dixie Browning
One look into Chandler Harrington's dark eyes and
Belinda Massey could refuse the Virginia millionaire nothing.
So how could the no-nonsense nanny believe the rumors that
he had kidnapped his nephew—an adorable, healthy little boy
who crawled as easily into her heart as he did into her lap?

BORN IN THE USA: Love, marriage—
and the pursuit of family!

BUSA4